PRINCESS
OF
THERMOPYLAE

Belinda Harrison

DEDICATION

For Renee – *my* vulnerable princess and my pillar of strength. I've loved you for twenty years, here's to the next twenty.

And for my parents – that Dictionary you got me for my 6th birthday has most likely helped me get to this point, but please don't read any further than this, it'll just be awkward for both of us (thanks for always supporting and believing in me though).

ACKNOWLEDGMENTS

It always 'takes a village' and my journey to this point is no different. I've had an amazing team from early readers Allan, Chrissie, Lisa and Keira, to the support of my book club (wine club) girls: Allison, Lauren, Trudy, Katisa, Amanda and Bridget, to my amazing editor Kristie who said she doesn't want to be acknowledged, but I said too bad! She has also been known to encourage, support, yell (in the comments section of the manuscript), roll her eyes, shake her head, remind me of awesomeness, ninja kick with excitement, ignore her family to keep my head in the game, edit, suggest and occasionally forget to read an important line that makes her put in an unnecessary comment soon after – thanks for everything you've done for me to this point. And to Jane Routley, whose comments and suggestions during her manuscript assessment made this the best book it could be – thank you so much for your honesty and support. I'm sure there are even more people I should thank, but I misplaced the piece of paper that had everyone's name on it so just let me know I forgot you and I'll fix it!

And most importantly, these acknowledgements wouldn't be complete without mentioning the two people who have been the most patient and understanding of my moods, my disappearance from them from hours (or sometimes days) on end, for agreeing to turn the TV down or knowing they need to tap me on the shoulder to get my attention because my headphones are in to tune them out: my favorite two people in the world (behind Skylar and Alexis – but let's not mention that) Renee and Ava. You know I love you guys and we all know that this wouldn't have been possible without you. But I have bad news… this is only the first book, there are still five-ish to go, so I'll be absent just a little longer.

And thanks to you – the reader, for buying this book and helping make my dream come true! I hope you enjoy my book and will tell me everything you loved or didn't about it.

1

Xirokambi, Southern Peloponnese, Greece
3rd waning, Moon of Gamelion, 528bc

The dark, three-sided shape burned bright against the pale olive skin of her left shoulder, mocking me with its presence. Her mark was the same as mine, the same as my mother's and her mother's before and her mother's before that, all the way back to the beginning of our line. I did not know how many there had been before me but I had wished, hoped, there would be none after.

I held her as she cried, so tiny and fragile. She quieted when Leandros wrapped her in a blanket. She was mine, ours, theirs; the knowledge of that last truth terrified me.

With eyes of the brightest blue, they matched her father's and she stared up, capturing my red ones with such intensity. Tendrils of dark hair lay across her brow and down to the nape of her neck, slick with the memory of her birth. She had the roundest cheeks and most perfect lips, both tinted in hues of pink. But that one symbol, that dark mark on her skin, haunted me. It reminded me of where I had come from, of who I truly was. Of who *she* might one day become.

Those who did not know of my past would assume it was a birthmark, matching the one on my shoulder. How many nights had I laid awake while Leandros slept, wishing and hoping that our child would not bear it? I had allowed his love, his words, to convince me that she would not. I had wanted to believe him, to believe that our union would alter the line. But it had not. I would always know the truth, as would he, and we could never tell our daughter what it truly meant.

Leandros' voice brought me from my thoughts. "She is beautiful," he whispered.

He gazed at our child with such adoration that for a moment I forgot my fears and simply basked in the ardor that shone from his eyes. He was my dearest love, the only man I had ever wanted. The only man I would have dared flee my family with. He was everything to me.

"She has your eyes," I said with a smile.

"And your mouth," he replied, returning my grin.

I dropped my eyes back to our child, my smile fading. "She also has my mark. We can only hope that with half-mortal blood, she is free of the curse."

Leandros drew the small blanket away from the baby's shoulder and nodded.

"We agreed that if she had it, we would never tell her what it meant. You *are* still prepared to keep the knowledge from her, are you not?" I asked desperately.

"Of course, Zita. We shall keep her safe and far from your family, protecting her no matter the cost," he said, resettling the blanket.

I exhaled. I should not have doubted him; he loved me as deeply as I loved him. He would do whatever he could to keep us all safe. The arrival of our daughter only strengthened that, I saw it in the set of his face.

"We should name her Skylar," I said with a smile.

"Skylar," he repeated. "It is as beautiful as she."

Fierce agony suddenly plunged deep into my back, high up on my shoulder blades. The mark on my shoulder burned hot. I screamed, thrusting Skylar into Leandros' arms. No! They could not know of her, they must not find her.

"What is it? What is wrong?" Leandros asked; his hand immediately at my shoulder.

"My family have found us, they are coming. I can feel it."

"How?"

"My mark. It burns with the knowledge."

"How did they find us?"

"I do not know. There is little time before they arrive. They shall make me kill you."

"They cannot, they gave their word to Ares th—"

I shook my head. There was no time to tell him all I could feel. I cried out again, clutching at my arm. "He has given them permission," I replied through gritted teeth.

"Do they know of our child?"

I shook my head, rocking back and forth against the pain. "I cannot tell, but they shall be here at any moment. You must take Skylar and go far away."

"But …"

"Take her. Keep constantly on the move, just as we have these past moons, never stay in one place for too long. Please. If they find her with the mark, they shall take her back and raise her as one of their own."

"Then you must join us as soon as you are able," Leandros said, lifting my chin with his finger.

"Of course," I replied, knowing it would not be so. Leandros handed Skylar back to me and rushed about, collecting items he believed we would need. "Hide the cloths from her birth," I added.

He only nodded in reply, throwing the bloodied material into the fire before returning to his task. I held Skylar to my chest, kissing her soft forehead and taking in the smell of her.

"I am so sorry. This is not how I wished for it to be. But you must know this: I shall never forget you. I love you my darling. Forever." I whispered the words to my daughter, knowing there would be no more between us in this life.

Leandros returned to my side. I passed Skylar to him. He bent down, kissing me fiercely on the mouth, and I felt the slight tremor as his lips pressed against mine.

"I shall see you soon," he said quietly.

I managed a smile, nodding as he crossed to the door. He looked back once, then drew a deep breath and walked out, the wood shutting behind him with a soft thud.

The sharp, stabbing pains at my back increased in intensity the closer my family got. Even from such a distance, I could hear the flap of their wings. Mine threatened to emerge in response, but something held them beneath the skin. I realized it was that action causing the torturous discomfort.

I screamed again, digging my nails into the earth beneath my fingers. The owner of the house, Sotiris, entered the room.

"What is it?" he asked. "Is it the baby? Where is Leandros?"

"You must run, please. Go far from here."

"What do you speak of? What is that noise?" he asked, lifting his head to search the empty air above him.

"Danger," was the only reply I gave.

My family arrived outside, announcing their presence with a deafening screech. The small room lit up. Through the window, tall flames leapt, and though I could not see their tops, I knew they would reach high into the sky. "Go," I told Sotiris again, and this time he did not hesitate.

The straw roof ignited above me, the unseen force censoring my wings and rendering me unable to move. Such power could only be wielded by our master, though I could not feel him nearby.

"Find them!" a voice commanded.

I did not immediately recognize the speaker but three of my kin entered the house. Two hoisted me up by my arms and dragged me roughly outside.

A large group had come, twenty at least; I looked for my mother, but she was not among them. With hair the color of ravens, long and as tangled as my own, their faces and bodies resembled women. Large black wings erupted from their shoulder blades, flapping as the wings of birds did, mine remaining trapped beneath my skin.

I was swept up into a vertical sphere of wind; my cousin Canace commanding the element (though I had never known her to be able to do so before) and the Keres around her.

"Where is the boy you defied your family to be with?" she asked, smiling wickedly, her hair whipping about her face.

I did not answer. Canace would take much pleasure in my demise, of that I was certain. We were of similar age, but Ares had said it would be *my* mother's line that would carry his Chosen One, not hers. Over the winters Canace had attempted to obtain my power for herself. I had always had Ares' protection from her. Clearly tonight I would not.

Canace turned to the gathered group. "Find him!" she shouted.

She had barely uttered the words when the third Ker who had entered the burning building emerged with Sotiris. The roof collapsed behind them, the walls crumbling beneath its weight as the fire consumed all with an unstoppable need.

"Forgive me," I whispered to Sotiris.

He did not hear me over his frightened pleas for life.

Canace approached, picking him up by the back of his ash-smudged chiton. "So, this is the boy you defied us for?"

"No, I am not the one," Sotiris said. "She came to me w–"

"He is my Leandros. My lover," I cut him off. "He is the one I defied my family and the proud history of the Keres for."

Grandmother Rizpah stepped forward, the usually black symbol on her left shoulder that marked us as kin glowing red. Canace gave her a triumphant smile. Grandmother nodded in return and sent two long flames to engulf myself and Sotiris. I writhed as the heat singed my skin.

"No!" I cried, attempting to call forth my wings and break free of the wind and flames.

Tears wet my cheeks. I knew this was to be my end. I hoped Leandros had gone far and fast. I prayed our daughter would grow outside the reach of my family, never to know what had been foretold.

My grandmother recalled the flames to her hand as Canace addressed me again. "You shall kill this boy who has brought you such shame and you shall experience his pain as your own. Do you understand?"

I nodded and Canace released me from the wind.

"Do it now," she commanded.

At once, my wings sprung from my shoulders. Sudden hunger flooded my veins.

"I am so sorry," I murmured.

I leapt, ripping apart Sotiris' flesh with sharp claws and pointed teeth. His blood filled my mouth, soothing and sating me at the same time as it scalded my throat and stomach. Where I drove my teeth into his skin, my own body stung, but I did not stop until his head and limbs were separated from his body.

Panting, I straightened, wiping blood from my face as my wings retreated again. The group clustered around me. Canace rested her hand on my shoulder. A sneer creased her features as she ran her finger across my collarbone.

"Pathetic," she muttered, ripping the amulet from my neck. "You do not deserve to carry the Chosen One's line. Kill her," she ordered.

The pack, led by my grandmother, dove on me in a frenzied feeding attack.

My kin. Those I had once called friends. Those I had spent days over the battlefields with. Those I had celebrated with. Those I had loved. They bit and tore at me as we had once torn at the mortals together. Charged. Feverish. Insatiable.

I felt the pain as their teeth shredded my body, but the tears in my heart were far greater than the physical wounds they inflicted. I screamed, kicked, scratched. I knew I could not overpower them, yet I fought all the same. I fought because once it was all I had ever known. I fought because I would never see my daughter grow. I fought because I would never kiss the man I loved or make love to him again. I fought for as long as I could, but soon my limbs were severed, my blood drained. My screams no more than gasps.

I closed my eyes, succumbing to my death with nothing louder than a whimper.

2

19 winters later
Spercheios River Valley, Region of Malis
3rd rising, moon of Anthesterion, 509BC

I kept my face as close as I could to the flapping of Skotos' dark mane above my shield. The winter wind rushed past me, chilling my nose and making my eyes water. The man behind me was gaining; I could hear his stallion's snorting pants. I gripped the reins tightly around the solid javelin in my right hand, my heart keeping time with Skotos', his movements steady and certain as I drove him faster.

The large rock ahead approached quickly, but the man and his horse drew almost level, the white streak covering its tan nose at my shoulder. I squeezed Skotos' flank between my thighs and he lengthened his strides again. We pulled ahead.

Finally we reached the rock and I smiled, sitting up and pulling hard on the reins at Skotos' neck, drawing him to a standstill.

"That run was far closer than the last two," my father said with a wide smile as he pulled up his own horse.

"Indeed. Had it been much further to the boulder, I believe you would have overtaken us," I replied.

"Perhaps I shall be victorious the next run."

"Perhaps," I agreed as we dismounted. "But the animals deserve water before we attempt another."

It felt good to be back atop Skotos after the laborious travelling over the Evrytania Mountains the past four days. The highest elevations of the mountains were covered with grasslands, as opposed to the forests that dominated the lower areas, but they were slippery with snow and hidden obstacles and we could not ride our stallions. Had either Skotos or Skaris become lame, we would have had to leave them there to die and neither me or my father were prepared to do that. I had almost moaned in delight when I saw the Spercheios Valley spread out in front of us when we woke with Helios' light that morning, immediately challenging my father to a race.

"The run shall have to wait for another day," Father said, covering his face with water. "We shall find Trachis up ahead on the other side of Mount Oetaea." He pointed to the named peak and I followed his gaze as I took my shield from my arm and lay it beside my javelin on the grassy bank of the river.

"Are the paths over the mountain well-travelled?" I asked as I knelt down. I splashed the freezing water over my cheeks and rubbed it along the back of my neck beneath my hair.

"I do not know but we do not have to traverse the mountain; we can follow the valley around it to the town."

"That is welcome news. Are you still in agreeance that we leave at the first sign King Agrias intends to do us harm?"

"I am. If he truly is allied with the Epirotes who fought against us at Stratos, you know it is easier to take revenge on a small number of belligerents, rather than a larger army. He may do so to send a message to Cleomenes and the men who fought with us at Stratos."

"I hope his true intentions do not remain hidden for long," I nodded.

"As do I," Father agreed. "Come, allow us to continue."

"What do you know of Trachis itself?" I asked as I stood and readjusted my cuirass.

"Not much, though I understand it is far smaller than either Athens or Sparta. Where those cities house up to one hundred and twenty thousand citizens and slaves, Trachis has perhaps only twenty thousand."

I picked up my weapons and took Skotos' reins, giving the chestnut stallion a gentle tug. He followed obediently, black tail swishing, his breath no longer ragged with the exertion of his exercise.

"There is a temple outside the town between the Asopos River and the famed hot springs, I believe you shall enjoy those. The river that runs down from the mountains is said to be as hot as a bath; I expect I shall find you there as often as time permits," he added with a grin.

"I always enjoy the heat of a bath when the opportunity arises," I agreed, returning his smile. "How far are they?"

"A candlemark or two from the palace. We shall explore them togeth–"

A scream split the air, followed immediately by the sound of metal against metal. Without thought, I fisted my hand in Skotos' mane, jumping up and kicking my heels in before I was properly astride him. Father mounted Skaris in the same manner and we galloped away from the river.

I pulled Skotos to a halt as we rounded the base of the mountain and dismounted beneath a large laurel tree. Positioning my shield at my left side, I felt for the xiphos at my thigh should I require it instead of my javelin.

My focus sharpened, my senses livening as I stood in the shadow of Mount Oetaea, surveying the scene. The voices and metallic echoes quieted, though men still battled in front of me. The distinct spicy-sweet smell of rosemary drifted up from the trampled bushes to my right, slightly masking the scent of wet grass and another fragrance I could not name. Sparse vegetation of olive and laurel trees dotted the area, the mountain's base lined with large rocks and boulders.

A soldier lay on the ground, his eyes wide as though surprised with the suddenness of his death. His spear and shield were still in his hands; his grip slack on both. I was surprised to find I recognized his clothing and armor; a short chlamys over linen body armor that reached his mid-thigh, leather greaves covering his shins, feet dressed in scuffed sandals. He was an Epirote. A large hole split the armor above his heart, allowing blood and life to drain from his body. I studied his face but did not recognize him as anyone I had faced or seen flee from the battle at Stratos.

Nearby, two soldiers parried and defended against the other, their feet sliding in the dirt beneath. Their swords met, one obtaining the advantage over his opponent before being pushed away again. They stood, watching and waiting, deciding whether their next move should be one of attack or defense. Both held shields with mirroring designs – an eagle standing proudly in the center. Another indication they belonged to the same Epirote tribe.

A man, dark-haired, handsome and obviously important sat on the ground, kept in place by the end of a long spear held at his throat. A cut above his eye bled furiously, meeting the blood of his sliced lip and dripping over the end of his chin. He wore a long, woolen himation of brilliant orange, bordered with an intricate design along its lower hem. I could not make out the exact pictures, but they appeared to depict some sort of hunting scene. His eyes met mine briefly before returning to the last pairing of the group.

A long himation was gracefully wrapped around a slender body and I did not need to see the face of the wearer to know that the body belonged to a woman. The yellow cloak covered her from head to ankle, joyfully embroidered with vines and long leaves, secured at her waist with a slender girdle. The design favored her curves in a way that only came with having the finest materials, and the knowledge of how to wear such a garment. The cloth draped her head, concealing the color of her hair, but a veil had been pushed back, revealing an off-white length of fabric across her eyes.

The woman appeared to be cowering before the soldier who stood in front of her. He was either fastening or attempting to remove the material covering her eyes. I could not tell exactly which his intent was, though the set of his face did not lead me to believe he was aiding her, and the man on the ground appeared to fear for her.

I counted the stamping, snorting horses nearby. There were eight. I counted only seven people before me. Someone was missing.

I scanned the area, but saw no one else. I returned my eyes to the man and woman. The scene did not appear to make sense. The soldiers all wore the same uniform, and had the same shield designs, but there was clearly division amongst them.

The external noises returned as the soldier with the woman turned, catching sight of Father and me.

"By the gods," he whispered.

His dark hair lay low on his brow. A long scar ran from his hairline, down his cheek and over the point of his chin in an angry, raised line. His face resembled that of the man on the ground and I realized they must be closely related.

He pushed the woman behind him in a gesture akin to possession rather than protection, drawing a sword from his waist as he regained his composure. "To whom do you claim your allegiance?" he demanded as the woman stumbled and fell awkwardly to the ground.

It was not the first time Father and I had been asked such questions. Father's height of almost seven feet and mine of six, often caused fear or resentment amongst those we met.

"The king of Trachis. King Agrias," Father replied, arriving beside me.

"He sent you?"

"Yes," Father answered. "And you would be?"

Before he could answer, the man held in place with the spear at his throat grabbed it, jamming it back into the stomach of his captor, doubling him over. The finely-dressed man got to his feet and charged toward the scarred soldier.

Brothers perhaps, I thought, as in profile they appeared even more akin to one another. He relieved the soldier of his sword and rammed into him, both falling to the ground, screaming insults and unintelligible words.

One of the soldiers to my right dropped to the ground, blood spurting from his throat. The other began in our direction, sword raised.

Father adjusted his shield, preparing to meet his attack. "Get the girl, Skylar. Head for Trachis," he yelled.

I nodded, shook my shield free of my arm and took off. The winded soldier was on his feet again, the scarred man's sword in his hand. I gripped my javelin tighter and thrust it towards his stomach, then his chest. He evaded both, bringing the sword down and chopping into my weapon. The wood did not split, but the sword stuck deep. I released the end I held and as he attempted to free his blade, I took advantage of his distraction, drawing my own sword and driving it deep into his stomach. Leaving it where it was, I continued on, reaching the woman and scooping her up off the ground.

"You shall be safe now, I give you my word," I told her. She nodded and wrapped her arms around my neck.

The scent of her invaded my senses; a combination of flowery sweetness and a spicy undercurrent. I breathed it in, closing my eyes as her body trembled against my own.

"Thank you," she whispered, her fingers knotting at the nape of my neck.

I opened my eyes again, dropping them to the exposed arm wrapped around me. Across the light-colored skin of her forearm were four long, purple bruises, ugly and harsh against the smooth flesh. I drew a sudden breath as my anger rose.

I stepped towards the nearest horse but before I could place her atop the beast, the two grappling men crashed into us. I reeled back, steadying myself and setting the woman down again.

I reached for my xiphos, momentarily forgetting it was no longer at my side. The men stood, arms wrapped around one another as they wrestled. I approached, tearing them apart and pushing each to the ground, hard.

The woman screamed. I turned. Her hands were beneath the hood on her head but it was not that reason that caused her panic. The man with my xiphos stuck in his stomach held her by the ankle. She shook her foot, but could not break his grip. I rushed to her side, slamming my foot down on the soldier's forearm, the bones snapping as his fingers sprung open. He screamed in pain and I lifted the woman once again. I carried her back to Skotos, returning her to her feet and reaching out to wipe the tears from her cheek.

"I shall take the cloth from your eyes then take you and your friend to Trachis on my horse."

She nodded her reply. I slipped my fingers beneath the warm material, careful not to catch them in the fine strands of brown hair that escaped and tickled my bared arms as I attempted to undo the knot. I loosened it as her cold hands covered mine.

A rustling caught my ear. I looked up, barely having time to push the woman out of the way before a body descended from the tree above, bringing with it the sharp point of a spear. It found its mark deep in my flesh between my neck and the protection of the armor at my right shoulder.

I cried out, falling to my knees with the agony. My vision dimmed. The ground shimmered as tears sprang to my eyes. Were those hooves approaching? Perhaps it was just the clatter of my own heartbeat. Blood rushed in my ears, drowning out the panicked voices of those around me. All sound outside my body began to fade and I could no longer make sense of anything.

The woman. The heady scent of her perfume. The trembling of her body as I held her. The color of her hair as it lay across my arm; image after image flashed before me.

My pain was gone. My limbs heavy. My eyes drooped. I could not stay awake any longer. My eyes closed. I fell forward, unable to protect my face as I slammed against the ground.

There came a shout of "No!"

It was the woman with the beautiful brown hair. I could not open my eyes.

Darkness claimed me.

3
Palace of Trachis, Region of Thermopylae

Dim, flickering light jumped outside my closed eyelids. My head pounded, limbs heavy and unwilling to move. The pain at my neck was excruciating, hot where the rest of me was cold.

"I have seen injuries akin to this before," a deep voice said.

"And?"

A pause.

"Not one of those men survived the night."

A sharp intake of breath.

"I shall send for our finest healer, a man by the name of Gnosidicus. She shall not die here Leandros, not this day."

The darkness came again.

*

The sweet smell of flowers and spices tickled my nose. Fingers skittered along my arm. Warm breath fluttered the hair at my ear with soft words.

"Do not die. Please. You cannot. You must not."

*

"I have learnt much about Trachis since we have been here. Though we are in an Athenian region, it is not a city-state of Athens. King Agrias is

Macedonian born and has brought many of the customs of his people to the south.

"The Macedonians name kings in each town or village they conquer and call their own. There is still a degree of responsibility to answer to the king of Macedonia at Aigai, but ultimately each is responsible for his own territory.

"To the north-west, Epirus is divided into a number of smaller tribes; the Athamanes, Thesprotians, Chaonians and the Molossians. The Illyrians are further north of Epirus and have their own tribes, including the Taulantii and Dassaretii."

*

A voice, slightly rasping, an urgent whisper. "You must see past the broken mortal body. See what is inside her, feel her blood running through you. You see how she differs from all others of our kind as it was said she would." A hand touched my shoulder. "She carries the mark. She *is* the one you have waited for. We cannot allow her to die, Master. Not when you have waited so long."

"Why did we not know of her when she was first born?" a deep, male voice asked. "How was she able to live without our knowledge all those winters?"

"I cannot say for certain, though perhaps the mortal bloodline masked what we feel each time one of our line is birthed."

"There can be only one to whom she belongs," his voice was cold.

"Yes, Master."

"Your daughter," he noted.

"Yes, Master," she repeated.

"And the Bessoi tribesman; he is also alive. He hid this child all along."

"I should have gone myself that night but I … I was weak, sending my mother to do the job I could not. I beg your forgiveness, Master, if I had known …"

"It matters not now," the man replied. Leather creaked. A breath of air brushed my face. Warm fingers closed around my left arm just below my shoulder. Beyond my closed lids, brightness lit the room. I gasped as the tingling sensation swept through my body. "We shall know soon enough," he murmured.

*

A long, purple himation entered my blurred vision. Bared feet, large and dusty; a man's. Smaller ones beside, neat, feminine with more purple above them. My throat burned with thirst but I could produce no relief for it when I attempted to swallow, the movement sending waves of pain down into my chest. I closed my eyes against it.

Warm fingers caressed my forearm and hand.

"Shall she wake soon?" a melodic voice asked above me.

"I do not know. In truth I did not expect her to see out her first night here, but she has proven herself strong. Perhaps a few more days shall see it so."

"She must wake. She cannot die," the soft voice answered.

"Gnosidicus has done all he can, the rest is up to her."

Their conversation ended and one set of footsteps receded. The second person made no noise, nor movement for many moments. Not until warm skin brushed my cheek.

"Please wake up, I beg it of you," the woman whispered.

I caught the sweet aroma of flowers. The scent familiar, but I could not place it before I fell into the darkness again.

*

Voices. Two females, speaking softly, friendly. The throbbing in my head had dulled, but still my limbs would not obey my commands to move. Footfalls approached and a third voice entered the conversation; sharp and accusatory.

"You keep Melanthios waiting. Go now and visit him and your father."

"Melanthios can wait, she needs me," the melodic voice I had come to recognize replied.

"She has not woken in almost a week, indeed she may not wake at all. You cannot aid her in her recovery. You have other matters to attend."

"I shall spend as much time as I wish with her. What is *your* sudden interest in her?"

"Alexis, go. I shall stay with her. Do not anger Melanthios," the second voice soothed.

The third voice answered as though the second had not spoken.

"She grew without a mother's guidance. If she wakes I shall teach her to use a loom, to find a husband and a home."

"You cannot truly believe such tasks would interest her?"

"In time I believe they shall."

"Why now show concern as a mother should?"

I wanted to speak, but my mind clouded and I joined Hypnos' realm once again.

*

My father's voice drifted into my slumber. "We find ourselves within the greater region of Thermopylae. The name Thermopylae means 'Hot Gates' and refers to the springs I spoke of on our way here. You may recall when we travelled through the Isthmus many winters ago, I mentioned the town of Thermae. Its name means hot and it is also home to a heated spring. I never had the chance to tell you how Thermopylae's water came to be that way, so I shall do so now, though I still do not know if you can hear me.

"It is said that long ago Heracles jumped into the river in an attempt to wash off the hydra poison infused in the cloak that he could not take off. The river turned hot and has stayed that way ever since."

"I feel as though I have been bitten with hydra's poison," I said, hoarsely.

I opened my eyes to find my vision finally clear. Father was by my side, a chuckle escaping his lips as he squeezed my hand. I lay on my stomach on a hard bed, my ankles and the top of my head overhanging each end, my arms dangling down the sides.

I raised my neck; it was painfully stiff, but thankfully obeyed my wish. A marbled wall stood not two feet from my head, a small window high above.

"Thank the gods," he whispered.

"Or someone," I replied, the unfamiliar rasping voice I had heard flittering in, and immediately out, of my mind. I gripped my father's hand and rose.

"Steady," he murmured, taking my elbow.

A second pair of arms circled my waist and I swung my legs around to sit upright on the bed. The floor was patterned with mosaic tiles, partially obscured in one corner by a large pile of bloodied cloths and a clay basin.

A woman moved into my line of vision. Dark haired, brown-eyed. Regal.

"Welcome to Trachis, Child," she smiled. Hers was the third voice I had heard when I last woke.

I managed a smile, though my face was stiff to do so. "Thank you," I replied, clearing my throat.

"I shall fetch you some wine," she said.

I nodded and she moved away.

"Are you warm enough?" Father asked. A thick himation draped the bottom half of my body. My cuirass had been removed; bandages replacing the bronzed armor around my torso.

"My shoulders are a little cold," I replied. "Are you well? Are we safe?" I added in a whisper.

"I am and we are," he replied just as quiet before fetching a second himation and settling it across my shoulders.

I reached up to gather it at my chest, surprised by the discomfort in my sides. I sucked in a deep breath.

"Allow me to aid you," he said, drawing the ends of the himation together. "The healer says you have several broken ribs."

The woman returned and placed a full skyphos to my lips. I covered her hands with my own, tipping the cool liquid quickly into my mouth, choking slightly as I gulped it down, which sent more sharp pain through my sides.

"How did I come by those? Last I remember, the soldier dropped from the tree and speared me," I asked when I had drunk all I could.

"After you were felled he kicked at you until I drove my javelin through his neck," Father replied.

"I understand that warriors enjoy discussing their wounds and speaking of how they eluded Hades once again, but speak no more of it for the moment. Your daughter must focus on her recovery."

"Apologies, Queen Melina," Father said, lowering his head slightly in her direction as she sat the cup on a nearby table.

"Apologies," I echoed, wiping specks of escaped wine from my lips. "Tell me, the young woman in the yellow himation, the man dressed in orange, do they join us here?"

Father hesitated, but finally nodded. "The woman, yes. She is well, no more than cuts and bruises."

"And the man?" I prompted.

"He could not be saved."

I dropped my head, disappointment settling stone-like in my stomach. I had failed him, I had failed them both. I pushed myself off the small bed, pain shooting up my arms, across my back and down my legs as I did so. I drew a shallow breath and limped across the cold floor.

"Sky, please, return to bed, you are weakened," Father said, his hand at my elbow again.

"I should have aided him further," I insisted, my pace increasing. "I should have placed her on the nearest horse and sent her away. I could have saved them both. I should have."

I replayed the scene in my head; the blindfolded woman in the woolen cloak, the soldier's grip at her ankle. The swordsman with his throat slashed. The tumbling men. The soldier dropping from the tree. I squeezed my eyes shut, reeling as a wave of sickness washed over me.

"You saved *her*," Father countered.

"It was not enough," I shouted. "I should have …" I managed nothing further, collapsing into my father's arms as Hypnos claimed me.

4

I woke to a darkened room. A torch flickered against the wall, throwing long shadows across the floor. I was on my stomach once again but my head no longer spun and my pain had diminished considerably.

Soft footfalls sounded and I closed my eyes, uncertain I wanted anyone to know I was awake again yet. Warm fingers worked deftly, holding out the length of material wrapped around my upper body and changing the cloths at the wound between the nape of my neck and my shoulder. My attendee moved around the small bed, the familiar scent of flowers, *roses* I realized, and that spicy undertone following. The blindfolded woman.

I opened my eyes. Dainty feet stood facing me, exposed beneath a long, green chiton. They did not move and I wondered if it was the length of my body she stared at or something else in the room.

I inhaled deeply, raising my arms to grip the edges of the bed. The discomfort I had experienced at my sides the last time I woke was no longer shooting; reduced instead to a dull ache.

One warm arm wrapped around my waist, breasts pressing against my shoulder. "Thank you," I murmured.

The woman stepped back, though her hand remained on my arm a moment longer.

I raised my eyes to hers and met a shade of the deepest green I had ever known. I could not breathe as I took in the sight of her, the swift grip of arousal surprising me. The light of the torch danced in the emerald depths, making them sparkle. Her dark brown hair was clipped back in an elaborate twist, lips plump without being overly so. Her thin nose complimented the rest of her features and a pink hue appeared high on the fine cheekbones under my intense gaze. A soft gasp escaped her lips, parting them ever so slightly.

"You are the one from the fight," I eventually said, my heart hammering in my chest.

"Yes," she replied.

I swallowed, still unable to take a full breath of air. "What is your name?"

"Alexis. Princess Alexis of Trachis."

"You are the Princess? I ... of course," I stammered, dropping my eyes from hers.

There could be no denying her lineage. I had observed the way she carried herself that day in the valley. I attempted to bow in her direction, but my ribs announced that they had not completely healed yet. I put a hand to them as she laid hers against my shoulder, halting my progress.

"Do not injure yourself further for me, please."

I straightened, but did not meet her eyes, my father's words about the man's death reminding me I must make amends.

"I must ask your forgiveness, Princess. I could not save the man who was with you in the valley," I said, the pulsing between my thighs slowing.

"Basileios," she supplied. "My husband."

"No," I whispered. "My deepest apologies." I closed my eyes again, bowing my head as bitter disappointment flared in my stomach. I had allowed not just a man, but a prince to be killed, someone's husband, a mother's son. Perhaps even someone's father. I shook my head.

"You must not hold yourself accountable for what happened," Alexis said, her finger gently raising my chin.

I hesitated before opening my eyes and meeting the princess' again.

"The blame of Basileios' death does not lie with you, but with the one whose sword ended his life," she murmured, holding my gaze.

"I doubt King Agrias would see it the same way. He sent for my father and I specifically and I cannot imagine he shall be impressed with me when I could not even save the Prince from a handful of soldiers," I said, anger heating my blood.

"To me, what you did was everything. You did not know who we were, or the circumstances of the fight, yet still you aided us, me, without question."

"I knew one soldier was absent, I counted the horses. I should have searched for him. I should not have been injured or surprised so easily, I am better than that," I countered.

"Skylar," she said, taking my hand firmly in her own. "I do not hold you responsible for Basileios' death and neither does my father."

I opened my mouth to challenge her, but faltered when she squeezed my fingers. She said I did not carry the blame for Basileios' death, but how could I not? From the moment I had heard her scream, she and her husband had become my responsibility.

"Do not remain here, Princess. I do not deserve your company," I finally said, retrieving my hand and turning my face and body from her.

Alexis did not leave, reaching out to draw her fingers over the mark on my left shoulder instead. I shivered slightly at the touch. "What is this?" she asked quietly.

"It has always been there," I replied, wishing the gentle caress did not serve to both soothe and send fire through my blood in equal measures.

"It is unusual," she murmured. "Just as you are a very unusual woman," she added, tapping lightly where her fingers lay.

I frowned, uncertain of the intention behind the remark. "If I am so unusual perhaps you would be wise to keep clear of me, as girls have always been advised to do … and why do you attend me, why am I not tended by one of your slaves?" I asked sharply.

Alexis drew an audible breath before answering. "We Macedonians are not as fond of using slaves as the Greeks are," she replied.

I opened my mouth again but the bustling entrance of a short old man and a well-muscled soldier prevented further words.

"Ah, Alexis, here you are. I told Melanthios this is where I suspected you would be. And I see our patient is also awake, that is happy news," the older man said with a grin.

The soldier named Melanthios only grunted in reply, his face darkening as our eyes met – both of us recognizing the other from the fight the day I was injured. Father had said we were safe, but I still did not know if Agrias was allied with the Epirotes who invaded Stratos. I searched my memory, but could not remember seeing Melanthios there.

"Come, Alexis, you and I are due to have words," Melanthios said, placing a hand at her elbow. "There is nothing for you here."

I bristled at his tone, my senses further heightened when Alexis stiffened at his touch. I wanted to apologize for my words to her, and to keep her in the room, if only to learn of Melanthios' relationship to her. But before I found suitable words, Alexis increased the pressure on my arm and I met her eyes.

"I shall call on you again soon," she promised.

"There is no need now she is awake. Gnosidicus knows what he is doing," Melanthios growled.

"You know where to find me," I nodded, watching as Alexis allowed Melanthios to draw her away.

"The princess has watched over you closely, barely leaving your side since you arrived. I only hope it does not cause her issues with Melanthios," Gnosidicus mused. "Allow me to inspect your wound."

I was surprised by his frank admission, yet I knew his words to be true. Her gentle voice and perfume had always been there when I woke. Even in my weakened state I had known of her, though I did not know who it was that kept me company.

"She should not have," I muttered. The old man either did not hear me or chose not to reply, concentrating instead on what he saw.

"Lift your arm," he directed.

I did so slowly so as not to aggravate my ribs. "How long have I been here?" I asked.

"A little over a week," he replied. "Good, you may lower it again. You gave your father quite a scare, yet I shall admit that to me you are something of a wonder."

"Why?" I asked, returning my arm to my side.

"This injury is not one that any person – soldier or commoner – recovers from, yet you not only appear to be recovering well, but I believe you shall have almost full use of your arm again."

"King Agrias asked me here for a reason and I shall not disappoint him any more than I may have already."

"If that is your intention, you must allow your body time to heal and rest. You cannot engage in training with your father or our soldiers for at least a moon."

"A moon?" I cried.

"At least," he nodded.

"What am I expected to do until then?"

"That is not for me to decide, but if you do not rest the arm you favor to hold spear or sword, you may find you can never use it again in the same manner."

"Fine," I agreed grudgingly. Being rendered unable to ever raise a weapon against an enemy was worse than the thought of staying still. But only just.

"I shall return in a few days to see how you are healing. Lie down again. For now, Hypnos is your friend."

"I do not believe I shall be able to sleep any more tonight," I replied, but did as asked and returned to my stomach.

The old man covered me with a himation, tucking it firmly around my legs and shoulders. "Rest is what your body requires. Gift it with that and it shall reward you with what you ask of it in return."

"Thank you for seeing to me since I arrived."

The healer only nodded before leaving.

I watched the torchlight flickering across the wall and floor of the room as I had before Alexis – before the Princess of Trachis – had arrived.

Those brilliant green eyes swam before me. My heart quickened and my body warmed as it had when I had met her gaze. The way her lips had parted and how soft they appeared. I wondered how it would feel to kiss them. I knew I should not consider such ideas, but I was helpless to deny the desire; I had never been as stirred by the very sight of a woman before. I already knew how her scent affected me; I had paused to savor it, albeit momentarily, in the valley.

She was beautiful and obviously kind, tending me even though I had not saved her husband. Her *husband*, I felt the slightest hint of jealousy at the word. He had been allowed to kiss her, to hold her, as I found myself wishing I could. The purple bruises on her arm; had he inflicted them? Anger heated my skin at the idea. I knew there were those who took pleasure in harming beautiful women, some because they could, others because they believed it was their right. I hoped her clothing hid no other such injuries. I wanted to ask her if they did, desperate to hear that melodic voice when she answered.

Of course I knew I could never ask her such personal questions. She was a Princess and it was not my place to request the answers from her; she would confide in those she called friends. Personal secrets had only ever been afforded to my care when the knowledge was directly related to the task I had been assigned.

I sighed. I called no one friend except my father. I must rest as Gnosidicus insisted and when King Agrias revealed his plans for us, I would be ready to stand and fight. My place was amongst soldiers and men as it had been for the past seven winters. There was no reason to attempt to engage the princess further, no matter how much I desired to feel her warm hand on my arm again or how her very presence invoked my body to react.

Alexis and I did not travel similar paths and I had failed in my duty to protect those who belonged to King Agrias' kingdom. I would do well to remember *that* truth, as well the fate that had befallen Kuria when I had shared her bed. I would not seek the princess out while I found myself in Trachis.

5

"You should appear to her; it is time she knew who she was, who we are."

"No. She requires more time to heal. She must build up her strength if she is to aid me in what I seek."

"Can you not simply heal her fully and give her the strength she needs?"

"We do not wish to make the mortals more suspicious than they are. You know her wound was not one she should have survived; we can do no more for now."

"Bu–"

"I said no! I feel the strength in her bloodline. She belongs to us, there is no denying that, but it shall be another few moons until she is ready. You shall wait until I tell you it is time. Do not approach her before. Is that understood?"

"As you wish, Master."

6

I turned from the high window as my father entered my room. "You said we are safe here, you have had words with King Agrias about why he asked us to come?" I asked without preamble.

"We have spoken some and I have shared my worries regarding his alliance with the Epirotes," he replied. "Whilst it is true that they find themselves intertwined, we need not fear he seeks to take revenge for any deed in Stratos."

"Do you think it wise to have spoken so openly with him?"

"I found no hint of lie in his answers, and he wished to wait until you woke to provide us with all the specifics," he nodded.

"I have indeed, for my own daughter has spoken of little else but you since she returned," a second voice replied, the speaker following my father inside.

A purple cloak, elaborately adorned hat and thick boots complimented fine features and dark hair. Eyes several shades lighter than the ones that had sparked my imagination when I woke met mine.

"King Agrias, allow me to introduce my daughter: Skylar."

I held out my arm, intending to take his in the customary Greek grip, but he clasped my hand tightly between his palms instead.

"Skylar, I am pleased to see you awake and recovering so well," he smiled.

"I am pleased to meet you, King Agrias and am most grateful to you; your healer has cared well for me. But I must beg your forgiveness for the loss of Basileios. I asked it of the princess …"

"But she would not accept it?" he finished.

"No," I confirmed.

"And neither shall I," he said, continuing to smile.

"I do n–"

"There is nothing for us to forgive. You returned my daughter safe to me and, as I hope my days are many until I meet Hades in the Underworld, I am grateful I can thank you in person for rescuing her for I would not have wished to wait until then to do so."

I opened my mouth to speak again, but he squeezed my hand and released it.

"My initial intentions for asking you here have altered, but are you well enough to discuss matters?"

"Absolutely," I replied. The king closed the door to my room and I offered both men a space on my bed as I stood opposite them, eager to question the man and form my own opinion on his truth or lies. "Father says you are allied with the Epirote tribe we faced at Stratos."

"The Molossian tribe from Dodona, yes," the king confirmed. "We have been aligned with them for a number of winters through Alexis' marriage to Basileios."

"And how did that come about?" I asked.

"I had wanted to betroth Alexis to my dear friend Thaddeus when she came of age, but he counselled me against it."

"Why? Did he not believe she would make a good wife?" Father asked.

"He believed she would make a fine wife, but all Macedonian betrothals are formed with a specific strategic alliance in mind. Just as mine was to Alexis' mother, so Alexis' had to be when it was her time," Agrias replied. "I once called Macedonia home, and we had always had a peaceful relationship with the Molossians, though they themselves are not a peaceful people. Most of the tribes in Epirus have fierce reputations, but they had never dared challenge the might of Macedonia. For a time, it was the same when I came south."

"And then?" I prompted when the king paused.

"When Alexis was three winters old, we received word that the Molossians had begun to negate their nearest rivals, gaining strength and intending to take the Greek lands to the south of their own. Thaddeus told me the Macedonian betrothal custom was one we should not leave behind and convinced me to go and meet with Andreas – Basileios' father, and head of the Molossian tribe. I proposed an alliance that would ensure he did not attempt to take Trachis or the area around it."

"Alexis' marriage to his son," Father supplied.

"Yes," the king nodded. "Andreas accepted and said he would send his eldest son, Basileios, for Alexis when she reached thirteen winters. The boy was fifteen at the time, and I chose him over the other four."

"As eldest, did he not already have first claim?" I asked.

"Andreas allowed me to meet with each son and decide which I favored. I did not know at the time that he was the eldest, and perhaps Andreas would not have allowed me my choice if it had not been so. But it was decided and when the time came, Basileios arrived and took Alexis back to Epirus as his wife."

"So you remained safe from the Epirotes?" I concluded. The king nodded in reply. "But that is no longer the case?"

"No," Agrias replied with a shake of his head. "The attack at Stratos was the first phase in the Molossian plan to gain more land and influence outside Epirus. Basileios however, wanted none of it. He was not akin to his father and brothers. He was considered weak by them – a failure as he had not been able to give their father an heir by his *Princess wife*. He did not fight when their tribe went to war. He was more peaceable in nature and wanted to relocate to Trachis and sever ties with his family."

"And Melanthios?" Father asked.

I raised an eyebrow at the mention of the warrior's name.

"Ah, yes, in stark contrast to Basileios, is Melanthios, second eldest of Andreas' sons by a single winter and far more barbaric and ambitious. He is the favored son, and closest confidant of the old man." I frowned at his words, but allowed the king to continue. "He seeks glory and power, as well as territory and has been able to successfully convince the Illyrian tribes of the Taulantii and Dassaretii to ally themselves with him. The Macedonian history with our Illyrian neighbors is a long and bloody one, we have battled them for many winters, my great-grandfather killed in one particular war with them."

"Did the Illyrians join the Epirotes at Stratos?" I asked.

"Some of them did, yes, and the intention was to move against us once they controlled Stratos and its lands."

"You are not prepared to stand against them?"

"I am, though if the four tribes marched on us, I do not have the capability to hold them off for long."

"Is that why you sent for us?" Father asked.

"It is," Agrias nodded.

"We are only two people. You command an entire army so what use can we be to you?" I frowned.

"Melanthios was to go to Stratos with his brothers, until he learned of Basileios and Alexis' intention to escape Dodona while the army was gone. He pretended to leave with the rest of the men, but headed east rather than west. He placed two soldiers loyal to him within Basileios' confidence so he would know exactly when they were leaving, and the path they would take."

I recalled the soldiers who stood against one another in the valley – they had all held shields with the same facing designs. The scene now appeared to make sense, as I could not make it when we first arrived. "I remember Melanthios standing before Alexis. At the time I could not tell whether he was working to free the blindfold from her eyes or attaching it."

"He was most definitely tying it," Agrias confirmed. "Melanthios ambushed them and it was he who killed Basileios so he could claim Alexis for his own and force us to become his vassal, rather than his ally."

"I should have killed him then and there so Basileios lived," I murmured.

"Sky, it is not in your nature to kill without unerring proof of injustice or wrongdoing," Father said, shaking his head. "You would not have harmed Melanthios in the valley, not even if you had not been injured. He would have given you no reason to, as he gave me no reason."

"So you did not see Melanthios kill Basileios?" I asked.

"No, I was battling the soldier whose spear stuck you."

"But there would have been no other explanation when Basileios went down," I frowned.

"Be that as it may, I was far more concerned about you. There was much confusion during the scuffle and he appeared genuinely upset that his brother had been lost when Agrias' men appeared soon after. He claimed another of the disloyal soldiers killed Basileios and I had no proof otherwise."

"And what of his behavior since? He appears able to come and go within the palace freely; I cannot believe you have not seen him or had conversations with him."

"I have seen, and spoken to him, on a number of occasions but he has given me no reason to be suspicious of his actions."

My frown deepened as I considered my father's words but I said nothing further on it for the moment. "How can Melanthios claim Alexis as his?" I asked instead. "And how did you learn all this?"

"It is their custom," the king replied before answering my second question. "Alexis; Melanthios spoke of it the day you arrived here."

"So why did you ask us to come?"

"Through messengers, Basileios and I discussed how we might free him and Alexis from his father's tribe, and from the claim his brothers would have on Alexis upon his death. We both knew that the dissention would cause a war between our towns, but he was hoping to convince the other two largest tribes of Epirus – the Thesprotians and Chaonians – to join with us."

"Why do you not simply ask Macedonia for assistance? With their army and yours, would you not be far more powerful than a few small tribes?" Father asked.

"I am not as closely allied with the Macedonians as I once was, and they have joined with another, larger army, and are often too busy doing their bidding to assist me here."

"That does not answer why you sent for us," I noted.

"You speak true," the king nodded. "Before Melanthios arrived, I had intended to offer you coin to go to Dodona and kill him and his younger brothers. The entire tribe if it was needed. I did not want it to be known that I had instigated it, which is why I did not want to send any of my own men."

"That is not a particularly commendable act," I noted.

"No, and the decision weighed heavily on me once I had made it. But I did not believe there was any other choice if I wanted to avoid war for my people."

"You said it *was* your intention to send us to Dodona. What now do you propose?"

"Unfortunately, I do not know. If Melanthios' action to kill Basileios had been known only to him, then I would still ask you to kill him for me. But, his father sanctioned the murder and encouraged Melanthios to claim Alexis and take Trachis."

"He comes with no army and it sounds as though all those in his confidence were killed in the valley, so the risk does not appear too great to me," I mused. "I would still be prepared to go through with your request."

"You are not well enough to carry out any such request," Father growled. "Besides, what of the other brothers? If Andreas ordered Melanthios to kill Basileios, then why would he not give the same request to the next brother, and the next and the next?"

"That is my thought as well," Agrias nodded.

"I need to make amends for allowing Basileios to die, and even in my current state I could slit Melanthios' throat with ease. As you well know," I added, holding my father's stare.

"She is as determined and loyal as you described her to be," Agrias laughed.

"She is," Father acknowledged, though he did not appear as pleased with the knowledge as the king. "Have you discussed the matter with anyone else?" Father added before I could speak again. "The general of your army perhaps? Or another trusted advisor?"

"I have. It was at our recent assembly that I was finally convinced to send assassins into Dodona to negate the threat rather than my own men."

"Who sits in on those proceedings?"

"The assembly is made up of the army if we are at war or the people of our town if we are not. If I were in Macedonia, the council would consist of the most important generals of my army, noble Macedonians known as somatophylakes or personal guards, and others from Macedonian aristocracy I had named as friends or companions of the king for life. Here it is a little different, though I still have my personal guard – Thaddeus – attend, we have only two other Macedonian-born men with us."

"Were they sent by your brother to ensure he knew what was happening here?" Father asked.

"No, Epiktetos and Stavros grew up with Thaddeus and me and once we were settled here, they joined us. Their fathers are Macedonian nobility, so their place on the small council is expected by their families, and as I have continued with that particular tradition also, I have no hesitation in having them form part of it."

"Do they make up the entirety of the small council?" I asked.

"No, the remainder is made up of native Malians; men who were leaders of their tribe before we arrived. Melina's father is amongst the number and I promoted one of their own as a general for our army. You have already met Moeris, Leandros."

"A good man and a fine leader from what I have observed," my father acknowledged.

"Indeed," Agrias nodded.

"You shall recognize him when you meet him also," Father noted, addressing me. "We met him in Sunium when we were last there, amongst other places."

"Ah," I nodded, recalling the named man after a moment.

Sunium was not the first time I had noticed Moeris, but I had confronted him there, demanding he tell me who he worked for and why he was following us. He had not given me the answers I sought, though perhaps it explained how Agrias knew we would be in Stratos when he sent his messenger. I set the knowledge aside for now; there would be time for conversations on the matter later.

"So you shall discuss this new information with your council?" I asked.

"Not with all of them, but with those closest to me certainly. And now that the two of you are aware of how things stand, perhaps we can find a solution together."

"The solution appears simple – kill Melanthios and convince the other Epirote tribes to join you and stand against Andreas if it comes to that. Father and I could leave immediately to organize the alliance," I shrugged.

The king smiled. "I am warmed by your determination, but as your father notes, you are not ready for such travel or exertions. You must allow your body as much time as it needs to heal. Without the knowledge that you can trust your body, you cannot have the strength of mind to defeat an enemy."

"But ..."

"Rest, Skylar," Agrias said, placing a hand on my arm. "Allow us to think the matter over and discuss it together in the coming days. If we are unable to avoid war then I shall delay it as long as possible to ensure you have recovered."

I sighed but nodded, knowing he spoke the truth. Having now heard his words, I could not deny that I felt he spoke true and held no love for the Molossians, just as my father had said and I knew I wanted to aid him however I could. I just had to hope Melanthios would hold off any attack *he* had planned so I could stand against him as Agrias needed when the time came.

7

"May I enter? I have figs and the last piece of bread sweetened with honey," Alexis asked.

I turned from the window, unable to resist a grin. My father had brought me some of the honey-sweetened bread several days ago; it had become an instant favorite. "Please," I nodded, indicating Alexis join me on the bed with her treats.

I had seen the princess only from a distance since both Gnosidicus and Agrias had told me to rest, and despite my earlier resolve to push thoughts of her from mind, I had not been able to. Having her sitting so close reminded me acutely why that was.

I inhaled sharply as she returned my smile, handing me a fig and turning her eyes to the package in her lap. I ate it quickly, eager for the bread. Alexis broke it in half, passing me the larger piece when she realized the fruit was gone already.

I closed my eyes, barely stifling a moan as I bit into the fleshy dough which was still warm from the baker's fire. The bread itself was something I was accustomed to, but the addition of the honey made it appear somehow exotic and new.

"I believe I have found your weakness," Alexis chuckled.

"Mmm-hmm," I replied, opening my eyes to find hers twinkling before me. I felt the heat rise to my face, swallowing quickly as she held out the other half.

"You have it," I said.

She shook her head. "You are the one who needs to regain your strength, I brought it for you."

"I appreciate that, but it is so good, it must be shared. I insist," I replied, closing my hand gently around hers so as not to squash the food she held.

"I shall bring more next time," she promised.

I nodded, releasing her hand as the image of feeding it to her popping unbidden into my head. I cleared my throat and found a loose thread on my tunic to occupy my hands instead. "I saw you riding in the field below the balcony yesterday. The horse was beautiful, is it yours?"

"Yes and I have sorely missed Calla since I left for Epirus. I was not permitted to take her," Alexis replied, finishing her mouthful.

"Calla? That means beautiful, does it not?"

Alexis' cheeks tinged as she nodded, but she smiled. "Most beautiful, yes. I was only six winters old when she was gifted to me, and even then I believed she was the most beautiful horse I would ever set eyes on."

"Ah. She was a present from your parents?"

"Yes," Alexis nodded. "The soldiers found her wandering near Mount Oetaea, lame from a thorn in her foot. They were going to kill her, to put her out of her misery, but my father was with them and said there was no need. He freed the thorn, applied some herbs and when she had made a full recovery, he presented her to me as an early birthing day gift."

"I have seen many horses, though none with her exact coloring," I nodded, recalling the light tan of Calla's body and the brilliant white that covered each leg between hoof and knee and her long mane and tail. "Are there many in the north that share it?"

"I have never seen another," Alexis replied. "Your steed is also very fine."

"You have seen Skotos? Was he injured in the valley?"

"Yes I saw him, he has the pen beside Calla's for the moment and no, he was not injured the day you were."

"I am relieved to hear it. As soon as I am able I shall visit him."

"How did you choose his name?" Alexis asked.

I hesitated, having never shared the story before. It was not that I kept it secret, rather that no one had ever asked it of me before, and I was not accustomed to sharing details of my life with others.

"Skotos means darkness. I found him in the dark when I was almost eight winters old," I finally replied.

"Perhaps I could accompany you now to the stables; you could speak of how you came to have him as we walk."

I hesitated again. "Gnosidicus says I must remain here for the moment, but I thank you for the offer. Perhaps another day." There was nothing I wished for more than to leave the small room, but Alexis' offer felt as if it belonged between friends rather than two people who had just met.

"Oh. Of course, you should rest," she said, putting aside the cloth that had held the bread. She appeared almost disappointed with my answer and, briefly, I considered sharing the story and going to the stables after all.

"Do you visit the agora often?" I asked instead.

"At least once a week," Alexis replied. "Perhaps when Gnosidicus allows, you would join me there for the day?"

"I could," I found myself replying.

"May I ask you something?"

I nodded.

"I have never met anyone as tall as you or your father. All the stories I was told as a child spoke of heroes – of Heracles – who stood taller than any man in Macedonia, but until you, I never met anyone who came close to those stories. And your eyes, I have never seen a shade as brilliant and blue as you both have."

"That does not appear to be a question," I smiled, my cheeks coloring slightly with her words.

"Where are you from? Where were you born? Where do your parents call home?" she grinned.

I drew a deep breath, my smile fading. Though I knew her question was asked only out of curiosity, I had not been asked about my past for many winters. My father had insisted we never speak of where he had been born. I had wondered why he was so adamant but had not questioned his reasons when he first commanded my silence.

"I am from Greece; I do not call anywhere home. My place of birth was not my parents' birthplace and my father and I have no ties to the place that was," I replied stiffly.

"Oh," Alexis murmured. "I wondered if perhaps you were from Thrace, I have heard the Thracians are very tall, but your hair being so dark does not match with what I know of them." I frowned. "The Thracians are Macedonia's closest neighbors to the east, but few of them make their way to the south so I never witnessed it myself," she added.

"I … I did not realize Thrace was so close," I murmured.

Alexis nodded. "It is less than a week's travel from here."

My father's tribe of the Bessoi were indeed Thracians and when King Agrias' messenger had found us in Stratos, my father had hesitated for a long moment before agreeing to travel this far north.

"Skylar?" Alexis asked, reaching for my hand and threading her fingers through mine. "What troubles you? I did not mean to upset you."

With effort I relaxed my brow. "You did not," I assured her, tightening my hand against hers. The feeling of our entwined hands was so natural, so comforting. The skin of her palm was soft where mine was calloused from winters of holding spear and sword. I knew I should not so enjoy the easy touches she bestowed, but neither did I draw my hand away.

"You have travelled much whilst I have only ever seen Trachis and parts of Epirus where Basileios' family is from," she admitted, drawing her thumb across the skin atop my hand.

I drew a breath and though the mention of her husband pierced at me, I allowed it to pass without reference. "You do not enjoy living in a palace, being a Princess?"

"There are aspects I enjoy certainly, but in Epirus I did not live in a palace. Basileios' father is not a king," she replied. "They are a simple tribe, they do not have grand palaces or homes. But there are those who want for more than they have."

"Melanthios," I supplied.

"Yes. He sent men to take Stratos so as to control the lands from Illyria in the north to the Gulfs of Calydon and Corinth in the south."

"It would have been a large victory, that is certain, but we kept Stratos from them. It remains ruled by the Acarnanians with aid from the Aetolians."

"I did not realize you were at Stratos. You fought with them against Melanthios' men?"

"Yes, we were there when your father sent a messenger asking us to come."

"I am glad the Epirotes did not win. It would have spelled trouble for more than just the people of Stratos," she nodded.

"Yes," I agreed.

"I believe the west, and Stratos specifically, to be pretty. Was it?" Alexis asked after a moment of silence.

I shrugged. "Perhaps it could be, though what I saw of it was not. Blood stained dirt, houses and crops burnt to the ground, severed body parts floating down the river."

Alexis sucked in a breath and dropped her eyes. I instantly regretted my uncensored words. I must not speak of such ways with her – it was doubtful she would be accustomed to hearing of them. And, I reminded myself, that even though I had not saved her husband, still she tended me in my recovery and wished to see me; my words must speak of more enjoyable things.

"Apologies, Princess, I did not …"

She shook her head. "Do not be concerned, I understand the world is not always pleasant."

Silence dragged out between us but she did not take her hand from mine, her thumb still caressing me when finally I offered further words.

"Father and I followed a tributary of the Achelous River through the Evrytania Mountains and over Mount Tymphristos on our way here, I found it to be beautiful; clear and gently flowing. I have found Trachis to be the same, the little of it I have seen from my window."

Alexis recovered herself, the eagerness returning to her face. "It is. Have you been to Sparta? To Athens? What are they like?"

I smiled, instantly charmed by her fascination with towns far from where she had grown. "Big. A lot of people, a lot of noise, a lot of politics," I replied, thinking of Athens.

She nodded, taking her fingers and settling them on top rather than between my own. "I imagine you have seen much, met many fascinating people. I have never met a woman who was also a warrior or has so much freedom to travel wherever she wishes and does not have to marry or behave the way other women do. It must be wonderful to be that free."

There was a wistful tone in her voice and I watched her curiously, asking two questions I had told myself I would not. "Your life with Basileios, was it not harmonious? Did he mistreat you?"

Her eyes found mine, holding them as she considered her answer. I was struck by not only her beauty, but her fragility. I did not wish to hear that he had hurt her; knowing I could not do the same to him if he had. My heart beat loudly in my ears as I waited for her answer.

"Our betrothal served its purpose, for the most part," she finally said.

I swallowed, my eyes finding her lips as her tongue moistened them. "You did not answer my second question."

"He did not harm me. I did not fear him." Her chin dipped towards her chest and I followed her line of sight, watching her fingers skim across the tops of mine. "Do *you* wish for a husband? A lover?" she asked quietly.

I could not catch my breath. I raised my eyes and she met them. The green depths pinned me in place as I struggled to form an answer. "I ... I do not wish for a husband," I stammered.

I could not admit to her that the lover's arms I sought did not belong to a man, that they never had. She slipped her fingers between mine again.

"You are fortunate you are able to choose such a path for yourself," she whispered.

I wanted to kiss her, to make her understand my words and show her what I could not say. I enjoyed the feeling of her fingers between mine, the warmth that radiated from her skin. She did not appear afraid to lay hands on me, though I had not paid her for such a privilege. I wanted to know how her skin would feel as it slid against mine.

No, I told myself firmly, dismissing the images. Alexis was a Princess, not a woman who allowed herself to be used for pleasure by men or women. I could not take her to bed. It would spell only danger for her if I did so. I could not allow her so close.

I stood. Alexis followed me to her feet, our hands still twined. "I ... I must ..." I did not know how to finish my sentence, but I knew if I did not move away from her I would do something I should not. I took my hand from hers, but her eyes remained on mine. I could not read all that was on her face, but I could see she had questions.

"Skylar," she said quietly.

I shook my head. "You should go. I must rest," I told her, closing my eyes in an attempt to calm my raging blood.

"Shall I fetch Gnosidicus?" she asked.

"No," I replied, shaking my head once more.

"I shall visit again soon," she promised, her warm hand finding my arm and squeezing briefly before she moved away.

I clenched my jaw to keep my lips shut, desperate to ask her to stay, yet not daring to.

"Oh! Mother, what are you doing here?"

"I could ask the same of you," the queen answered. "Come."

I heard the exchange, but the words were distant. My body was alive. Blood pounded in my ears, my stomach, between my thighs. The yearning radiated to the deepest reaches of my soul. I wanted to run my hands over my body, to imagine they were Alexis' as I rose to the highest point of desire. But my wound would prevent full range of movement and how would I explain what had happened if I caused it to open again? I squeezed my hands into balls, digging my short nails into my palms and attempting to quell the desire flowing through me.

8

When I could no longer hear Alexis and the queen's footsteps, I opened my eyes. I blew out a long breath, realizing that someone leant against the door of my room.

"How long have you been standing there?" I frowned.

"Long enough to see many things," my father replied with a smile. "She cares for you."

"She brought me some honey-sweetened bread that is all."

"So did I, but I do not remember getting the same reaction," he laughed, pushing off the frame and entering the room. "You have always favored the prettier ones for pleasure."

"Do not speak of her as if she is one of them. She is the Princess of Trachis. I would nev–"

"Sky," he said, resting a hand on my shoulder. "I apologize. I meant no disrespect to Alexis, or to you."

"I know," I sighed. "But I would never pursue her, not after … after what happened with Kuria."

"Mmm," he said. "You still think of her; of Kuria?"

"Not as often as I once did, though she has been on my mind since we arrived here."

"You are afraid something similar may occur?"

"No. I would never allow myself close enough to anyone again to invite such an act. Besides, I race to be well enough to assist Agrias in whatever he needs. I do not have time for such dalliances."

"What about simple friendship with Alexis? Would you deny yourself her company because you fear the actions of one man three winters ago?"

I hesitated, taking in a deep breath. I had not considered a friendship with anyone in many winters. I had been content with only my father for company for longer than I could remember.

"Alexis reminds me of Kuria in some ways; she asks many questions about my life," I murmured.

"And do you give her answers?"

"No. Just as I denied Kuria of them, so too I keep them from Alexis, though part of me *does* want to share them with her."

"That is new for you," Father mused.

"Yes," I agreed. "But I am not comfortable with it. What if–"

"Perhaps it shall be a welcome change," Father interrupted gently. "Perhaps you should allow Alexis to know you a little. You cannot live fearing what may never come to pass. If you feel an attraction or wish to spend time with Alexis, then allow yourself to do so. Enjoy the moments you have with her whilst you have them."

I frowned again, but said nothing.

"Perhaps it is time we stopped being so alone. Perhaps we should allow ourselves to remain in one place and find friends; even if they are not those we have spent much time with previously."

"You mean those of royal blood?"

Father nodded.

"Why do you suggest this now?" I asked. "Why are you not concentrating solely on what we came here to do?"

He sighed loudly, sitting on my bed. "I almost lost you, Sky."

"It is not the first time I have been injured during a fight."

"It was not the same as the other times and you know it. You almost *died*. It made me realize we cannot do this forever. *I* cannot do this forever. It is time for a change."

My frown deepened. "Are you ill?"

"No."

"Then I do not understand. I cannot be friends with a princess. I do not belong in a palace. If we were to stay we should be in Trachis itself, or in the barracks with the soldiers. Or perhaps we should be in Thrace."

Father went still. "Thrace?" he repeated.

I nodded. "Is it your home you wish to return to after all these winters?"

"How did you learn we were near Thrace?"

"Alexis. The Thracians are the nearest neighbors to the Macedonians."

"You spoke of my tribe with her, my past?"

"Of course not. But I remember where you told me you were born."

Father exhaled loudly, but did not respond. I pressed ahead, needing to understand his sudden change of heart.

"You and Mother fled Thrace because her family did not approve of your union. But what of *your* family? How did they react? Have you never wanted to return to the mountains you once called home? Have you never wanted them to meet me?"

"I can never return."

"Of all the villages and towns I have seen, you never showed me where you and my mother fell in love, the place you were brought up in."

"I said I can never return," he yelled, rising from the bed and pacing the floor. "A tribe such as the Bessoi is no place for a child who has not been trained in the art of axe or javelin since she could hold one."

"I am no longer a child. I am a warrior as you are. Why do you hide me from them?"

"I am not hiding you from *them*," he replied.

"Apologies for the interruption, but did I hear correctly? You are a Bessoi tribesman, Leandros?"

Father stiffened, but stopped his pacing as he nodded in response. King Agrias entered, and though I kept my eyes on Father's face, I could not read the look on it.

"If I am not mistaken, the Bessoi are the only Thracian tribe to have never submitted to enemy or neighbor."

"It is a long time since I called Thrace home," Father muttered, nodding again.

"You must pardon my fascination, but the Bessoi are something of a wonder. They have always been known as a wild and savage mountainous tribe, inhabiting the region north of Hellas. Bloodthirsty, always in a fight, impossible to bring to heel, no matter the size or fame of the army that attempted it."

"It has been so for many, many winters," Father acknowledged.

"Though some of your accent remains, you speak Greek as fluently as I do with. Did you learn to speak it alongside your Thracian language?"

"No. We knew some of the Greek language, the rest I learnt once I left."

"You have been gone many winters?"

"Since before Skylar was born."

"What position did you hold in your tribe?"

"I was a peltast; a warrior."

"A peltast," the king repeated. "I believed Thracian warriors to mark their skin with patterns, yet you do not appear to have them," he added with a slight frown.

"That, as with many other Thracian customs, were not observed in my tribe," Father replied.

"Other customs?"

"Yes. I am certain you heard that the Thracians sold off their young girls for the highest price?"

"I had hoped they were only stories with no truth behind them," Agrias nodded.

"Unfortunately not. They were true for many Thracian tribes, but not the Bessoi."

"In what other customs did you differ?" Agrias asked, and I could see where Alexis got her curiosity from.

I watched with interest as my father responded. It appeared I was not the only one who had considered sharing words of days past with those in Trachis; though Father did so with less hesitation.

"The pairing of children from our tribe was decided the day each of us was born, we were not allowed to choose a partner for ourselves."

"But you did not agree with those ways? Is that why you left Thrace?"

"Partly, yes," Father replied.

"You did not teach Skylar to use weapons as soon as she could walk, as you and your ancestors were?"

"No. Skylar's upbringing was a mixture of Spartan and Athenian ways."

"I did not hold a sword until my twelfth winter," I added.

"Indeed? Your mother was Greek-born?"

"No. She was not of my tribe either," Father replied before I had the chance, a flash of pain creasing his forehead for the briefest of moments. I did not miss it and neither, it appeared, did Agrias.

"She has passed from this world?" he asked.

Father nodded.

"I am sorry to hear that," the king said, laying his hand on Father's shoulder.

"Thank you," my father responded.

I had never known my father to speak so freely of the ways of his tribe, or of my mother to anyone before. He had rarely spoken to me of the woman who had birthed me and as I had no memory of her, I had not found questions to ask him of her. I knew a little of his homeland, but only from a conversation we had had after I killed for the first time.

He appeared to already trust the king very much. Perhaps he truly did want for friends and to remain in Trachis once we had aided Agrias. I was not certain that was what *I* wished for, but Alexis' smile came to mind with unnerving ease and I wondered what she was doing.

9

The sun had long since fallen behind the mountains to the west of the palace as I stood outside its walls, my back to the entrance as I faced the east. The town, agora and Malian Gulf stood somewhere below, but aside from the occasional flickering torch, which I presumed lit rooms in the houses, I could see none of the area.

"Skylar, what are you doing out here?"

"I could not stay in that room any longer, Gnosidicus. I crave the breeze on my face, the open spaces," I replied, turning to the healer.

The old man sighed. "You have been most patient, I have treated many soldiers and the one thing you all have in common is your inability to stay still for days upon end. I can only imagine with your wandering nature it has been harder for you than most. But your body *must* stay warm else your wound shall not heal."

I allowed him to settle a himation around my shoulders and pulled it tight against a sudden gust of cold air.

"I have visited cold regions before," I assured him.

"I am certain that is true, but you did not suffer an almost fatal wound whilst there, did you?"

"No," I conceded.

"Come," he said, offering me his arm with a smile. "If you insist on being up then allow me to give you the tour." I looped my arm through his, smiling as I matched his slow footsteps across the stone balcony.

The grand entranceway was an elaborate portico almost six-and-a-half feet wide with four Doric columns, two at either end, inviting us to make our way to the entrance proper.

"The palace here in Trachis is taken from the design of King Agrias' brother, King Amyntas of Macedonia. Of course the palace in the capital is far grander, having many more rooms, but our entrance faces the east, looking out over the town, agora and the sea as Aigai does."

"Agrias' brother is the King of Aigai – as in the King of *all* Macedonia?" I asked, surprised Agrias had not mentioned it when he spoke of him.

"Oh yes," Gnosidicus confirmed.

"Oh," I murmured, uncertain what else to say.

Gnosidicus and I walked beneath the red tiled roof, which was twice as high as the buildings either side of it, and he took his arm from mine to shut the set of wooden double doors. They were at least four daktyloi thick; the width of my palm from my wrist to the base of my smallest finger. Two strips of bronze broke up the dark wood at the top and bottom, another across the middle.

"May I aid you?" I asked as Gnosidicus reached for the wooden bar to hold the door closed.

"No. I may be old, but my limbs are still capable," he replied with a grin. I nodded, but ensured I was close enough to catch the timber if required.

When the lock was firmly in place, Gnosidicus spoke again. "I am certain you have come across many courtyards in the Greek homes you have visited, but they are merely functional spaces, unlike here in Trachis. *We* use the courtyard as a place where one can enjoy the beauty of a garden," he said, indicating the greenery before us. I nodded in reply, all too familiar with one particular courtyard in Corinth. "Though it is dark, do you see the four statues in the torchlight?" he asked. Again I nodded. "Our gods, goddess and hero protect those who come to the garden, and provide answers to those who seek them. Artemis guards the south-east side," he said, pointing to a marble statue to our left. "Zeus the north-east corner, Heracles the south-west and Dionysius the north-west."

"You worship Greek gods?" I asked, surprised.

"Some," he nodded. "As King Agrias began to favor more Greek ways, he incorporated a wider variety of their pantheon into our lives." I was about to ask him to elaborate when the old man held his arm out again. "Come," he instructed.

He turned left, guiding me away from the wing I had spent the entirety of my stay in, to a room with no door, only an opening eight feet wide to enter through. We stood in the doorway and I realized that, though the outside of the room appeared to be square, the inside was circular.

"This is the Throne Room," Gnosidicus supplied, though his

description was not necessary; three gold thrones gleamed in the torch light to our left. "Many wars have been decided from this room. Alliances as well," he added. He took my elbow, escorting me along the veranda and down a walkway to the next room. "We have five banqueting halls in the palace, this is the one most often used by the royal family, whom inhabit the apartments on this south side. The first apartment belongs to Agrias' favored guard, the next two the king and queen and the princess, though they are only accessible via the central room between. Shall we?" he asked, inclining his head in that direction. I nodded.

"There is another banqueting hall beside the great entrance, and the kitchen leads off that," he continued, pointing them out. "Along the north section, where you have found yourself, are four guest rooms and two walkways – one at either end – which lead to the north and east balconies. You can make your way down into Trachis or to the Black River via the plain from either. I personally enjoy watching the sun rise over the Malian Gulf from the eastern balcony each morning when I find myself here at the palace."

"The Black River?" I asked, frowning.

"Apologies. You would know it as the Melas River," he replied.

"The Melas," I repeated, continuing to frown. "I believed it was the Spercheios River that flowed so close to Trachis. We were following it when we came across the princess and her husband."

He smiled. "No, the Spercheios is further to the north-west, the Melas and Asopos Rivers are our closest, one to the north, one to the south, our town in the valley between."

"Oh," I murmured. I had re-lived the moment I first saw Alexis standing before Melanthios a thousand times, and believed I was looking out onto the place where, for all my winters of training, my instincts had failed me, almost costing me my life.

"On the farthest side – the west – are three apartments for the men, you would know them as ..."

"The andron," I supplied.

"Indeed," Gnosidicus acknowledged with a smile.

Columns stood at regular intervals beneath the entire roofline of the palace between the rooms Gnosidicus pointed out and the garden courtyard. They matched the columns of the portico and gave the impression of conformity and unity to the rectangular space which was not displeasing to the eye.

"Many an infamous banquet has been held in their depths," he added.

"I can only imagine. Where does the walkway ahead lead to?"

"Ah, well spotted. If you follow it, you shall find yourself at the soldiers' barracks, though I cannot allow you there just yet. The palace bathing area is to the left just before the walkway, I encourage you to visit there instead."

"Instructions from my father no doubt?" I asked with a grin.

"Yes," Gnosidicus nodded, returning my smile. "Did you notice the intricate pattern of the tiles in your room?"

"I did," I replied. "It is an amazing picture."

The enormous amount of time I had had to spend on my stomach since waking ensured that I noticed not only the design on the flooring, but the number of individual black, white, grey, red and yellow tiles it took to create such a picture. Female figures carrying baskets on their heads appeared to walk around a large flower in the middle. The women were in black, no discernible features bar the flowing ends of their chitons, their baskets in grey and the large flower a brilliant yellow.

"I am curious about the flower; it is unlike any I have seen with its many layers and points. What does it symbolize?"

"You notice much. Most people see only a flower, yet it is actually a sixteen-pointed sun, the symbol of Agrias' proud homeland; Macedonia."

"It is beautiful."

"The king shall be pleased to hear you speak such words. He spent much time and coin building his palace so each room acknowledged his heritage through either the mosaics on the floors, or tapestries on the walls. He is fond of hearing that both were well spent. The palace back in Aigai is as magnificent as any found in Greece."

"I am certain there are many Greeks who would disagree," I grinned.

"Oh, I have no doubt of that," Gnosidicus nodded.

"Perhaps I could pass on my regards to King Agrias personally? Do you know where he or any of the royal family are this evening?"

"Last I saw, the king was with your father. The queen has guests she entertains. As for the princess, I am afraid I do not know, perhaps she is with her friend, Hesper."

I nodded, suddenly wishing for company just as everyone else appeared to be enjoying.

"I believe it is time I saw you back to your room," Gnosidicus said, nodding towards the north wing of the palace.

"Could I visit the stables before I return? I have not had the chance to visit Skotos since I arrived."

"Of course, though I shall not be able to accompany you as I am expected elsewhere."

"I am certain I can find the way if you give me directions."

Gnosidicus did so and saw me as far as the walkway between the banqueting hall and the room belonging to Agrias' guard.

The stables were not far from the palace itself and the path was well worn, lit with torches either side. The door stood open and I entered, finding Skotos in the third pen along.

He was an impressive sixteen-and-a-half hand high stallion, dark bay in color. The hair covering his face and body was such a deep brown that most of the time it appeared black. The only break in the darkness was a small teardrop shaped off-white patch between his eyes.

"Apologies it has taken so long for me to visit you, my friend," I whispered, stroking his nose. "I am pleased you were not injured the day I was." Skotos nuzzled at my hand and I took an apple from a nearby basket. "Have you made friends with Calla since arriving? I hope you were polite to her, her owner has taken good care of me."

My steed snorted in response, crunching the fruit between his teeth. I ran my hand over his flank, wondering if father had laid me across his back to bring me into Trachis.

"There were too many casualties that day," I mused.

"Thankfully, I was not one of them," a voice murmured, startling me.

I turned, finding Alexis in a pen further down the row on the opposite side.

"Apologies, I did not mean to interrupt nor encroach," she said, ducking between the two lengths of wood that kept the horses inside.

I noted there was no animal in the enclosure she exited from. "You are not here to visit Calla?" I queried, nodding at the empty space behind her.

"I fed and groomed her earlier," she said, pointing to the lightly tanned mare, who stood happily munching on long lengths of straw in the pen beside Skotos. "Now I am simply happy to enjoy the solitude."

I raised an eyebrow, but said nothing.

"Skotos appears pleased to have you visit," she said with a smile, joining me and patting him in long strokes.

"I am glad to finally be allowed leave my room to come visit. I would have gone to the barracks, but Father made me promise I would not."

"Why?"

"He knew I would attempt to pick up weapons and train with the men."

"And your body is still incapable of attempting such feats?" she ventured.

"Unfortunately," I nodded. "It has been many winters since I spent so many days without training or fighting. It does not sit well with me."

We had been in Trachis for sixteen days, though admittedly I could not recall much of the first eight or so, and though I was not allowed to lift my weapons yet, I had not been completely idle in attempting to keep my strength up. At first I could not lift much more than a skyphos of water, but now I could bring a full amphora almost level with my shoulder, and hold it there for quite a while before it became too much.

"Perhaps you could speak of how you came to have Skotos? Currently you cannot partake in physical pursuits but I suspect you worked hard to have him; you said you found him, did you have to tame him?"

"Yes," I confirmed, drawing a deep breath. "Why do you ask to hear of it?" I asked, though not unkindly.

Alexis shrugged. "Just curious. I have never seen an animal being tamed before, but I have heard it is not always easy."

I hesitated, inhaling another long breath. Alexis had been prepared to share truths with me about her marriage to Basileios a few days before, perhaps I could share the one story with her. Besides, had I not wished for someone to spend time with as I walked with Gnosidicus? I blew out the breath I had taken and began.

10

"We were in a small town outside Sparta. My father was with the other men enjoying one of their celebrations and I could not sleep with all the laughter and noise. I snuck out and walked for candlemarks through the olive groves and the fields. Are you aware that the Spartans are as famous for their horses as they are for their military prowess?" I asked.

Alexis shook her head.

"Many of the breeders live outside the city itself and they supply the finest horses to those who enter the chariot races at the Olympic Games."

"Oh," Alexis murmured. "Was Skotos at one of those homes?"

"No, he was a wild stallion. He had probably come down from the mountains of Taygetos to the west, though I cannot be certain. It was almost dawn when I saw him, his dark coat gleamed in the moonlight as he pawed and stamped at the ground, his black mane and tail swishing as if in warning to me.

"I approached anyway, reaching out to pat his nose, but he would not allow me to touch him, throwing his head back and rearing up on his hind legs. My father and another man arrived – having come looking for me when father realized I was not in my bed. The man said he had seen the stallion before; several men had attempted to capture and tame him, but none had succeeded. My father told him that if anyone could, it would be me."

I smiled at the memory; in that moment proud and determined to prove his words true.

"Clearly you did," Alexis said with a smile of her own.

I nodded, resting my hand on Skotos' nose.

"Skotos was stubborn and strong, but my father fetched a rope and aided me to loop it around his neck. Several times I managed to leap onto his back, but he always threw me off."

"Is that where you got this?" Alexis asked, reaching out.

Out of habit, I raised my hand to deflect the blow, quickly realizing Alexis had no intention of harming me. "Apologies," I murmured, lowering my arm again.

She smiled, pausing only a moment before continuing in her movement to trace the small scar in my right eyebrow. I swallowed loudly when her warm fingers touched me, willing the adrenaline increasing my heart rate to dissipate.

"No. I have never favored helmet during battle and I was not fast enough to dodge a sword. Once," I replied, returning her grin with a tight one of my own.

She nodded and withdrew. "Continue your story," she said.

I cleared my throat. "Over the next few days, Skotos managed to throw me from his back several times and I lost grip of the rope. On the occasions it remained in my hand, he dragged me along behind until my father managed to halt him. I had scrapes and bruises all over my arms and legs, the skin torn from my palms, yet I was fortunate not to be more injured.

"The men of the town spent much time watching, many questioning my father's sanity at allowing a young child such a task. He ignored them, tending my scratches and offering advice for the next day."

"When you slept, were you not worried Skotos would flee?"

"Of course, so I tied him to a tree so he could not. Each morning we would resume our battle, neither of us willing to be the first to break. After five long, frustrating days, my father urged me to give up, believing the attempt to be futile, but I could not allow Skotos to beat me. I decided to change tack.

"When the sun went down that night, I returned to the tree Skotos stood beneath. I told him I did not care to tame him any longer, untying the rope that held him in place so he could run away if he wanted. I spun on my heel, intending to return to the house Father and I were staying at, but I had barely made it three paces when Skotos' warm breath tickled my ear. His nose lifted the hair at the nape of my neck as he attempted to get my attention. I continued to walk away, but he followed, nuzzling my shoulder and pushing his head beneath my arm. When he took several strands of my hair in his mouth and pulled on them I finally stopped. He took another step until his flank was level with me and stood completely still, allowing me to stroke his back as I asked him for permission to ride him."

As if confirming the truth of my story, Skotos pushed his nose beneath the hair at the nape of my neck, his breath warm as it lifted it.

"Skotos dipped his head, snorting in response and I fisted my hand in his mane, jumping atop him and settling myself in place. I stroked his neck and course hair, allowing him time to get used to my weight. I spoke soft words, feeling his heart calm beneath my hands until eventually we began to trot across the grass."

"You won," Alexis said simply, her eyes bright as she spoke.

"I did," I replied. "And Skotos has been a loyal companion ever since."

"Did you ever doubt your ability to beat him?"

"Never," I said with a grin as Skotos took his head from my shoulder again.

She regarded me silently for a moment. "Do you always get what you intend?"

"Not always," I replied, dropping my eyes from hers and drawing a deep breath.

She laid her hand on my arm. "Well, perhaps even the best warriors have their off days," she said, squeezing my arm. "Something tells me you do whatever you can to ensure it does not occur often."

I swallowed loudly, nodding in response as a shiver ran the length of my spine both from her words and the sensations that having her hand on my skin gave. I swallowed again, needing distraction from the heat that suddenly announced itself in my stomach. *Do not wish for more than there can be. Do not repeat past mistakes,* I told myself firmly.

"I thought I might find you here," Father's voice announced. I took a step back from Alexis as she removed her hand. "I am pleased to hear you have not visited Moeris this day," he continued.

"I gave my word I would not," I replied shortly.

Father reached Skotos' pen and realized I was not alone. The corner of his lip lifted. "Princess, it is good to see you again," he added, bowing slightly in Alexis' direction.

"So this is where you are, Alexis," King Agrias noted, appearing beside my father. "Your mother seeks you. She would not think to look for you here."

"That is why I chose this place," Alexis murmured, her eyes on Skotos' back as she bestowed a long stroke.

I watched her with interest; her easy manner gone.

"Go now, Child. It would not do to have her upset with you," the king continued. Alexis only nodded and took her hand from Skotos.

"Thank you for ensuring Skotos was comfortable. I am glad you were here to speak with," I said, reaching out and placing a hand on her shoulder.

She lifted her eyes to mine and gave me a small grin. "I enjoyed hearing your story."

I nodded, dropping my hand to my side again as she left the stables. I watched her go, wishing I could join her in whatever it was the queen asked of her, if only to remain in her company for a little longer.

"On our way here, Agrias and I were discussing the statues in the courtyard, how they are of the gods *we* worship rather than Macedonian ones I have heard of," Father said.

I drew my eyes from the doorway and settled them on the two men. "Did he also happen to mention that his brother is not a King such as he is here in Trachis, but King of *all* of Macedonia?" I asked.

"He did, which is how the discussion of the statues came about," Father nodded.

"Gnosidicus said you began to favor the Greek ways after you left Macedonia. Why?" I asked.

"We find ourselves deep in Greek territory and I have adopted many of their ways over the Macedonian to separate ourselves from them somewhat. My brother does not begrudge the changes, understanding that to keep Athens and Sparta from my door, I must be seen to live as they do – to celebrate the same festivals or worship the same gods."

"That cannot be easy, to disregard all you have known and believed in," I murmured.

Agrias shrugged. "Sharing some of the same gods has certainly helped, though I have not begun to celebrate the same festivals yet. I seek more information on them and the correct ways to go about honoring the particular god they represent."

"Perhaps now we are here, we could teach you; we have been to many a festival over the winters," Father offered.

"I would appreciate that," the king grinned. "I believe you were in Athens during the Apaturia, aiding the Spartan King, Cleomenes, to expel Hippias."

"We were," Father acknowledged with a nod.

"You recall when we spoke the other day and I told you that my brother was allied with another large army whose bidding he often does?"

Father and I nodded in reply.

"Well, I referred to the Persians. I did not agree with my brother's decision to submit to King Darius of Persia's envoys when they landed in Macedonia three winters ago. He bowed to them without hesitation as he did not want his soldiers to face the Immortals of Darius' army."

"There are gods who fight with them?" Father asked.

"No. The Immortals are the elite fighters of their army, said to have never been bested in battle. Fierce and strong, sometimes it is they who are sent to demand tribute, for no one is brave enough to deny them."

"Oh," Father murmured.

"Amyntas agreed to become a tributary vassal expecting that, as his kin, I would do the same. But I have never cared for the Persians and their ways and refused the request."

"So you turned your back on your brother and homeland for good?" I enquired.

"Not entirely. But, getting back to Hippias – my brother offered him the territory of Anthemus on the Thermaic Gulf after he fled. He knew Hippias had kin in Sigeion and as Athens had discarded him, believed he could make himself and Hippias powerful allies for Darius. Hippias refused the offer, along with the offer of Iolcus by the Thessalians and continued on to Sigeion where his half-brother rules. Whether it was through conversations with my brother, or some other reason, Hippias has since made his way to Darius' court in Ecubana and has allied himself with the Persian King."

"If Hippias calls himself friend of the Persians, then perhaps it is best he was expelled from Athens. He deserves all which befalls him whilst he finds himself in Darius' court," Father said bitterly.

"You have faced the Persians in your travels?" Agrias asked.

"Not personally. But I know of the cruelties they inflict when jealousy beats beneath their breast. I would never call myself friend to them," Father replied.

My father could only be referring to a woman named Nasrin whom we had met in Hermione, in the south of the Peloponnese a few winters before. She had once called Babylon, and then Persia home, though her memories were not fond and she had fled to Greece just before we met her.

"I am pleased then that I did not ally myself with those you would consider enemy," the king nodded.

"As are we. Hippias' rule was not one of kindness and compassion. His ways I am certain would be welcomed in Persia. You though, appear to lead your people in a far kinder manner, and find yourself with a heavy heart when you are counselled to take lower actions."

"I do. Come, allow us to enjoy some wine whilst you tell me how you managed to exile the tyrant of Athens," the king offered with a smile.

"Of course," my father said, nodding. "You must ask Skylar about her felling of King Cleomenes," he added with a laugh.

"I imagine he did not take kindly to such treatment," Agrias commented, eyebrows raised as he half-turned towards me.

I rolled my eyes but gave Skotos another apple before following the two men from the stables. "He did not hold it against me for long," I replied.

11

I stood at the doorway of my room looking up at the tiny lights dotting the night sky high above the courtyard. There were so many and, though I attempted to count them, they were too numerous and I lost my place before I was anywhere near done.

I lowered my eyes to the opposite side of the palace; the central chamber was brightly lit by torches along its walls. Being that our conversation was cut short the night before at the stables, I had hoped to see Alexis again during the day, but so far I had not.

I spent most of the morning watching the soldiers train, and finally meeting Moeris properly. My father and the king's guard, Thaddeus, put on quite a show for the younger men by sparring with their actual weapons, rather than the wooden equivalents they were supposed to.

I was not alone in assessing the skill of the soldiers; Melanthios and another man appearing on the opposite side of the training area soon after I arrived. They appeared almost the same age, though the stranger was dressed simply in a tunic and sandals and he held no weapons and bore no scars from battle. Melanthios meanwhile stood in his armor, sword at his thigh, and his hand going to the pommel of his weapon when his eyes found mine.

With the two men appearing friendly, I asked Moeris who it was who joined Melanthios, the General advising that his name was Antigonos, and that he was originally from Dodona. He had travelled with Basileios when he came to collect Alexis, and remained afterwards.

I had questioned Moeris if Antigonos had been left behind to keep an eye on Agrias, to ensure the king could not rally a large enough defense against Melanthios if the time came. Moeris said he had always been loyal to Agrias, but agreed he would keep an eye on him, just to ensure it was so, when I asked him to.

When the display was finished, I queried my father as to the whereabouts of my own weapons. *Safe* had been his only answer, and though I attempted to convince him to allow me to have them, he would not be moved. Part of me knew he was right to deny me of them – my body still needed time to heal before I picked them up again – but I longed to feel the grip of the wooden handle of my xiphos and the weight of the bronze shield on my arm as I battled against an opponent.

The afternoon I spent walking on the plain beside the Melas River. The few trees there were large and shady and I had no doubt that in the heat of the summer would provide instant relief from the sun. I considered asking Father to take me to the hot springs he spoke of before we arrived, but again, I knew my body would not be up to the ride if it was indeed two candlemarks away.

I blew out a breath, deciding I may as well go to bed, though gods knew I was sick of the small room I found myself housed in. The past few nights I had stretched out on the ground to sleep; the short bed uncomfortable now I did not have to sleep exclusively on my stomach.

I took another look at the lights above before turning to go inside. As I did, Alexis emerged from the central chamber, catching sight of me immediately. I held my hand up in greeting and she returned it, her instant smile matching my own. She changed direction and started across the courtyard, though her progress and smile faltered as she noticed Queen Melina emerging from the bathing area.

I watched with interest; the queen headed in my direction while Alexis stealthily retraced her steps, remaining behind one of the larger shrubs until she believed Melina would not see her. She gave me another wave and walked quickly to the door Gnosidicus had said belonged to Agrias' guard.

I turned my attention to the striking figure of the approaching Queen, automatically extending my hands when she reached out hers; the skin over my shoulder blade protesting only slightly when I lengthened my arms.

"I wondered if perhaps it was time for you to enjoy a full body bath. I cannot imagine washing from a small basin as you have been is very satisfying," the queen said, smiling widely as she squeezed my fingers. "Gnosidicus agreed that your back has healed well enough so I had the water prepared for you."

"Thank you, Queen Melina," I replied, smiling at the idea of a long soak in a bath.

"Come," she directed, keeping one of my hands in hers as we made our way to the baths.

Now that I was upright, I stood taller than her by at least half a foot and I realized she was almost the exact height of her daughter, though her scent was not the same, eyes brown rather than that brilliant green, and her hair was a light brown whereas Alexis' was dark brown. The princess' features more closely matched her father's, though perhaps the women shared similar dispositions.

My thoughts remained on Alexis' hasty retreat when she had seen her mother and I attempted to recall the conversation I had overheard between the two of them as I lay recovering on my bed. They had exchanged words about Melina's interest in me and what she wished to aid me with should I wake. Alexis had been upset; I had heard it in her voice and I wondered what had transpired between them prior to my arrival to cause such hurt. I had never heard those exact matters spoken of between mother and daughter before, but then I had few conversations to compare it to. The Greek daughters I had met would never consider questioning either of their parents in such a manner; it was not the Greek way. Though perhaps Melina was not Alexis' birth mother; perhaps she was Agrias' second wife. I found myself with yet more questions I wished to ask Alexis, should the chance arise, and I truly hoped it would.

"Skylar?" the queen's voice interrupted my thoughts.

"Apologies," I replied, bowing my head ever so slightly in her direction. "I was contemplating the thought of a warm bath."

"Come, I have laid out a new chiton for you already," she smiled.

"Thank you," I said again.

The bathing area was made up of two separate rooms. Bathers in the first room were hidden from the view of anyone passing through the walkway outside by a single door, similar to the one at the entrance to the palace. The bath was placed towards the back of the room, opposite the door, but concealed by a marble wall that stood as high as my hip.

"I have prepared the second room for you," Melina said, continuing through another single door on the right.

I followed. A small table stood to the left. To the right, a warm fire was built into the wall with an empty three-legged stand above and a thin shelf filled with jars and pyxides cut into the marble at a height level with my shoulder. The cauldron that had sat atop the flames to heat was on the floor; the water it had held now in the marble cistern in the middle of the room.

"It is perfect," I whispered, noting the length of the vessel; I would have no trouble stretching out my legs when I got in.

"Allow me to aid you with your clothing," Melina said.

"That is not necessary," I replied, not used to having others do so much for me.

The queen stepped closer as I reached for the clip that held my tunic together above my left shoulder, her hands beating mine there. She smiled as I lowered my arm again.

"You are fiercely independent by nature, a product of your upbringing I suspect, and whilst independence has its advantages, it also has its downfalls." I frowned slightly, but said nothing as she continued. "A woman must learn when to allow others to make decisions for her; when the decisions should be left to her father or husband."

I drew a breath, choosing my next words carefully as the queen freed the material at my shoulder and I held it against my breasts. "What is it exactly you wish to speak of, Queen Melina?"

She smiled. "You are direct, I respect that quality."

"In my experience it is often the best way to obtain answers," I replied.

"Indeed," she agreed, stepping back a pace as her eyes assessed my body and face. "I believe it is time you found yourself a husband, someone to protect you, to care for you when you are ill. Someone to begin a family with."

I took in another deep breath, blowing it all the way out again before I spoke. "This is about the princess," I said, a statement, not a question. "You do not wish for her to spend time tending to me."

"She has other, more important matters that require her attention," the queen acknowledged.

"Alexis cared for me well after I was first injured; but I am certain you know she has not visited me for days, not since I woke properly."

"No, she has been kept terribly busy with her future husband and the plans we must make."

I allowed no emotion to show on my face at the mention of Melanthios and Alexis' future, folding my arms across my chest instead.

"You cannot truly want her to return to Epirus with Melanthios," I noted. "But why speak of it with me now?"

"Because Alexis must do what is expected of her. If she wastes any more time with you, she may drift from those expectations."

"You are warning me to stay away from the princess?"

"Not warning, simply suggesting that your time be directed towards *other* women whilst you are here in Trachis."

"You do not believe that Alexis could influence me in the ways you wish, that she would not set an example of how a woman should behave?" The queen paused, evidently considering my words, but I pressed on. "You take many liberties suggesting such plans for my betrothal and future, yet you are no parent of mine. What encourages you in such matters, for I am certain it is not my father who has made such wishes known to you?"

"No, he believes that you do not need a husband. But he shall not be in this world forever; you must find another to walk your future with."

"If indeed I *sought* any kind of permanent arrangement with another, I would wish for one whom did not want me to change in any way. Who would accept me for who I am, who would be my equal and have the strength of character to stand beside me without fear that they had chosen wrongly; that they would not be harmed for choosing such a path.

"I do not seek a lover for protection, I have been taught in the Spartan ways; to defend and be accountable for myself both in battle and in life. I survived an injury most say I should not have. I am far stronger than I appear, even without full use of my body," I said, drawing myself up so that our height difference was more obvious.

"Your father says you have also been taught many of the Athenian ways, yet Athenian women tend their husband's homes and bear many children."

"You speak the truth, but I do not follow their ways as closely as the Spartans. I admire and enjoy Athenian poetry and plays, but not all their beliefs. Spartan women are as strong as the men, they are taught to fight and defend their home as children; their training is the same as that of their male counterparts."

"But you are no longer a child. Those Spartan women you speak of still marry at a young age and produce children to continue the great Spartan traditions. Yet you have borne no children, you have no husband to continue your own line."

"How can you be certain I have never birthed a child?" I asked, my words soft, yet forceful.

Melina stepped forward, her hands unfolding the arms at my chest. My tunic fell to the floor and I stood exposed before the queen. Her eyes travelled the length of my body before meeting mine again. The warmth of her fingertips played across my stomach, her palms smoothing their way up to my breasts, cupping them firmly.

I could not speak; too stunned by the action and the way her hands felt on me. I was all too aware it was the Queen of Trachis who stood before me, rather than a hetaira or slave I had engaged for pleasure, but that did not diminish the sudden fire in my blood.

She leaned close, the soft material of her clothing brushing against my thighs. For a moment I believed she would kiss me, but her breath lifted the hair at my ear instead as she spoke.

"This is not the body of a woman who has birthed a child," she whispered.

I swallowed loudly, unable to prevent my nipples rising beneath her hands, my breath keeping time with my heart. Her scent was more floral than her daughter's, not stirring me as Alexis' did and too sweet to be truly inviting, but I drew it in anyway.

The queen appeared almost smug as she released my body from her grip, one finger skimming over the bruise above my ribs. I inhaled sharply, desire smoldering between my thighs.

"Your body gives away your true desires Skylar. So now I shall give you that warning; stay away from Alexis."

I could not reply, wishing to deny her observation, though it was true. Despite my thoughts and my own words to my father that Alexis and I could not be friends, the queen's insistence that I stay away from the princess made me want to do the exact opposite.

Without another word, Melina withdrew from the room, closing the door behind herself. I reached out, placing my hand against the marble of the bath as I attempted to catch my breath.

It had been moons since I had enjoyed the touch of a woman – the last a slave girl King Cleomenes had sent to me in Sunium. I had enjoyed both she and some very fine wine that night and I easily recalled the way she had used more than just her hands to bring me the pleasure I had sought.

It was not the queen whom I wished had touched me, yet she had ignited the desire that began the night I first looked into Alexis' eyes. I closed my own, skimming my hand down my stomach, imagining it to be Alexis' soft caress. I could not deny that I wanted to touch Alexis, to have her touch me as the slave girl had. Simple companionship was not what I most wished for with her. The deep green of her eyes floated behind my eyelids. Her soft brown hair tickling at my arm. Perfect pink lips. Her smile. I imagined her warm hands on my arms, my stomach, my thighs, wrapped around my neck as I drew her body against mine.

12

I sucked in a deep breath as my fingers found the place I wanted Alexis' touch; where she would draw screams of ecstasy from my lips as she took possession of my body. I stroked, the pressure building within.

After the battle in Stratos there had been no victory celebration, no offer of men or women for those who wished it, and then we had left. As we travelled over the mountains we had camped beneath the twinkling lights above. My father and I side by side. I had wished to find relief, to release the tension a battle always brought, but there had been no opportunity.

My breath grew shorter. I braced my legs, my hand squeezing the edge of the bath for support as I neared the peak, Alexis' face loomed large in my mind, lips parting as she spoke my name. I increased my movements, ignoring the protests from my ribs and back, driving myself higher until finally I fell over the edge, driving my teeth into my bottom lip to avoid her name escaping.

It was not as satisfying as when a lover brought me to my end, but still the shudders racked me and a sense of relief flooded my veins.

My eyes flew open at a sound from the doorway. The queen watched me. My chest heaved but I held her gaze, removing my hand from between my legs and placing it beside the other on the rim of the bath.

She gave me a satisfied sneer. "Stay away from her," she warned again, closing the door firmly.

I attempted to draw a full breath. Melina had remained to watch me pleasure myself; she must have known I would. She had wanted to incite my desire. Why? She obviously knew I preferred women lovers to men and did not come to that conclusion simply by placing her hands on me just now. She had wanted me to speak the words, and when I had not, she had dared to inflame my body, to have it speak the words I would not, and had no way of stopping.

I stepped into the marble cistern, the warmth of the water cool against my heated skin. I lay my arm along the edge of the bath, my cheek resting atop my forearm, my body still craving true release. At least the action Melina had witnessed had not been with Alexis. The princess would not be in any danger from what I had done. But it would not do to make the queen an enemy; I was only too aware of what could happen when I came between family members. I could not do so again.

*

My cheek still rested on my arm, the water around me tepid. I had been dozing lightly for some time and it appeared I had finally succumbed to Hypnos' realm. I stretched and stood, stepping over the side of the bath and shivering as my feet touched the cold floor. I warmed my body at the fire before reaching for the chiton the queen had left, crudely wrapping the soft linen about my body.

My vigorous activity earlier had not reopened my wound, but my body was stiff and sore from the movements and the fabric was far longer than I was accustomed to – reaching almost to the floor. I struggled to shorten it so it resembled the tunics I was used to wearing but I could not fasten the fibula at my shoulder. Leaving the material hanging at an odd angle, I gathered up my tunic and held it against my chest to prevent my current coverings from falling to the ground.

I did not wish to think of what had happened after the tunic was last separated from my body, for my skin still itched for the sating that could only be provided by another's touch, rather than my own. I swallowed loudly as Alexis' face appeared too easily in my mind again. It was not wise to allow such dreams of her when she could not share my bed; after all, she had already lost one husband and was promised to another.

Still, I craved her touch, more so now than before.

Content I had not left anything in the bathing room, I made my way back through the two single doors, almost colliding with the one person I had just told myself I must not think of.

"Apologies, Princess," I murmured, attempting to step around her. "I did not expect to see anyone out this late."

"Skylar," she said, sounding just as surprised at our sudden meeting.

Tentatively I raised my eyes to hers; it was a mistake. My blood instantly heated, the deep cravings rising to the surface and raising the hairs at the back of my neck and along my arms.

"I … we were … you have been for a bath?" Alexis stumbled.

"Yes, your mother had it prepared for me," I replied.

A look was exchanged between Alexis and the woman whose arm was in hers. The woman was beautiful in her own way with deep brown eyes and dark hair curled around her head, but my gaze barely settled on her before making its way back to the princess.

"You appear to have had some trouble redressing. May I?" Alexis asked, indicating the loose end of the chiton at my shoulder.

I could not allow her hands to touch my skin; not when I had just been fantasizing of her doing exactly that. I found myself nodding in response anyway.

"You have something to fasten it with?" she asked.

I fumbled beneath the tunic I held for my brooch, almost dropping both. The woman beside Alexis snickered. *Gods!* I rolled my eyes; anyone would believe I had never been in the company of a striking woman before. I retrieved the small silver pin and handed it to Alexis.

"Thank you," she murmured.

When Alexis had a secure hold on the ends of linen, I lowered my arms to my sides, the tunic gripped firmly in my left. She moved around me, settling the material into place over my shoulders and back, gentle when it came to the right side. I was still damp from the bath, the material sticking to several spots on my skin, but she freed them, smoothing the chiton expertly so it hung in the correct manner. Her spicy fragrance was not as potent, but it still clung to the air around her, invading my senses and inviting me to allow it to fill me.

Alexis returned to face me, the brooch still in her hand. Her body was bare inches from mine, her warm breath blowing onto my shoulder as she worked the pin through the material. I watched her, noting the small frown between her eyebrows as she concentrated. Her arm brushed my breast, the nipple hardening instantly at the touch. I attempted to stifle the gasp, but it escaped anyway.

Alexis' eyes whipped to mine. "Did I stick you?" she asked, concern written across her features.

"No," I replied, willing my heart to calm. As distraction from the assault of her aroma and close proximity I cleared my throat, settling my eyes on the statue of Heracles standing proud and tall in the courtyard.

"I must apologize for the abrupt end to our conversations," I began.

Alexis paused ever so slightly in her fixings.

"The day you brought the bread for me and at the stables," I added.

"Oh. It matters not. You know my mother wished for me to join her last night and I had something else to attend that first day," she replied, waving off my words.

"You did not," the woman behind her smiled. "You told me …"

"Hush, Hesper," Alexis scolded.

"Well you were in a temper when you came to the kitchen and you had been to se–"

"Hesper!"

Hesper gave me a wide smile and conspiratorial wink, wiping both from her face, when Alexis turned to face her angrily. I smiled back, immediately warming to the woman and enjoying the deep flush that colored Alexis' cheeks as she returned her eyes to the task at my shoulder.

The pin was firmly in place, yet Alexis did not take her hands from it, stroking the material it held as if it were not sitting perfectly already. She was gorgeous; even more alluring when embarrassed. I had to admit that the more time I spent with Alexis, the more I wanted to be around her. I had never wished for that before and it was both thrilling, and scary.

I met Hesper's eyes, mouthing the question 'slave' to her and indicating Alexis. She shook her head, smiling once again as she pretended to throw out a net and drag it back in. I understood and my grin widened. Wiping it from my lips, I hooked my finger beneath Alexis' chin, bringing her eyes up to meet mine.

"Your slave speaks with disrespect towards you, Princess. Perhaps she should be reminded of her place," I suggested.

"Oh, no, Hesper is not my slave, she is my friend, my best friend, we have been friends since childhood," Alexis blurted out.

"Indeed?" I asked.

Alexis nodded, continuing hastily, "Yes, we have always been close. What causes you to believe she is m–?"

"The warrior teases you, it is enjoyable to watch you color at her words," Hesper murmured, leaning close to us. "She does not appear as intense and serious as you claim."

I chuckled, allowing the smile to escape as Alexis quieted, the color in her cheeks deepening under my stare.

"So it would appear," she agreed.

It would be so easy to kiss her, standing as close as we were. I dropped my hand from her chin and took a step back.

"Thank you for aiding me with this," I said, indicating my clothing.

"Well you were barely dressed as you were, it would not do to have the men see you attired in such a manner."

"Indeed," I said, bowing my head to her. "I am in your debt, Princess."

"I shall remember that," she promised, wagging her finger and returning my grin.

"There you are Skylar," my father's voice drifted along the veranda as he hurried towards us. "Queen Melina told me she left you here candlemarks ago, yet I saw no evidence you had been back to your room, are you well?"

"I am fine, Father. Do not worry."

"I must admit, I wondered if you had decided to move your bedding to the bathing area, what with your love of a hot bath." He turned to the two women as he spoke. "I once found her squashed into a bath with a young betrothed couple just so she ..." he paused, realizing who stood with me. "Oh. My apologies, Princess, Hesper."

"Not at all Leandros, please go on, I would enjoy hearing how that story ends," Alexis said, shooting me a wicked grin.

Father's eyes lit up. "Excellent, well ..."

"Father," I warned.

He took no notice of me, edging his body between Alexis and I and launching into the tale with such vigor and jolliness that I could do nothing but stand back and watch. He had always had a flair for storytelling – other people's stories, rather than his own – and he never failed to keep his audience well entertained.

"Well, as I am certain you are aware, the wedding feast is a long, often drunken, affair. Whilst it begins as merriment and happiness, soon the new couple retires to be alone to begin their new life together, and to make a new life."

I rolled my eyes. "*You* appear to have indulged in a little merriment this evening," I muttered.

He ignored my words again. "The night I speak of was no exception. It was almost dawn and the young man and his new wife had been seen to the bridal chamber to enjoy each other privately. The celebration was at the home of a wealthy man and there was a bathing room attached to the chamber. They warmed the water in the cauldron and soon had the tub filled, and themselves inside it, enjoying one another as couples do.

"Now, I was charged with the task of keeping the space private for them, but I was momentarily distracted by a scuffle between two of the bride's brothers and when I returned to my post, I caught a glimpse of Skylar's long hair floating out behind her as she dashed into the bathing area."

"Oh no," Alexis cried, her hand going to her mouth, but hiding a smile.

Father threw a glance in my direction, his grin wide. I shook my head. When he spoke again, he lowered his head towards the princess, his voice quiet, almost secretive. "Skylar rushed in, stripped off her dirty clothing and proceeded to seat herself right between the astonished couple, ensuring their plans for privacy and creating a child were shattered."

"I would point out that I was barely seven winters old at the time. I did not know what they were doing … or attempting to do," I said, my cheeks warming.

Father straightened again, thoroughly pleased with his retelling as he crossed his arms over his chest.

"Wherever there is a warm bath *that* is where you shall find Skylar," he announced.

"I shall remember that," Alexis said with a laugh that was pleasant and full. "The baths we have here *are* larger than most, I am certain your daughter would find someone to share them with if that was her desire."

My father laughed loudly as my face burned. "Very good, Princess."

Alexis turned to Hesper. "Come, it is too late for bathing now, my mother shall send someone to look for *us* if we do not return to our rooms."

"Indeed," Hesper agreed.

"It was nice to see you again, Leandros," Alexis said.

"And you, Princess," he replied with a small bow.

She stepped forward, placing her hand on my arm. "I hope you enjoyed your bath, even if you had to have it alone. Feel free to use them as often as you wish."

I smiled, the skin beneath her touch tingling. "I have not bathed with another for many winters," I assured her. "But I thank you for the offer."

She squeezed my arm briefly then moved away. Hesper hesitated, looking between the princess and me before she spoke.

"I am pleased to finally meet you, for I have heard much. I am glad you have recovered so well. Shall we see you soon?"

"Of course," I replied, smiling as once again Alexis looked at Hesper in disbelief.

The two women made their way back along the veranda, hugging briefly before going their respective ways – Alexis entering the central chamber Gnosidicus had pointed out and Hesper the end apartment where the healer had said the king's guard lived.

Once they were out of sight, Father turned to me. "The princess has quite the sense of humor, and her friend is easy on the eye also."

"Father, I have no interest in Hesper."

"Nor she in you, I am certain. I was not suggesting such an idea. But I believe you have found two willing friends there."

"Did you seek me for a specific purpose this evening?" I asked before he could press me further about the princess, or my bath.

"Nothing specific, no. I was simply with Agrias when the queen mentioned you were enjoying their baths. But I did not miss Melanthios' cold appraisal of you at the barracks today, and with his room so near to yours, I wanted to ensure he did not seek you out this evening."

"For what reason would he have had? He is not aware I know of his actions against Basileios, is he?"

"I do not believe so, but given our thwarting of what he wanted, he shall not be pleased you are recovering quickly."

"I imagine not, but the longer it is until he learns I am a threat to him, the more time I have to heal."

"And to make friends," Father mused, his eyes settling on the royal apartments.

"Perhaps," I murmured, my own finding their way to the lighted torches.

Easy, familiar banter such as I had experienced with Alexis and Hesper was rare to non-existent outside of my father's company. If I was to give merit to his words about finding companions to spend time with, I was in no doubt who I wished for that companion to be, despite the queen's warning and my own ill-advised desires.

Friendship between Alexis and I was all we could have, and the haunting memories I held should be deterrent enough to keep actions for anything else at bay.

13

Two nights later, I made my way across the courtyard to Hesper's door, intending to find out where Alexis was so I could thank her for the gift she had left me earlier that morning. I had been surprised and delighted to find the small basket outside my door, the cloth cover barely disguising the smell of the honey-sweetened bread. I had eagerly opened it, finding the bread still warm from the fire as I shoveled a handful into my mouth. There was also a smaller package beneath the food; an amphora with a picture of a bath on the papyrus label. I had taken out the wooden stopper, drawing in the sweet aroma and noting it had undertones of Alexis' perfume.

I had decided it would be wise to seek out Hesper, rather than guess which apartment off the central chamber belonged to Alexis, as I did not relish the idea of encountering the queen again whilst alone.

I knocked and had to wait only a moment before Hesper opened the door, greeting me with a wide smile. "Skylar, it is good to see you again so soon."

"And you," I replied. "I wondered if you could tell me which room belongs to the princess, I wish to speak with her."

"There is no need to seek her anywhere else for she is here," Hesper said, half-turning to call to Alexis.

"What is it?" Alexis asked, arriving beside her friend.

"You have a visitor," Hesper replied, indicating me.

"Skylar," she smiled.

"Good evening, Princess," I replied, nodding in her direction.

"I shall leave the two of you to talk," Hesper said, moving back into the room.

"Thank you," I nodded.

Alexis stepped outside, drawing the door partway closed behind her.

"I wanted to thank you for the gifts you left me."

"You enjoyed the bread?" Alexis asked, her grin widening.

"Very much. It is quickly becoming a firm favorite of mine."

"I am glad. It is Hesper who makes it so well."

"I shall remember to thank her as well then," I nodded. "The oil for the bath is also pleasant. If I am not mistaken, it contains some of the same ingredients of the perfume you wear."

She lay her head to the side. "You have knowledge of perfumes?"

"A little," I replied with a shrug. "Does it indeed contain some of the same elements as yours?"

She nodded. "In both, marjoram is used as the top fragrance and cinnamon as a middle note."

"Yours is a far sweeter smell, what causes that?"

She smiled. "Labdanum is at its base. It brings out the cinnamon, but there is also some rose mixed in."

I nodded, forgetting that it had been the rose I first recognized when I awoke to find Alexis in my room.

"Neither the labdanum or rose are in this one though, are they?" I asked, holding up the small amphora.

"No," she confirmed. "Sweet rush is the other middle note and frankincense provides the base."

"It is an almost spicy scent," I noted.

It was her turn to nod. "It is exotic, different to any I have smelled before. As you are," she murmured, dropping her eyes momentarily as her cheeks reddened. She cleared her throat, raising her eyes to mine when she spoke again. "The trader at the agora said it comes from the far south-east, towards Egypt where frankincense is more popular."

"It is," I replied, pleased yet uncertain how else to respond to her admission of my being exotic. "Well, it is very pleasing, I shall enjoy using it."

A peal of laughter from inside made Alexis jump and I realized that she and Hesper had not been alone.

"Apologies Princess, I keep you from your guests," I said, inclining the top half of my body.

"Not at all, you are a welcome sight, I assure you," she replied, laying her hand on my arm. "Perhaps you would join us?"

"No. I … I do not belong at such a gathering. I must go." I backed away from the door, noting a number of curious faces turned in our direction.

Alexis' hand remained on me and though I moved, she did not take it away, her grip tightening ever so slightly. "Wait. Do you intend to use the oil now?" she asked.

"Yes," I replied. I lifted the hand she had on my arm, placing a light kiss atop it as I had seen my father do when hosts presented him with fine wine, good food, or both. "Thank you again for the gifts. You spoil me with them."

She opened her mouth to speak again, but I released her, giving a final wave and heading along the veranda to the bathing area.

I opened the door, entering the second room and pushing away visions of what I had done after my last bath there. I placed the amphora and my clean tunic on the wooden table by the door and crossed to the fire. The water in the cauldron was almost hot enough, but I suddenly wondered how I was going to get it from the fire to the bath without injuring myself. In my excitement to see Alexis, I had not thought that far ahead and I frowned at my ill thought out plan.

The scowl remained in place as I recalled the women at Hesper's apartment. Though I had not studied the five of them in depth, I knew they were all of noble blood; no doubt wives and daughters of powerful citizens. Gold fibulae had adorned their long chitons of blues and greens, hairpins in the same shining color holding their hair in place atop their heads. I did not belong in such company. They would not welcome me for I was not as refined as they were. I had not attended banquets and festivals, or partaken of parades as they would have. My experience of those events was from a male perspective rather than the girl I had been, or the woman I was.

I blew out a loud breath. They were just another reminder that I should not seek Alexis for company whilst I was recovering; our paths were too different. I was not worthy of her friendship.

The door suddenly opened and Alexis slipped inside, a smile finding her lips as she took in the look of surprise I obviously wore.

"Gnosidicus tells me your wound is healing well," she murmured, closing the door and leaning against the wood.

"Not as quickly as I would prefer, but well enough," I replied, unable to keep the grin from my own face. "What are you doing here? Shall your friends not miss you?"

"They are not friends of mine but women who have become influential in Trachis since my absence. My mother wished for me to meet with them."

"Ah," I said with a nod. "How long have you been in Epirus?"

"Five winters."

"Hesper appears to enjoy that you have returned. Your mother allows you to spend much time with her?"

"Yes, though I suspect she believes it a punishment for me to see

Hesper surrounded by her three sons whilst I have no children of my own," she shrugged, her smile disappearing.

"Is it?" I asked carefully.

"No," she replied, inhaling deeply.

"Are children something you wish for?"

"I have not been able to carry a child to term, though Basileios placed them inside me. After a time, other wives gave them to him."

It was not an answer to my question, but I did not press her – unable to determine if it was sadness or mere acceptance etched across her features.

"Apologies," I offered instead. "When I was in Athens I heard the story of the previous King of Sparta, Anaxandridas, and his Queen, Anassa, and their quest for children. May I speak of it to you?"

"Please," she replied with a nod and the hint of a smile; the curious nature I was starting to welcome resurfacing.

"For many winters, Anaxandridas and Anassa attempted to birth children of their own, but with no success. The healers said she was barren and the Ephors, who kept council with the king, urged him to set her aside and take another wife as she would never provide him with an heir. But Anaxandridas loved Anassa and would not discard her. The Ephors allowed him to take a second wife and she provided him with the required heir, Cleomenes.

"A winter later, Queen Anassa gave birth to a son, Dorieus. Winters later, she bore two more sons, Leonidas first and then Cleombrotus. Perhaps if Basileios had lived, you would have eventually provided him with the expected son."

"Or perhaps the queen's sons are not the king's children," Alexis countered.

"You may speak the truth," I conceded with a shrug. "But perhaps they are and it was only time the royal couple had to overcome."

"I believe some couples are not destined for children together," Alexis murmured, dropping her eyes again.

"Or perhaps there is another who is worthy of such a gift with you, if that is what *you* wished for," I offered. *If you truly wanted it and I could give it to you, I would.* The surprising thought floated through my mind and I swallowed loudly so the words did not leave my mouth.

"Do you wish for children?" Alexis asked, raising her eyes to meet mine.

I hesitated. "I do not believe that children are in my future," I eventually replied.

Alexis considered my words, but said nothing further, crossing to add some wood to the fire that burned low in the fireplace.

"Sometimes I wonder how it would be to stay in one place, have servants get me food, wash my hair, wear expensive linen every day," I mused.

"I imagine you would bathe every day if there was the option to do so," Alexis replied with a smile as she stood up again.

"Perhaps," I agreed, returning the grin.

"You wish for a place to stay, to call home?"

I shrugged.

"I do not believe that is in my future either. Father and I have never stayed anywhere more than a few moons and I have never considered changing that."

"Would you tell me of the places you have been, the people you have met?"

I smiled again at her thirst for knowledge. "I met Cleomenes, the King of Sparta last winter," I offered.

"Ah, so that is how you knew the story of his mother and father."

"Yes," I confirmed.

She frowned. "You said you were in Athens when you heard the tale."

I nodded.

"What was the Spartan King doing in Athens? I believed they were rivals. How did you meet him?"

"Father and I were ..." I paused. I could not tell Alexis where we had truly been or what we had been doing. I had enjoyed the company of several women that night, but I did not believe she would understand if I spoke of it. "We had been invited to a banquet at the home of a wealthy couple. There were many men and women there, Cleomenes being one of them. He and Father struck up a conversation; the two of them finding they both enjoyed their wine unmixed, as you do here in the north, and that led us to other discussions."

She dipped her finger into the cauldron of water above the fire. "It is ready," she nodded, when I raised an eyebrow in question. "I shall fetch Thaddeus to empty it for you into the bath."

"I can do it," I insisted.

"You shall not; your back is still healing," she replied, leaving the bathing room and effectively preventing me from arguing further.

I contemplated simply moving the cauldron myself anyway, but it would see me have to return to my room and wait for Gnosidicus to attend when I re-injured myself – and I knew I would re-injure myself. Besides, it was not fair for Alexis to have to return to Hesper's when she had followed me already.

I smiled at the thinly-made excuse and wiped the grin from my face as Alexis returned, a man not much taller than her, though a number of winters older, following. He nodded to me and approached the fire, gathering two pieces of cloth and wrapping them around his palms.

He picked the cauldron up by the bronze, nymph-shaped handles with ease, pouring the water into the bath and setting the cauldron on the ground beside the fire before discarding the cloths.

"I am Thaddeus," he said, offering his arm to me. "I saw you at the barracks yesterday, and am sorry we did not get to speak then. I am glad to finally have the chance to thank you for returning our princess to us safely. She has been sorely missed these past winters."

I gripped him tightly and nodded in return. Thaddeus smiled widely, his gaze finding Alexis with fondness, and perhaps something more. I squeezed him a little tighter.

His gaze returned to mine and he released me as I did the same. "It took both Moeris and I to lift you onto your horse to bring you back here, I was afraid that act would worsen your condition, but it does not appear to have hindered your ability to heal," he noted, holding my eyes.

"Apparently not," I replied.

"Well, enjoy your bath," he said, his smile never faltering as he turned from me. "You too," he murmured to Alexis in a voice so low I was certain I was not supposed to hear. He kissed her cheek, chuckling.

"Goodnight, Thaddeus," she said with a smile, pushing him through the door and closing it again behind him.

My nails pressed painfully into the flesh of my palms as I watched the exchange. Jealousy at the attention Thaddeus gave Alexis gnawed at my insides as I recalled that Agrias had once wanted to betroth Alexis to him. My jaw clenched.

"He appears fond of you," I grimaced. "Do you wish he was to be your new husband?"

"Thaddeus?" she laughed, leaning against the door as she had when she first joined me. "Oh no, he is Hesper's husband. I have known him even longer than I have known her. He is a loyal friend."

"And that is all?" I asked, unable to prevent the words slipping out.

Alexis regarded me, head tilted ever so slightly. "Friendship is all that has ever been between Thaddeus and me," she replied.

I nodded, unable to meet her eyes any longer, annoyed by the irrational possessiveness that ran through me.

"If you wish to undress, I shall gather the oil," Alexis offered.

"You ... you do not have to stay," I said.

"Oh. If that is what you wish."

I swallowed loudly but raised my eyes to hers. I should send her back to Hesper and the women. She raised too much conflict within me. I knew what had happened with Kuria and Stamatis and yet I still wanted Alexis to remain and spend time with me.

"I would enjoy the company, but ..."

"Then I shall stay," she replied firmly. "Do you need assistance with your pin?"

"No," I said, voice thick. "Thank you."

She nodded and made her way to the small table by the door, turning from me. I lowered my eyes, reaching for the silver piece at my shoulder.

"I was surprised your father recognized me even though I was not in my usual royal garments when we met outside the bathing area the other night," Alexis said.

"He has an excellent memory for faces," I replied.

"What about you?"

"I notice much also."

"Such as the aroma of the perfume I wear."

"Yes." I kept my gaze on my task and silence drew out between us as I struggled to free the pin from the material. "How can a simple object be so difficult?" I mumbled.

"Do you need some help?" Alexis asked and I did not need to look up to know she was smiling.

"No," I grumbled, the pin finally loosening. "I have it." A noise from the outer room caught my ear, but I did not pause in my task, gripping the end of the fibula tighter.

"Are yo–ah! Please. You are hurting me, Melanthios. What are you doing here?" Alexis' voice was quiet, scared.

"You are mine now. I shall touch you how and when I choose. You shall not deny me my wishes."

My head whipped up, my brow furrowing at Melanthios' response; the words familiar and haunting.

"No, leave me alone," Alexis insisted, attempting to free herself from the grip he had on her wrist.

With his free hand, Melanthios slapped Alexis across the cheek. She fell against the table, his other hand still around hers. Even from where I was I could see how tightly he held her. My blood boiled. I left the pin half in and half out of the material at my shoulder, crossing the room in three strides.

14

"Take your hands from her," I demanded; my voice soft and dangerous.

"This business is none of yours, just as it was not the last time," Melanthios growled, his free hand pushing at my shoulder. The attempt was weak and I captured his wrist, the scent of wine thick on his breath.

"I am making it my business. Now release her."

He made no move to do so until I increased the pressure, forcing his hand to open. Keeping hold of him, I swept Alexis behind me.

"It is time you took your leave," I said.

"You do not command me, Girl," he panted, attempting to loosen my grip. I released him and he stumbled backwards. "You should be dead. It is time I finished what my man did not," he continued, taking his sword from its sheath and juggling it between his palms.

"Alexis, go stand near the fire." She did not reply, but her long chiton touched the back of my legs as she obeyed. I braced my feet but kept my body loose, poised to defend or strike.

Melanthios staggered forward, sword swinging. I ducked, his wild swing almost overbalancing him. We turned at the same time. He approached again, sword held above his head, roaring in anger. He was almost on top of me when I stepped aside.

"Skylar!" Alexis cried as Melanthios' sword bounced off the marble wall, reverberating through his body and sending him stumbling once again.

I did not wait for him to recover; ramming my shoulder into his chest and driving him against the table. The jar of oil Alexis had given me rolled across the flat top just out of my reach and fell from the edge, smashing on the ground below.

Melanthios cried out and swept his sword in my direction. I jumped out of its path. He regained his feet, rushing towards me again. I ducked and weaved as his sword slashed the air around me. Aware that we were far closer to the princess than I was comfortable with, I drew my leg up, kicking out and catching him in the stomach. As he bent in half, I brought my hand down on the arm that held his sword. It fell to the floor with a clang and I grabbed the front of his chiton, pulling him upright. I drew my arm back and slammed my fist into his nose, satisfied when I heard the bone break.

He fell to the ground, screaming, hands flying to his face. Blood pouring between them. I stepped back, my body coiled, waiting to see if he would attack again. He did not.

"You shall pay for your interference," he spat. With his eyes still on me, he scrambled on his knees to pick up his sword, re-sheathing it as he got to his feet and backed out of the room.

My knuckles tingled, my flesh alive with the adrenaline of the unexpected fight. I was breathing hard, but the trembling body beside me instantly cooled the hunger I had to follow the fleeing man.

"You have reopened your wound," Alexis murmured.

I turned to her, wiping at the tears spilling down her cheeks. "Do not be concerned with it." I placed my fingers against her reddened cheek, my back protesting the movement. "I should not have allowed him to hurt you," I frowned, surveying the damage.

"It would have been worse were you not here," she replied, her breath catching as she added, "So much worse."

I drew her to my chest and placed a kiss on her head. "I know, but you are safe. He shall not harm you while I am here."

Alexis wrapped her arms around my waist and I stroked her hair until her hiccupping breaths slowed. The feel of Alexis in my arms soothed the pain of my opened wound and I knew that when Father and I had finished aiding Agrias, it would be very difficult to leave Alexis and the friendship that had so obviously begun to form between us.

Alexis' grip on me loosened and I reluctantly released her. "Apologies, your tunic," she whispered, her fingers smoothing the wet material at my chest.

"Do not allow it to concern you, it is only water," I told her, taking her hands in mine. "I am more upset about the bathing oil."

Alexis looked to the broken amphora, nodding sadly.

"Allow me to escort you back to your room." *Then I shall go to Agrias and tell him I intend to punish the man who would dare raise a hand to the princess, I* added silently.

"You need your wound tended to. Allow me to do that first. It is again because of me you have been hurt."

I wiped the last of the tears from her cheek and brought her chin up so her eyes met mine. "I shall be fine, truly. We both know I have suffered worse in a fight. It can wait until Gnosidicus looks at it."

Alexis shook her head. "I want to do it. I must," she pleaded.

The words tugged at my heart and I drew a breath, nodding my assent. "Very well, but you shall not leave the room alone should you require herbs."

"There are plenty kept here," she replied, pointing to the pyxides on the shelf above the fire.

Noting a dish set I knew to be a mortar and pestle – an essential item when preparing medicines – beside them I nodded again, satisfied.

With her hand still in mine, Alexis led me to the bath. "Sit on the edge," she directed.

The rim itself was barely as wide as my palm, but I perched as best I could at the end of the oblong shaped vessel. The back of my thigh was across the end and right side of the bath, my knee bent and clasping the side so I did not simply topple sideways.

"I need to unclasp your pin and take your tunic down," Alexis said quietly. I hesitated, but again nodded my agreement. She remained behind me, reaching over my left shoulder to take the pin the rest of the way out of the material.

With painful slowness, Alexis peeled the linen away, murmuring a quiet apology as one area stuck to the blood above my wound. The front fell at my waist, unguided by her hands, exposing my breasts to the cool air.

The adrenaline of the fight had not entirely left me yet, nor had the feeling of pure comfort of holding Alexis in my arms.

"I have to wash the blood away to see what damage has been done," she said, her presence behind me shifting.

I only nodded, closing my eyes as a familiar stirring began in the pit of my stomach. I heard several items being placed on the edge of the bath and a moment later she returned, dipping a small cloth into the water beside us. I drew a breath, anticipating the discomfort.

"You were again where I needed you," she said, dabbing at the area with surprising gentleness.

I attempted to dismiss her words with a wave of my hand, but the movement caused me to suck in a sharp breath.

"Keep still," she said; her hand atop my shoulder. "You were not afraid of Melanthios just now. Your father told me you showed no fear of him or the other soldiers in the Spercheios Valley that day either. You are admirable and brave. I am so fortunate that on both occasions you were here."

For a moment I did not know how to respond. Words of gratitude for aid were not uncommon to me, though hearing Alexis speak the words touched me on a far deeper level. "I have known no other way for seven winters," I finally mumbled.

"Is that when you first picked up a weapon; seven winters ago?" Alexis asked.

I nodded.

"What led you to do so?"

"A mercenary."

"Would you speak of it with me?"

"You want to know why I kill?"

"I wish to know how you came to choose your path in life, or how it chose you," she replied.

"Oh," I said.

I drew another breath, exhaling it slowly. I did not wish to find myself so drawn to Alexis, but there was no doubt I was; our shared stories of past days and my inability to do anything but ensure she was safe from harm again tonight cemented it. I wanted to know of her life, just as I wished to share who I was with her when she asked it of me – and I knew she would ask it of me just as clearly as I knew I would speak of it to her when she did.

"Father and I were at Anticyra, a small town half a day's walk southeast of Delphi. The people there were friendly; families of farmers and such mostly, a few fishermen. We had been with them a moon, aiding them to harvest and prepare the hellebore they are famous for."

"I have heard of hellebore before," Alexis said. "When I was a child, Gnosidicus told me of Cleisthenes of Sicyon using it against his rivals at Cirrha. Do you know the story?"

I gave another nod. "I do. I heard the tale whilst at Anticyra, though if you would speak of it, I should enjoy hearing it again."

"I believed it was *you* who was supposed to be telling me a story," Alexis said, though I heard the smile in her voice as she settled a hand on my upper arm.

I drew a quick breath and released it. "You have finished cleaning my wound, have you not?" I asked, turning my head to catch her eye.

Her smile disappeared and a small frown appeared between her brows. She did not meet my gaze. "I have. I ... I apologize for asking such questions of you. You do not have to share anything with me if it is not what you wish."

I regarded her, reaching out my left hand to capture the one of hers she was about to move away. She finally raised her eyes to mine and I gave her a smile. "I only meant I would enjoy hearing you speak, for you are no doubt about to insert herbs into my wound and it shall be painful when you do so. Being able to concentrate on your words instead would be much preferable."

"Oh," she said.

I released Alexis' hand and she nodded slightly, reaching for the pyxides she had retrieved from the shelf.

15

I squeezed my hand against the marble as I waited.

"Cleisthenes of Sicyon has a grandson, also named Cleisthenes. The younger man has been unofficially named as the new archon at Athens following Hippias' departure," I offered, hoping to encourage her to speak.

"You have met him?" she asked.

"Briefly. He is favored enough, though his family's name has not always been synonymous with great deeds. It shall be interesting how he is received by the majority of Athenians."

"Oh ... Is it true the story of the Cirraean war between the city of Cirrha and Cleisthenes of Sicyon began many winters before the actual battle?" Alexis asked, the smell of herbs being mixed together reaching me.

"It is," I confirmed. "Cirrha was a well-fortified city in the southeast of the region of Phocis, with a harbor into the Gulf of Corinth and lush plains around."

"And as their riches grew, so did their greed," Alexis said, taking up the tale. "It is told that the soldiers of Cirrha frequently robbed and tortured people travelling to Delphi to see the Oracle, as well as imposing enormous taxes on the citizens who called Delphi home. They claimed the amount was fair due to the number of travelers who came to the town each winter, bringing coin for the Oracle as well as purchasing food and provisions for their journey home.

"The Cirraeans also attempted to steal land from Delphi, extending their boundary ever so slightly each winter, believing that once close enough, they could take Delphi for themselves and extend their power as well as their wealth."

"Yes. Cleisthenes was from Sicyon, in the north of the Peloponnese, between Corinth on the Isthmus and Achaea in the north-west," I nodded as Alexis pressed the first herbs against my injured skin. "He was known as a tyrant in his own land, though he did not approve of what the people of Cirrha were doing and vowed to stop them. He gathered together some of Delphi's neighbors and formed an alliance, intent on protecting Delphi and its people and visitors."

I sucked in a breath, the wind whistling between my teeth when Alexis pushed the medicine in deeper. "Apologies," she murmured, pausing in her efforts.

"Keep going. With both," I directed, clamping my back teeth together against the pain.

"When the neighbors allied with Cleisthenes, they consulted the Oracle, asking how they should subdue Cirrha. Most were of a peaceable nature, but the Oracle declared that only fierce war would keep Cirrha from returning to their current ways. Cleisthenes used his army's ships to block the city's harbor, before the allied forces besieged the city itself. By accident, Cleisthenes found a water pipe which provided Cirrha with fresh water and a man named Nebrus advised him to poison the supply using hellebore."

Alexis paused in her speech to gather more herbs and I attempted to relax my hand against the side of the bath. She returned to her task too soon, though the stinging was not as severe when she placed hands on my skin again. "The hellebore in the water caused the soldiers to vomit and defecate until their bodies were weak from the acts. Cleisthenes waited until they could not raise weapons against him and his allies and attacked, capturing Cirrha and defeating its people."

"Cleisthenes slaughtered those who had not already died from drinking too much of the poisoned water; and it mattered not if they were soldiers or citizens, for it further proved he would severely punish any who stood against him, even far from home," I finished.

"I would not want to meet him if that was true," Alexis murmured, pausing a moment before she went on. "There is a much older story of the use of hellebore, though it was known then as melampodium after the ancient healer Melampus."

"Is there? I have not heard of that."

"They say Melampus once used hellebore to cure the King of Argos' daughters from madness caused by the maenads who were followers of Dionysius."

I inhaled sharply again as Alexis added more herbs at my back, wondering how easy it would be to get her to speak of that too if I prompted her. "I believe I owe you your answer about my time in Anticyra now," I said instead, taking another deep breath.

"Only if you wish to share it," she replied, lightening her touch.

With you I do, I thought as I nodded. "The men and women of Anticyra who grow the hellebore are very careful who they sell it to. They make their transactions in person to other healers they have known for many winters; healers they trust only to use it for its healing properties for mania and fever. They do not part with it easily and do not sell it for a small price, such is its potency and the potential for misuse.

"When father and I were there, we aided them to harvest the plants. Shall I tell you how that is carried out?"

"Please."

"The hellebore grown by the Anticyrian people is white hellebore and it has a yellowish-white colored flower. They harvest it in the spring, just after the flowers bloom, on a night when there is no moon to be seen far above.

"Only the root is required, but the entire stem and flowers are extremely toxic to touch so when Father and I were invited to help, we wrapped material around our hands so the poison did not soak into our skin and harm us.

"Each of us were given a stick to draw a circle in the dirt around the plants and the eldest woman of the town chanted prayers to Athena before lifting the roots of the first plant from the ground. When hers was extracted, we did the same, chanting and pulling at the thick stems until we had them all. The old woman then took them away to be hung, dried and cut into individual portions ready for sale.

"A few days after the harvest, Father and I were making preparations to leave Anticyra when word came that a mercenary and his men approached, intent on taking the entire hellebore crop for themselves to defeat an enemy.

"They arrived within a candlemark, cutting down the slaves in the fields, women, children, whoever crossed their path. When they reached the town itself there was panic; people rushed to their homes, mothers scooped up babies. No one was safe, and none of them were able to defend themselves."

I closed my eyes at the memory, seeing it as clearly as the day it had happened. I had watched the leader ride in, swinging his sword and cutting down those I had come to know and care for the past moon. For only a moment I was frightened, the next I was certain, changed.

"I could not stand by and watch those people be slaughtered, to lose what they had worked so hard to produce. If they lost their hellebore, they would not see another winter for they needed the coin its sale would bring to buy food."

"The fields their slaves worked did not provide them with enough to eat?" Alexis asked.

"No, the land is rocky and often more grass than crops grow."

"Oh."

"The leader began to set fire to the homes, forcing the people back out into the dusty street. He and his men jumped from their horses and removed heads from bodies, children from their mothers' arms. They laughed and smiled as the people of Anticyra met Hades one after another."

Alexis drew a sharp breath and I paused. "Apologies, I forget myself. I should not speak such memories with you, I–"

"No, please, go on," Alexis murmured, her hand at my shoulder. "I asked you to speak of it."

I drew another breath before I did. "Father and I stood in the middle of the street and I saw his hand go to his waist. He had always kept a sword tied there, though I had never seen him use it, I did not know if he even knew how. One of the mercenary's men descended, his own sword held high above his head. I did not consider my actions, but a fire burned deep within and I drew Father's weapon from its sheath, driving it through the approaching man's stomach before he could take my father's, or anyone else's, life.

"I had never held a sword before that day, but I felled a second man before Father found two long spears and joined me, the two of us almost single-handedly protecting those left in Anticyra. I cannot explain how I believed I could use a weapon of any kind, but as soon as I felt the handle of the sword between my palms, it was as though I had always held it."

"How old were you?" Alexis asked in a quiet voice.

"Twelve winters."

I could have sworn I felt her lips brush my shoulder blade before she spoke again and my heart quickened. "You witnessed horrific deeds that day, saw things children should never see, yet you stood unafraid. You were unwilling to allow it to happen. It speaks volumes of you."

"They could not defend themselves," I shrugged. "A few of the men attempted to save their homes, but they had never raised a weapon and too many met Hades before the sun set. I swore that day to myself, and to my father, that I would never stand by and watch innocent people be hurt, their homes destroyed or their livelihoods taken from them. I would stand for them when they could not stand for themselves. I would aid them when there was no one else. I would always be where I was needed …" I trailed off, chest heaving, embarrassed by long hidden words, and knowing that I had failed both Kuria and Basileios in my promise.

As if sensing my sudden discomfort, Alexis' hand tightened briefly. "As I said, you are brave."

I had not spoken of my vow with anyone except my father, and after we left Anticyra he told me of his own heritage; his tribe of the Bessoi. His words had surprised me somewhat, but when he felled the mercenary's men I knew as certainly as I had known of my own ability with a weapon that it was not the first time he had raised weapons to fight.

"All done," Alexis announced quietly. "But you shall need a clean tunic."

16

"I have one," I replied, indicating the tunic I had brought with me to the bathing area. It lay crumpled on the floor beneath the table, but Alexis gathered it up, refolding it when she found it tangled. I could not put the garment on alone. She would have to aid me with that also. My heartbeat increased to a dangerous level.

Renewed adrenaline coursed through me with talk of past battles, as well as my own in Anticyra. I remembered how the hot flames of anger had engulfed me and taken over as I drew my father's sword and ran it through the men. How their blood had covered my hands, my body.

Alexis returned to the bath, her eyes on my face as she stood in front of me. My breath caught in my throat when I met the emerald green. I stood, allowing the material at my waist to fall to the ground. I stood as exposed to her as I had Queen Melina, in the very same room, and just as it had that night, desire fired in my stomach, and between my thighs.

A craving ignited my veins and, as I had after many skirmishes, I wished for a lover's hands to calm the raging inside. I wanted to feel Alexis' lips on mine, at my throat, everywhere across my skin. I wanted her with nothing short of desperation, though without words of encouragement I could not, would not, touch her. I ensured my hands remained fisted at my sides.

Her eyes travelled from mine, down my throat, to my breasts. My chest rose and fell in quick succession as she moistened her lips. I swallowed as the black centers of her eyes grew the lower they travelled.

She reached out and every nerve ending in my body livened, waiting for her touch. I held my breath, waiting, watching. She swallowed, her arm reaching around me to meet the other, drawing the soft linen around my body.

I almost cried out with the need for her, the breeze of my exhaled breath lifting the few strands of hair at the top of her head which had come loose from her plait.

Her eyes betrayed her hands, wishing to touch where they did. I wanted her, yet I did not place my hands over hers, nor draw her hips to mine. Part of me still remained in the past with Kuria, with the knowledge that I could never be with anyone who was promised to another. But despite that, despite all I had experienced, I knew if Alexis touched me, I would allow her. I would encourage her.

I felt the tremble of her hands as she refastened the pin at my shoulder, and my body mirrored the action. I needed a distraction – I would find another way to relieve the tension sitting coiled in my stomach later.

"Your father says you are to become Melanthios' wife; that it is the Molossian custom for a younger brother to claim the wife of an older brother who dies. But what if they are already betrothed?"

"It matters not. In the north, multiple betrothals are common. That is how Basileios was able to father other heirs for his line," Alexis replied, her voice shaking slightly.

"But Andreas is not content with that? He wants an heir from *you* specifically, and now he shall attempt to get it by his second son."

"Yes."

"Melanthios shall take it by force if he has to."

"Yes," Alexis said again. I would not allow Alexis to become Melanthios'. Agrias had said he was not akin to Basileios and his actions, his words tonight proved that. He had spoken little, yet I understood what his purpose had been.

"I ..." Alexis hesitated, keeping her eyes from mine.

I waited for her to go on, but she did not. I cupped her chin, tilting her head until her green eyes met my blue ones. Her cheeks colored, but she held my gaze when I took my hand away, finding her fingers instead.

"What is it?" I asked. "Tell me, please."

"I have seen what happens to the girls he has to his hut for the night. Melanthios is cruel." Tears swam in her eyes again. My jaw clenched, but I said nothing. "If I resist, he shall treat me worse than any of them. He has told me as much already. You must not deny him of me again, I fear for what he would do to you," she whispered.

"He would not succeed," I assured her, taking my hand from hers.

"Promise me you shall not give him another reason to harm you," Alexis pleaded, her fist bunching the tunic at my waist. I looked down to her hand. The tremble had returned to it.

"He shall not harm me," I said, raising my eyes and my hand, stroking the soft skin of the cheek Melanthios had struck.

The ugly, raised shape of his fingers had mostly faded, though I could still recall it on her skin. *I would never raise my hand to you* the thought flew into my mind and I barely clamped my teeth together before it escaped from my mouth.

"He shall not get away with this. I cannot allow you to return to Epirus with him."

"I doubt there shall be a choice. His brothers lead their army and the Illyrian tribes he has allied with here."

The entire line would be in Trachis at once. "How long until they arrive?" I asked.

"He did not say."

"Do you believe they know Basileios is dead? That Melanthios killed him?"

"It is doubtful, they were in Stratos when Basileios and I left and Melanthios and Andreas would not want to give them any ideas should they seek their elder brother's new prize of Trachis. Of me."

"They shall not have you, I give you my word," I said, slipping my fingers between hers again and squeezing gently. "It is time I saw you safely back to your room," I added, though I wished I did not have to leave her.

Alexis only nodded in response and I led her back to the central chamber, catching sight of Thaddeus and Moeris positioned outside the Throne Room. Thaddeus raised his hand, indicating I should join them. I nodded in response but continued into the central chamber with Alexis.

"Mine is this one," she indicated the door to the right.

"Wait here," I told her, placing her against the wall.

I pushed the door; allowing it to swing open as far as it could before I crept inside. The room was dimly lit by a torch in a metal holder. I checked behind the door. There were few places someone could be concealed in the room, but I took no chances, searching the space beneath the bed and below the chair, small table and various pieces of material draped across them. There was no one. Satisfied Alexis would be safe enough, I returned to the chamber.

"Where have you been?" Hesper whispered urgently, casting a glance to the door opposite Alexis'.

"Melanthios found me at the baths. Skylar protected me from him. Again," she replied.

"Go inside. Lock your door if you can and do not leave until I have made arrangements with your father for a guard to stand watch outside your room," I told the princess.

"Can you not return to protect her? You have proven yourself capable enough on two separate occasions," Hesper asked.

Much as I wanted to, I knew that if Melanthios had not been halfway to drunk, I may not have beaten him so easily. "No," I shook my head. "I cannot give Alexis the protection she requires. Would you stay with her until one of the king's men arrives?"

"Of course," Hesper nodded as Alexis reached for my hand.

"I shall remain as you ask, but please, you must heed *my* warning about Melanthios."

I took her hands in mine and inclined my head. "Good night, Princess. Be safe."

"And you," she murmured, pushing up on her toes to place a kiss on my cheek.

I swallowed, my desire instantly reignited and I fought not to raise my hands to her face and draw her lips to mine.

She released my fingers and I nodded to her and Hesper, closing the door to Alexis' room once they were both inside. I pushed away the feel of Alexis' lips on my skin, straightened my shoulders and drew in several deep breaths. The twinge in my back reminded me I must tread carefully, but I would not allow Melanthios to get away with hurting Alexis. No matter how ruthless she claimed their tribe was, I could be more so. To save her I would be as ruthless as I had to be.

17

I left the central chamber and made my way to Thaddeus and Moeris. Through the open doorway behind them, King Agrias' voice, along with Melanthios' could easily be heard.

"Join them now and defend yourself," Thaddeus whispered.

I nodded in reply and stepped into the Throne Room. Melanthios' face was bound in material, the skin below his eyes was dark and blood seeped through the bandages across his nose. Agrias sat on his throne, waving me into the room when he saw me, Thaddeus close behind.

"Come, please Skylar. I understand there has been an altercation between yourself and Melanthios this night."

"There has," I agreed. "Given that I have arrived late to these discussions, I assume Melanthios has given you some context already?"

"He has, though I would hear *your* explanation as he requests severe punishment as compensation for his injuries."

"I see. And what exactly has he accused me of?"

"I spoke to King Agrias and told him my brothers and I are often away defending our lands, whilst Basileios and Alexis remained in Epirus. As such, I have not had the privilege of knowing the princess well since she arrived in Dodona, and was attempting to get to know her better, prior to our upcoming betrothal, when you arrived at the baths."

Though I wanted to deny his lies, I would not give Melanthios the satisfaction. I kept my face neutral and said nothing, allowing him to fabricate his story for the time being.

"Your intention in seeking out my princess tonight was to do her harm and force her against her will," he continued. "In my attempts to defend her, you struck me."

"And yet you fled, leaving the princess to fight me off alone. If you wanted to protect her, why did you not take her with you? Or indeed return to the baths with soldiers to assist you?" I asked, unable to help myself, and surprised Melanthios had not foreseen the error of his claim.

"I—"

"So you do not deny your intentions for the princess?" Agrias interrupted.

"I did not touch the princess as you fear," I replied. "Melanthios does speak the truth though when he says I was at the baths, and that I struck him."

"I see," the king frowned, looking between the two of us.

"You have heard her confession, King Agrias. I ask now that she be held accountable for her actions. I do not believe it unwarranted for her to be stoned to death as is your Macedonian custom for betrayal."

Agrias raised his eyebrows at the suggestion, and I fought the impulse to speak before the king made his reply, raising my chin and meeting his gaze when he sought it.

"Whilst I follow Macedonian customs for many punishments, I do not believe *that* particular one to be warranted in this case," Agrias replied, addressing Melanthios and holding his hand up when the man opened his mouth to protest. "The punishment you suggest is reserved for those found guilty of plotting to kill the King, and I have heard no accusation of the same."

"You speak true, of course, but Skylar struck a member of the royal family, certainly it proves that she is not loyal to you, to your people," Melanthios continued.

"Until you and Alexis are officially betrothed, you are not a member of my family," Agrias replied.

Melanthios scowled above the reddening material but he was smart enough to keep any reply to himself, allowing Agrias to continue without interruption.

"I shall not call a capital trial, but I shall conduct my own enquiry into events. You were afforded discussion alone with me, so now I shall have the same with the woman you accuse. Moeris," he called. The General stepped into the doorway. "Take Melanthios into the courtyard, but do not venture too far; our business here is not yet at an end."

"Yes, King Agrias," Moeris nodded, waiting for Melanthios to join him.

"Our healer should be along at any moment to see to you, but before you leave with him, you shall receive my answer on the punishment you have requested."

"I thank you, King Agrias," Melanthios replied, bowing low and turning from the regent. As he made his way to the door, he bumped my shoulder, causing me to suck in a breath as the hit reverberated into my wound. "Consider carefully what you tell the king for my response shall be swift and harsh," he whispered, leaning close.

"As you found mine to be when you disrespected the princess," I growled, watching until he was out of sight.

"Approach," Agrias ordered. I returned my gaze to his, doing as asked and bowing respectfully before him. "Tell me of my daughter, where is she, is she well?" he asked, leaning forward.

"She was not harmed, and is in her room. Hesper is with her."

"Were you injured when you fought Melanthios?"

"Not as much as he," I shrugged. "Alexis saw to me."

"I am glad of it. Melanthios' version of events do not appear to ring true. Would I be correct in making that assumption?"

"You would," I nodded. "As Thaddeus can attest to, it was the princess and I who were speaking at the baths earlier, not her and Melanthios."

"It is as she says," Thaddeus confirmed, stepping forward.

"Understood. Continue."

"Melanthios arrived with the intention of having Alexis submit to him in whatever rough manner he chose."

"But you would not allow it?"

"Absolutely not," I growled. "When Alexis resisted, he raised his hand to her and I did not stand by and allow him to treat her so. We fought and when I bested him, he left."

"You already know they are to be betrothed; once that occurs, Melanthios can treat her as he pleases," the king said.

My mouth dropped open as I stared at him in disbelief. "You cannot allow it. She is your *daughter*. You must protect her from him."

He held up his hand and I paused. "I do not wish her to be subjected to such treatment, but it is the truth of the situation," he said.

"It should not be," I murmured. "She does not deserve that."

"No. She does not. From my first meeting with Andreas and his sons, I saw the differences between Basileios' manner and that of Melanthios'. I believed by choosing Basileios for Alexis that I had made the correct choice for my people, but now …" he sighed. "Now we find ourselves bound to Andreas and his family until Alexis' *death*." He shuddered as he said the word.

"By choosing Basileios over Melanthios you protected Alexis from many cruelties by his hand these past winters. We shall find a way to continue to protect her, together," I assured him.

"I thank you for your kind words."

"Alexis … Alexis told me …" I hesitated.

"What is it?" Agrias asked, in a voice that left no room for refusal of answer.

Thaddeus stood beside the king, his brows pulled together as he waited for what I was going to say next. I did not know anyone in Trachis well enough to know if they worked for the king or against him and his family, but Agrias needed to know about Melanthios' brothers.

"What is it?" the king asked again.

I considered the little I knew of Thaddeus; his actions towards Alexis and of his words to me since I had met him. I made my decision, addressing him first.

"Alexis trusts you, so I shall also, but know that if you betray her, I shall punish you just as harshly as any other."

"I love her as a sister, you may speak in confidence," he assured me.

I saw no flickering of lie behind his words. I nodded and wasted no further time informing the king and his guard of the imminent arrival of Melanthios' brothers and the Illyrian tribes he had allied with.

"It is as you said when we first spoke of them – they intend to take Trachis, even though they lost Stratos," I finished.

"So his entire line shall be here …" Agrias mused.

"Yes," I nodded, pleased his thoughts mirrored what I had considered when Alexis first spoke of it.

"We shall discuss this further, once the matter of your disagreement with Melanthios has been settled," Agrias said. "Given your answers already, I am afraid I must request two things which shall not be easy for you to accept, though I ask them of you to keep my daughter safe." I exhaled deeply but said nothing, waiting for him to go on. "First, I must ask you to stay away from Alexis, for a few days at least. I do not want to give Melanthios any reason to suspect you hold her confidence in what he has done, or what is to come."

It was a reasonable request, and with the warning Melanthios gave me to consider what I told the king, it could work in our favor; my body needed time to heal before I could face him again.

"Would you speak with Alexis of our agreement? I would not wish her to believe I had abandoned her after what occurred tonight."

"You care for her a great deal already," Thaddeus noted.

"Yes," I replied. "What is your second request?" I added, facing the king again.

Agrias hesitated before replying. "I shall ask you to apologize to Melanthios. I must be seen to punish you somehow or he shall seek his own revenge against you and I do not wish for that. You do not have to be sincere; just say the words so he does not suspect we know his truth."

I ground my back teeth against one another. "Fine," I replied, the words grudgingly torn from my lips. "But I do it to keep Alexis safe, not myself."

"I understand, and I thank you. Thaddeus, fetch Melanthios and allow us to be done with him for now."

"You trust him?" I asked quietly, watching Thaddeus cross the room.

"With my life," the king replied. "Thaddeus has been my most loyal friend, agreeing to join me when I wished to leave our homeland, both of us barely thirteen winters old."

I nodded again, finding that I too felt Thaddeus' loyalty and love for the king and his family. Melanthios trailed Thaddeus to stand beside me in front of Agrias.

"It appears Skylar has indeed wronged you, Melanthios," the king began. Melanthios looked smugly at me, as though he truly believed I would submit to him. I held his eyes until he returned his to Agrias. "But, and I hasten to make this *very* clear: there is to be no stoning, no retribution of any sort on your behalf towards this girl. She shall make her apologies but it goes no further. Understood?" Melanthios' smile faltered ever so slightly, but he inclined his head in agreement. "And Skylar, you shall not strike Melanthios again, you shall keep well clear of him. The princess is, until further notice, to be left alone by all involved here tonight," Agrias warned, holding Melanthios' gaze. "The queen has asked that Alexis teach Skylar to be more lady than warrior; which I assure you is well within the princess' capabilities. So, when it pleases the queen, Skylar shall accompany Alexis to all common places the women of Trachis populate."

"I would not wish to incur the queen's ill favor. I understand, and shall allow it," Melanthios agreed. "For now," he added, sliding a glance my way.

Clearly the king had not spoken to his queen recently about her intentions for my spending time with the princess, yet I was not about to correct him if it meant I could see Alexis sooner rather than later and ensure personally that she was safe from harm.

"Good. Skylar, you have words to speak to Melanthios?"

I nodded, turning to the man I had quickly come to despise. "Melanthios," I began.

"Should Skylar not kneel before me to make her apology?" he asked.

"I d–" Agrias began. I gave a subtle shake of my head and, drawing in a deep breath, got down on my knees, face upturned I met the arrogant smile above as anger boiled in my blood.

"I apologize that I did not do more damage when I had the chance," I muttered.

"Skylar," Thaddeus cautioned as Melanthios' hand clenched into a fist.

I blew out another deep breath and began again. "I apologize for striking you, Melanthios. I should not have done so. I ask your forgiveness and thank you for the opportunity to present myself at your feet."

"I accept your apology," he said, lowering his face to mine. "Though in future, I caution you to stay out of concerns which are not your own, and away from my property." The stench of wine and blood mixed together on his breath, blowing into my face as he panted. I clenched my jaw again, holding back the retort I was desperate to make.

"As it pleases you," I replied, dipping my chin in acknowledgement.

He straightened and turned to Agrias. "I shall go with your healer now, if you do not seek me for further words."

"That is all for now," Agrias nodded. "Gnosidicus is our finest healer and shall see to you well."

I got to my feet as Melanthios bowed briefly and left the room.

"Thaddeus, fetch Leandros, there is much to discuss before we retire," Agrias directed.

"King Agrias, would you ask Moeris to stand watch outside Alexis' room until you are able to speak with her?" I asked.

"Of course. Thaddeus, see to that also please." Thaddeus nodded in reply before making his way out the door. "I shall have Gnosidicus tend to your own wounds afterwards as well," Agrias said.

"Thank you," I nodded.

18

"You told Melanthios that the queen wished for the princess and me to spend time together, but I can assure you that is not the way she feels," I said to the king as we waited for Thaddeus to return with my father.

He smiled, waving away my words. "I am aware of what the queen wishes, better perhaps than she believes I do. She shall not deny Alexis of her desire to see you, nor you to see her or spend time with her. Trust me in this."

I only nodded in reply as the other two men arrived. A brief recount of the night's events ensued, and I repeated what Alexis had told me of the arrival of Melanthios' brothers, the army, and the Illyrian tribes he had allied with for my father's benefit.

"Alexis does not know when they shall arrive, or if they know it was Melanthios who killed Basileios. Indeed, they may not even know their eldest brother is dead," I told them.

"Do you know much about the younger men?" Father asked Agrias. "Are they more akin to Melanthios or Basileios?"

"Truthfully I do not know, though I believe they are closer with Melanthios being that they are warriors."

"Perhaps we should simply go ahead with our original plan and have Skylar and Leandros kill Melanthios, and then his brothers, when they arrive," Thaddeus suggested.

"No, there would be too many questions if all the brothers died here when there was no war," Father countered. "Their deaths would be too obviously traced back to Agrias, especially as Andreas sent Melanthios specifically after Basileios."

"So we encourage a war to begin and stand and fight with Agrias' army," I argued. "Any father who loves his child would not hesitate to stand against as many as needed to ensure her safety."

"I hear the words coming from your mouth, but I cannot believe I am hearing them," Father growled. "We do not *incite* wars, Skylar. We never have and we shall not begin to do so now. We have been in the midst of too many where innocent lives have been lost, the same is bound to happen here to people Agrias and his family love."

I drew a deep breath, knowing that my father spoke true; the war at Stratos so recently was one that had certainly taken too many innocent, young lives.

"If I can avoid a war with the Epirotes and Illyrians, it is certainly the course I would prefer to take," Agrias nodded.

"What if the brothers learn it was Melanthios who killed Basileios and can be convinced to turn against him and kill him?" I suggested. "That way his death would not fall back onto Agrias."

"Better," Father agreed. "They may fear he shall do the same to them given the chance, and seek to eliminate the threat."

"We need to know how much they know about Melanthios' journey here. What reason he gave them when he told them to meet him here. Why do they believe Basileios was coming to Trachis?" I wondered aloud.

"Exactly," Father nodded. "But how can we get the answers?"

"Alexis?" Thaddeus suggested.

"Not a chance," I immediately replied. "I am not prepared to have her in such close proximity to Melanthios. To get those answers from him she would need to..." I trailed off, unable to speak the rest of my thoughts.

"Agreed," Agrias nodded. "We cannot put her in such a dangerous position."

"What if you or Leandros were able to convince Melanthios you were just mercenaries, loyal to no one and easily bought?" Thaddeus continued.

"It may have worked, had Skylar not stood against Melanthios in his attempt to get to the princess earlier this evening," Agrias replied with a shake of his head. "There is no way he would believe it now."

"True. We need someone else who could get close enough without raising suspicion," Father agreed.

"Moeris," Thaddeus offered after a moment. "He is Malian born. He could convince Melanthios that he has never been happy having to serve under Agrias and his Macedonian ways."

"And as head of Agrias' army, he has influence to convince other soldiers to join him and strengthen Melanthios' numbers," I nodded, warming to the idea. "If he is able to gain Melanthios' confidence, he would gain access to the brothers and find out where they stand as well. Would he agree to such an assignment?"

"I believe so," Agrias replied. "I shall speak to him and gauge his interest. If he agrees, we can talk specifics with him in the morning, if it is not too much to ask you to wait until then? Alexis will be impatient to hear what has happened since you left her and I wish to have Gnosidicus see you before he leaves; I suspect he will advise you to rest for the remainder of the night, and I believe we could all do with some of that."

"As you wish," I replied with a nod, fatigue seeping into my limbs at the mere suggestion of sleep. "Until the morning then."

"Until the morning," Agrias echoed.

Thaddeus raised his hand in farewell and Father accompanied me to my room. I hugged him briefly and prepared to close the door behind me when he placed a hand on the wood to prevent me from shutting him out.

"I heard your words to Agrias, but I also recognize that look in your eyes. You must *not* go after Melanthios. If he is killed here and his brothers *are* loyal to him, you know who they shall target first in retaliation."

"Alexis, Agrias and Melina," I replied.

"Exactly. Be smart. We can protect them, protect *her*. But Agrias needs your mind, not your sword right now. It must be as it always is – we wait until we have all the information before we attack."

"I know," I nodded. "I shall stay away from him for now. I give you my word."

"Good," he said, allowing me to close the door.

I sat heavily on the bed to await the healer's arrival, my thoughts firmly with Alexis. I had always cared for those I protected, but with Alexis it was more than that. I wanted to protect her from all the cruelties of the world but I also deeply desired her. I wanted to know how she would feel when I kissed her, when I held her – not in comfort as I had at the baths – but in passion. How would it be to hear her say she felt the same?

With little more than kind gestures and gentle caresses, she had easily drawn words of my past from my lips. That I was willing to speak of so much more if she asked it of me was almost addictive. Alexis touched me far deeper than I had ever imagined someone could; than I had expected anyone to. It was becoming difficult to accept that once I left Trachis, I may never see her again.

I blew out a deep breath. I could not keep considering more with Alexis. I knew only too well how that would end. Kuria had been betrothed to Stamatis but had spoken words of my remaining with her, even if her wish had only been for the evening. Alexis was promised to Melanthios, and though she did not wish for him, neither did she speak words of wanting to be with me. I hated that she was to be Melanthios' but if I had any chance of changing it, Father was right; I had to be smarter than him. I could not allow my feelings for Alexis to put her in danger. I *must* keep away from her so she remained safe until the queen, or king, felt it time we were reunited. As hard as that was going to be.

19

I opened the door to the king and Moeris late the next morning, admitting them inside and offering them wine and a seat on my bed as I took up a place beneath the window.

"Moeris has agreed to aid us with Melanthios," Agrias announced.

"Agrias spoke of what you need me to find out, and by using my heritage, I believe I can convince Melanthios to tell me everything we need to know," the General said, returning the nod I gave him.

"Subtly, though," I cautioned. "We do not want him to suspect Alexis has shared anything he told she and Basileios."

"Of course," Moeris agreed. "I thought to ask him to come stay at the barracks; that would afford the two of you some space from one another, and allow me to speak with him more easily."

"Melanthios is currently housed in the room at the end of this wing," Agrias offered as way of explanation.

"He has always known where I was, indeed when I first met Gnosidicus he came to this very room. I am surprised he did not attempt to finish what his man began in the valley before," I mused.

"Perhaps he was waiting to see if you were a threat before he approached you," Agrias shrugged. "In any case, he now considers you either an enemy or a problem to be overcome, so the idea is a good one."

"Indeed," I agreed. "Moeris, you mentioned your heritage to be an advantage in gaining Melanthios' trust, as did Thaddeus last night, how do you plan to do so?"

"Allow me to share the story of my upbringing before Moeris answers," Agrias said. I nodded that the king continue. "I am the first-born son of Alcetas, King of Macedonia, of the Argead line. When I was six winters old, my father died. On his deathbed, he named my younger brother, Amyntas, as his successor. Amyntas was barely ten days old at the time so knew nothing of the arrangement for several winters."

"Why did your father not name you as successor – you were the older sibling?" I asked.

"In Macedonia, the King is free to choose whichever of his children he wishes to succeed him, regardless of birth order. He named Amyntas over me because my mother was not his favored wife; she was not his Queen."

"Your father had more than one wife?" I asked.

"Yes. Another Macedonian custom," Agrias agreed. I nodded, wondering if perhaps it was an 'all over' northern custom, rather than just a Macedonian one as Alexis had also mentioned Basileios had other wives apart from her. "I was not pleased with his decision, but could do nothing about it. Many feared I would attempt to kill my half-brother and claim the throne for myself, and perhaps I would have if there had not been those to guide me to another path.

"I remained loyal to my brother, to the wish of my father that Amyntas be the one to rule the capital. But when Amyntas took the throne in his own right at seven winters, I left. He attempted to change my mind and I have no doubt there were those who told him to keep me close lest I take up arms against him."

"Did you intend to do so?" I asked.

"No. I wished only to find somewhere to call my own, to be master of my own people, my own destiny. With my dearest friend, Thaddeus, I travelled for several winters through Macedonia, Thrace and parts of Epirus before turning south. When we arrived in Trachis, I knew I had found my new home. I loved everything about the plains, mountains and rivers and returned to Macedonia immediately to make arrangements."

"Those arrangements included how Agrias would conquer the people of the area – the Malian tribe I belonged to, and recognizing him as our King," Moeris interjected.

"You did not want to rule somewhere in Thessaly? I have heard the Thessalian plain is beautiful also."

"No, the Macedonians have an understanding with the Thessalians. We never fought them, nor sought their lands, as they have not ours. We have lived peaceably with them from the beginning. Indeed we share many similarities, including several of the gods we worship. Besides, the fertile lands, the sea, the uniqueness of the hot springs, the beautiful mountains behind our city … as soon as I laid eyes on Trachis, I knew the area must be mine."

"So did you bring an army from Aigai to fight the Malians? Did you eradicate anyone who stood against you and enslave the ones who agreed to remain?"

"Not at all. There are few instances where I would not attempt negotiation first and as I was almost twenty winters old, I sought a betrothal and a family, as well as a new home. I formed an alliance with the Malians, taking one of their own as my wife and promising that they would not be sent from the place they had always called home.

"There was a little resistance at first, but when I spoke of my vision for the palace and explained the strategic trade position they possessed with the Pass of Thermopylae, they saw the opportunity I brought. They welcomed me and aided me to build the magnificent palace you see now."

"And we have remained loyal ever since," Moeris added.

"The Malian woman you took as your wife, was that Melina? Or do you have others, as your father did?"

Agrias smiled. "I have only ever been betrothed once. It was not my intention for the longest time, there were other women I could have taken as my own, not only here but from other nearby tribes or from Macedonia itself. But I fell in love with the strong, beautiful girl recommended to me. With her in my bed, I never wished for anyone else, and when we had children, I never sought another."

I noted the king used the plural when speaking of children, but did not press him for the details. "So when you returned to Aigai, you struck an agreement with your brother that you would become King of Trachis?"

"I did."

"So, you understand how I could bend the truth of what happened, as you alluded to, in how our people were subjugated under Agrias, to convince Melanthios of my unhappiness, and worth to him?" Moeris asked.

"I do," I nodded. "It appears you are indeed the right man to approach him."

"And if it pleases you both, I shall go to him now and begin our charade. I shall find a way to keep you updated with my progress so as not to draw his suspicion."

"Very good," Agrias nodded, dismissing Moeris.

"Be careful, and good luck," I added as he left my room.

"Thank you," he replied.

"He appears loyal to you. You do not fear there is too much truth in his story?"

"No. From the very beginning, Moeris supported me in convincing his people to allow me here, and to join with me to make Trachis as prosperous as ever. It was he who chose Melina from the other girls to become my wife, though I know he was fond of her himself." I nodded.

The king's head dipped to the side in a manner that matched his daughter's as he regarded me. "May I ask you something?" I nodded again. "Your shield does not bear the picture of a specific town, does it? You do not align yourself with a specific tribe or people."

I shook my head. The face of my shield bore a dark, kneeling figure – neither male or female, adult or child – face upturned and arms outstretched as though pleading for something from the one who would have stood above it. "No. It is my own design."

"What does it symbolize?"

"That I fight for those who cannot fight for themselves, that I shall protect them when they cannot protect themselves."

Agrias considered my answer. "So, you do not fight exclusively for one particular person, for one particular people?"

"My father and I have always gone where we were needed," I replied with a shrug.

"And therein lies my worry. I have grown fond of you, and of your father, since you arrived, but I fear for what I have heard."

"And what is that?" I frowned.

"You have fought both alongside *and* against the Athenian army. You were offered coin on both occasions, just as I offered for your aid here."

"If we believe the cause to be just then yes, we accept coin and stand beside whoever asks it of us," I agreed.

"But do you feel no sadness at fighting and killing those you may once have stood beside in battle?"

My frown deepened. "Of course, but I cannot stand by and do nothing when those they fight are undeserving or when more people would benefit if the side I chose at that time was to be victorious."

"So it is not the amount of coin that determines who you stand with? For example, if Melanthios was to offer you double the amount I did, you would not aid him in his pursuit of Alexis and making Trachis his?"

"Never," I assured him. "There is nothing I wish for less than to see Alexis return to Epirus as Melanthios' wife. I give you my solemn word on that, King Agrias. My father and I are *not* mercenaries who simply kill for the enjoyment and coin we receive. We care for those we aid."

"Yes, I am starting to understand that," Agrias replied. "And though I sought cold-hearted killers when I sent for you, I find myself glad you are quite different."

"If we were just hired killers, we would not be concerned about what happened once we had killed Melanthios and his brothers, even if that occurred here rather than in Epirus. We would kill, collect our money and leave you to your fate without another thought. But I give you my word here and now that I shall not leave Trachis until I am certain that you and your family are safe from Andreas and the Illyrians. Indeed, even when it comes time for us to move on, I do not know how I shall leave thoughts of you all behind," I added, Alexis' face coming to mind as my heartbeat increased.

"I have no doubt that it shall be the same for certain members of my family also," Agrias nodded, holding my gaze. "But allow us to turn our thoughts to other, more pleasant matters, tell me more of your time with the King of Sparta."

I grinned and nodded, spending the rest of the morning entertaining the king.

20

The knock at my door was quiet but still it startled me. I put the amphora of water down, pleased I was now able to lift it above my head; my solitary training coming along well as I attempted to find ways to amuse myself confined to my room the past three days. I crossed the floor and swung the door open, finding Alexis on the other side looking furtively about.

"Princess?" I enquired, my heart lifting at the sight of her.

A smile lit her face. "May I come in?" she asked, her eyes continuing to dart towards the central chamber behind her.

"Of course," I replied. I stepped aside and quickly closed the door behind her as I saw Melanthios leaving the andron with Moeris, heading for the barracks. I had pictured Alexis many ways the past few days – mostly as the subject of Melanthios' cruelty, quickly followed by the ways in which I would make him pay for those brutalities and how I would soothe her injuries; both inside and out. "What are you doing here?"

"How are you healing?" she asked at the same time.

"I am well," I laughed. "Though it is a pity you could not have come to inspect your work earlier."

"My mother has kept me otherwise occupied during our separation."

"Ah," I said, nodding. "The queen has certain … expectations for you and they do not include tending to me. I expect she is pleased your father asked me to keep away from you in light of the incident with Melanthios." Alexis lay her head on the side, regarding me. "What?"

"What did she say to you about me?"

"I do not understand your question," I replied, smoothing the front of my tunic to cover my evasion.

Alexis stepped closer and laid her hand on my arm. "Tell me what she said to you," she insisted.

"Your mother and I spoke of much. I cannot recall all of the conversation," I shrugged. Alexis' eyes captured mine and she raised her brows as she stared me down. "She may have mentioned that we should not spend as much time together now that I have recovered," I eventually replied, unable to prevent the words spilling from my lips.

"I cannot believe her," Alexis frowned, dropping her hand and pacing back and forth before me.

I reached for her wrist and halted her steps, grinning when she looked up at me. "I did not tell her I would heed her words."

"There are few who would dare deny my mother what she wishes."

I shrugged and released her, wondering if it was a daughter's respect Alexis showed for Melina or fear for what had come before. "If that is so then I am surprised Hesper does not have to accompany you everywhere to ensure you do not sneak a visit akin to this to me," I said, attempting to keep the conversation light.

She held my gaze. "Now that you have spoken of it, I would not be surprised if my mother suggested it."

"But we are alone here, Princess. What causes you to believe your mother would find out?" I asked, leaning closer and enjoying the faint blush that crept up Alexis' neck.

Deep desire sprung to life and my heart beat wildly beneath my chest, all good sense and reason leaving me as Alexis' tongue ran along her bottom lip.

"Somehow my mother knows all that I do."

I wished there was a timber locking device on my door as there was on the front doors to the palace. I craved to be alone with Alexis, to enjoy her company without interruption or fear of discovery. Our days apart had only served to fuel my desire for her rather than dampen it.

"Perhaps she listens at doors, should I check?" I asked, though I was half-serious.

Alexis' eyes slid towards the door, but she shook her head. "I believe we are safe enough. My mother retired early this evening," she replied, her gaze resettling on mine.

"So you snuck from your room? Very devious, Princess," I said, unable to resist walking my fingers over her forearm and past her elbow.

I did not miss the shiver that gripped her, or the way her skin prickled beneath my fingers. She did not move away, her chest rising and falling in quick succession. I trailed my fingers back to her hand. She turned it so our palms rested against one another's as they had in this very room so many nights ago.

"I wanted to see you," she said quietly.

Need for her stirred in my stomach and I was once again struck by how different Alexis was to anyone I had met before. The way she laid her hands on me so often, how she had allowed me to trail my own over her just now. Perhaps I could have her as I wanted. Perhaps she wanted to be with me too.

"I am glad," I murmured.

Alexis lifted her arm, spinning her hand so her fingers slid between mine. My breath shortened as areas lower than my stomach tightened.

"You do not appear close with your mother."

"No," she replied, swallowing.

"Would you speak with me of what it was to grow with a mother's guidance and love?"

"I have no idea." Alexis replied, stiffening.

"Oh, I believed ... apologies. Is Queen Melina not your birth mother?"

Alexis blew out a breath, taking her hand from mine. I instantly missed the contact and my blood cooled at the look on her face. "She is, but she has never treated me as her daughter. Her child. I am just ... I," the princess paused again, but I saw the hurt cross her face.

I lifted her chin so our eyes met. "Tell me, please."

Alexis swallowed again, but did not look away. "I am but a disappointing replacement for her son," she murmured. I took my hand from her face, wrapping my fingers around hers as another tremor ran through her. She drew a breath before she went on. "I had an older brother; Alexander. From those who knew of him, who knew my parents at that time, I know my mother doted on him, spoiled him; loved him more than anything else in this world. Her entire life revolved around him until he died of illness when he was almost two winters old. My mother was heartbroken, insisting that she and Father immediately have another child to replace the one she lost so unfairly. My father would not deny her, for he wanted only to make her happy, and I soon grew inside her.

"But when I was born, I was not the son she had so desperately wished for. I did not have my brother's dark hair, or the eyes that matched hers. I was inadequate. She shunned me, leaving me to be fed and cared for by a wet-nurse and my father. She did not visit me or hold me. For the longest time I knew her only to be the woman who sat beside my father when we ate. I did not know that by calling her mother she was supposed to love me and spend time with me as my father did."

Tears welled in Alexis' eyes and swift anger and sadness gripped my chest. It was not the first time I had heard a tale of a child being rejected by a parent, yet knowing that Alexis had had to endure it pierced at me deeper than any before. How could Melina have treated her own child so? She had not received a son, but did that not mean their bond would be stronger, that she could teach her daughter the ways of the world? Of men and women and what was expected from her? Did Melina's own mother not do the same for her? I held tighter to Alexis' hand, wanting nothing more than to take her in my arms and relieve her of the hurt she carried.

"Did they attempt to have another son after you were born?"

"Yes, but my mother was never able to carry another child to term. When they no longer made attempts, Father forced Mother and me to spend time together, to have her teach me as a mother should," Alexis continued. "But we did not enjoy it, arguing and finding ways to avoid each other more than anything. Soon I was betrothed to Basileios and left Trachis, which I believe was a blessing to us both."

"I am sorry," I said quietly.

"Do not be, sometimes mothers and daughters are not meant to be close, it is best for all if they are not together ..." she trailed off, instantly squeezing my fingers between hers. "Skylar. Apologies. I speak out of turn. You have never known of your mother and here I speak of how awful it is to have one."

I gave her a small smile and placed my fingertips at her cheek, caressing the soft skin. "Do not apologize, it was I who asked you of your relationship with the queen," I assured her. "I only wish it had been different for you, that I had the power to change it. To grow without knowing your mother's love when she was so near is far crueler than to never know her at all."

Alexis closed her eyes, leaning into my touch. I too reveled in the simple feeling of her skin against mine. There was no doubt she wanted to spend time with me, despite our forced separation and her mother's insistence we not see one another, just as I wanted to see her. "Thank you," she whispered. She drew another breath as she opened her eyes. "Leandros says your mother was lost to the two of you the night of your birth."

"Yes," I nodded, taking my hand from her face. "It was my entrance into the world that ended hers."

Alexis nodded, catching my hand between both of hers and settling them against her breastbone. "Would you speak of it with me? If it is not too painful."

I inhaled deeply before I replied. "It is not painful, for you cannot miss someone you have never known."

"You truly believe that?"

I shrugged. "The idea of having a mother fascinated me somewhat when I was a child, but I did not *miss* her exactly. It is not as if I knew her, then had her taken from me; that was my father's pain to endure and I am certain the knowledge of such is far worse." Alexis' fingers stroked mine as I spoke; calming and encouraging me to speak words I had only ever thought. "It was because of me that they were so far from their homes and a healer. My mother's family did not approve of my parents' love so they fled while I was still in her belly. The night she birthed me, her family found them, my mother had passed into Hades' realm already but father was terrified her parents would take me from him, so he wrapped me in a blanket and slipped out in the middle of the night, running until he reached Sparta. We have never stayed in one place for more than a few moons since. I believe he still holds the fear that they may come for me." I inhaled deeply before I spoke again. "But I am grown now, I do not need them to raise me and I cannot forgive them for condemning my father to walk alone in this life without my mother. I would never leave him in favor of them for he sacrificed so much just to allow me to live; he cared for me and loved me when he could have turned his back on me."

"Skylar," Alexis whispered. I looked up to find tears in her eyes. I smiled and dried the one that escaped down her cheek.

"Do not be sad. If my life had been different I would not have found myself here now, with you, and I would not change that for anything," the words were out before I could censor them.

"Still …"

"Perhaps that is enough about mothers for one evening," I said, touched by her tears. "I am certain we can find better things to speak of. Or do," I added, my grin widening as my fingers traced the line of her jaw. Her cheeks colored again and the pulse point in her neck jumped. My heartbeat matched hers as I waited for her response, my body heating as I considered exactly what we could do.

She cleared her throat, wiping the last of the tears from her eyes and I reluctantly dropped my hand from her face when she took a step back. "I wish I could stay, but I had best return to my room in case Mother decides to check in on me."

"You believe she would?" I asked, raising an eyebrow.

"Perhaps," she replied with a shrug. "Though since returning I have ensured I keep the locking device across my door when I am in there."

"A wise idea," I agreed with a nod. "Though it is not only your mother I worry would pay you such a visit."

"No," Alexis agreed. "Thank you for what you did for me with Melanthios at the baths. Father said you had to apologize for striking him."

"I spoke the words he wanted to hear," I agreed with a nod.

She returned it and took a step towards the door before turning back, keeping her eyes from mine when she spoke. "Would you meet me tomorrow night? Late, at the baths?"

"Another clandestine meeting, Princess? Perhaps I am becoming a bad influence on you?" I grinned.

"A welcome influence, I assure you," she replied, meeting my eyes again. "I … I thought I could wash your hair, unless my mother did that for you."

"She did not," I replied, my breath catching. "But I am capable of such a task, you do not need to."

"It would be my pleasure. I have always found it extremely relaxing and enjoyable. As a princess there was always someone charged with carrying out the task for me."

"Perhaps they too enjoyed their task for they were able to glimpse the princess in her gloriously naked form."

The words were out before I could stop them. "I, uh, apologies."

Alexis laughed, taking my hand and squeezing it as she spoke. "There are few I allow to see me in such a manner these days."

I attempted, and failed, to draw a full breath. "I would be honored to allow you to wash my hair for me," I murmured.

"Good," she smiled, opening the door and taking a peek out. "Sleep well, Skylar."

"And you," I replied, holding open the wood and watching until she was safely across the courtyard and in the central chamber. She held her hand up in a wave and I returned it, waiting another moment before going back inside.

I lay on my bed, our conversation replaying in my mind. Alexis' tears at hearing of the night my mother died surprised, and yet comforted me. Perhaps if I had ever shared the tale with another their reaction would have been the same, though I could not be certain. Her own tale of birth and subsequent treatment by the queen inflamed outrage beneath my breast; I did not understand how parents who were fortunate enough to live to see their children grow could treat them in such a manner.

I have begun to care deeply for you, Alexis, though there are so many reasons I should not. I believe it is the same for you too and it has always been dangerous for others to feel that way. My mother wanted to keep me, but died attempting to have me. Kuria too.

I could not bear the same fate to befall Alexis, and I knew that, foolish as it was to wish for, I wanted more with her than simply sharing her bed for an evening. I wished tomorrow was already upon us for an entire day felt a long time to wait to see the princess again.

21

I reached the bathing rooms, my footsteps as light as my heart. I hoped the candlemark was late enough for Alexis, though I wanted to arrive before her and have the water almost warm by the time she arrived.

"Skylar, it is rather late for bathing, is it not?" the queen's voice greeted me as my fingers reached the handle.

I turned, meeting her with a cool stare. "It is never too late to enjoy a bath," I replied.

"Skylar, there you are, I believed we were going to meet at the kitchen *before* you bathed," Hesper said, arriving beside Melina.

I raised an eyebrow, but the look on Hesper's face told me I should play along. "Oh, my apologies Hesper, I must have misunderstood."

"Skylar is to join you at the kitchen?" the queen asked skeptically.

"Yes, she wishes to learn how to make the honey-sweetened bread she has so enjoyed since coming to Trachis."

"And it is *you* who intends to teach her? At this candlemark?"

"Of course, my Queen. Unless you wish to?" Hesper replied, bowing slightly in Melina's direction.

"You are more than aware that my talents do not lie in the kitchen, Hesper," Melina replied pointedly.

"Yes, Queen Melina," Hesper acknowledged, and I caught the hint of a smile as she inclined her head again in the older woman's direction.

"Well, do not allow me to keep you from your baking," the queen sniffed.

"Thank you," I nodded, stepping around Melina and allowing Hesper to loop her arm through mine. We cut across the courtyard and entered the banqueting hall beside the palace entrance. It was a large room, the same width and length as my own with windows high in the wall looking out to the east.

"Apologies, Melina has been keeping a close watch on Alexis," Hesper murmured.

"Alexis sent you to escort me here?" I asked. She nodded, unthreading our arms and indicating I precede her through the door and into the kitchen. I noted the small door to the left and realized it would lead out to the walkway Gnosidicus had mentioned.

"She still intends to meet then?" I asked, hoping Hesper would answer positively.

"Of course I do," Alexis replied, the smile evident in her voice. I turned, a grin breaking out on my face as she materialized from a small space which appeared a cupboard, full of bags of grain and flour.

"Good evening, Princess," I said, bowing slightly in her direction.

"I am pleased to see you again," she replied, crossing to my side and laying her hand on my arm.

"The mixture is ready in varying forms, just as we discussed," Hesper said. I raised an eyebrow again, looking between the two women for explanation.

Alexis smiled. "We intend to keep up the pretense of cooking in case Mother wishes to check on your progress."

"You two have put some planning into this," I noted, grinning.

"A well-made plan is always vital," Alexis agreed returning it.

"Indeed," I nodded.

"I shall leave you to speak," Hesper said, closing the door between the kitchen and banquet hall only halfway as she left.

"Thank you," I called after her.

"You did not take new clothing with you to the baths?" Alexis asked, pointing to my empty arms.

"No, I have not found myself in need of such, confined to my room as I have been. Though I hope to be able to join the soldiers soon; I must train with them in readiness for the Illyrians or any other enemies who intend to come this way. I must learn their formations, and their strengths and weaknesses."

"It sounds as though you also enjoy planning when it comes to attack."

"It is vital," I replied, mirroring her words. She smiled again as I leant against the table. "I would have taken bathing oil, but after Melanthios' visit the other night I have not been able to go to the agora to find a replacement." Alexis dropped her eyes and I chided myself for having brought it up again. I pushed off the table and crossed to her, lifting her chin. "It was a thoughtful gift. I am only sorry I did not take better care of it."

She raised her eyes to mine, a tight smile crossing her lips.

"Was Hesper going to wash your hair when we met the first night I experienced the excellence of your baths?" I asked, lowering my hand to take hers.

"Yes and then I would have washed hers, as we have many times."

"She is a close friend? You care for her?" I asked, jealousy swirling in my stomach at her words.

"I love her very much. She wishes I could stay here with her in Trachis."

"Oh," I murmured, my stomach dropping with a wave of disappointment. Alexis loved Hesper. She may have been betrothed first to Basileios, but her heart belonged to another. She treated me kindly and wished for my company, but she would never care for me as I did her.

I believed I had already received my punishment for allowing Kuria to take me to her bed, but perhaps the gods were not done with me yet and I would be fated to want the affections of someone I could not only never have, but who would also never return my feelings. My chest ached as I drew a deep breath. Melina must know of Alexis' love for Hesper, for women in particular – why else would she have warned me to stay away?

Alexis continued to speak as the knowledge settled heavily in my stomach. "Hesper was my first friend at the palace. She has always been my dearest friend. Her mother and father worked in the kitchen, as she does now. You know how well she bakes the honey-sweetened bread, if anything could make me stay here, it would be her bread, do you not agree?"

I nodded, taking my hand from hers, eyes downcast.

"Skylar, what is it?" she asked, her fingers finding their way to my arm again.

I swallowed around the lump in my throat. I could not tell her the truth, I would not. Besides, would it not make it safer for her if she did not have feelings for me? "It matters not. Please go on," I replied, though I wished to hear no more about the woman Alexis loved.

"When Hesper was betrothed to Thaddeus we were both overjoyed, for it meant she would move into the palace and we could pretend we truly were sisters, as we had always wished."

I blinked, wondering if I had heard correctly, and raised my eyes to Alexis'. "You love Hesper as a sister?"

She nodded and smiled. "Yes. Hesper has four brothers, no sisters, so we grew close from an early age. Of course I was soon betrothed to Basileios and moved to Epirus, but for a time we both lived here and she made it bearable."

The fog covering my heart lifted and I dared to entertain thoughts that her heart did not hold feelings for another.

"Melina comes this way," Hesper hissed, swinging the door open again.

"You should go," I suggested, covering Alexis' hand with my own.

"There is no time," Hesper replied, opening the cloth covered mixture on the table. "Hide. Both of you. I shall deal with her." She spread it out and began kneading.

Hide? Where? I wondered. Remembering the cupboard, I wrapped my arm around Alexis' waist.

"What are y–?"

I clamped my other hand over her mouth, lifting her as I took the two steps across and into the space. It was small and dark, my back pressing against the shelving on the wall as we stood huddled together. Alexis' stomach was warm beneath my hand and I could feel the quick beats of her heart. I loosened my grip against her face and she settled against me, my chin resting against the top of her head.

"Where is Skylar?" Melina asked.

"She is not much of a baker I am afraid. Just as yours do, her talents lie elsewhere."

Alexis' stomach rippled and I recognized it as the beginning of a laugh. If she allowed it to escape, we would be found. "Remain silent," I whispered at her ear, feeling the shiver that ran through her when I tightened my arm around her waist again. Alexis nodded and slipped her fingers between mine on her stomach.

She leant her head back against my chest, her eyes finding me in the dimness. A quick burst of pleasure surged through me and I grinned down at her, my eyes drifting to her lips when I took my hand away. I wished she would turn so we stood face to face, that she would press her body the length of mine. I swallowed and looked away as the queen spoke again.

"Where is she now?"

"She spoke of going to the stables to visit her horse," Hesper replied.

"Hmm. And where is my daughter?"

"She was feeling unwell and retired early."

"She did not answer when I knocked at her door."

"Apologies, I do not have answer for you. Perhaps Alexis has met Hypnos already and did not hear you?"

"Hmm," the queen repeated.

As much as I wanted Melina to leave so Alexis and I could continue to speak, I had to admit that having her leaning against me so intimately pleased me, especially when she drew both my arms around her tighter.

"She is gone, you may come out," Hesper said several moments later.

Alexis' fingers tightened against mine and she looked up at me again, offering a smile. I returned it, but did not take my arms from her. "You should go, it shall not be long before Mother finds you are not visiting Skotos," she said. Reluctantly I nodded and released her, stepping out of the dim pantry and into the brighter kitchen.

"You should return to your room as well," Hesper advised Alexis. "I would suggest answering when she knocks."

"Be certain to look as though you have actually been asleep," I offered with a grin, tugging at Alexis' chiton.

"I shall answer the door in what I always wear to bed – which would be nothing," Alexis replied with a wicked grin.

I almost choked, my mouth falling open briefly before I composed myself. "It appears I learn more about you each day, Princess."

She laughed and Hesper shooed the two of us towards the small door. She opened it, looking in both directions before indicating the queen was not near.

"Perhaps the two of you shall soon be able to meet without so much secrecy," Hesper murmured. "I do not wish to incur Melina's wrath, for I have come to enjoy my life here at the palace."

"I would speak to my father on your behalf. He would not allow you or Thaddeus to be sent away," Alexis assured Hesper, giving her a quick hug.

"As would I," I added, laying my hand on her shoulder and squeezing.

"Thank you. Now, go on, both of you," she insisted, pushing us out the door.

I smiled and took Alexis' hand, pulling her out into the walkway. "Come, Princess, I shall deliver you to your room."

"You should probably return to your own, we are not supposed to see one another," she replied, though her grip on my hand tightened.

I pulled her to a stop, my eyes searching the courtyard and verandas, finding neither friend nor foe to discover us before I turned my gaze on her, a slight frown creasing my forehead. "We are not, yet you invited me here tonight. It was you who came to visit *me* last night."

"True. Do you wish I had not?" she challenged, placing her free hand on her hip as the hint of a grin lifted her lips.

"That is not what I said," I replied, realizing she was teasing me.

"Good. Come then, you may see me safely to my room." She led me to the central chamber and opened her door. I unclasped our hands, entering first to give the room a brief check. I stepped aside and allowed her to enter.

"Thank you for meeting me tonight," she said.

I leant against the door frame, reaching for her hand again as I spoke. "I am glad you asked it of me, though I find myself disappointed it was for such a short time. Perhaps I could come in?"

"I do not believe it wise, my mother has almost disturbed our plans twice this evening. I fear we may not be so lucky a third time."

I nodded, blowing out a deep breath. "You may speak true, but know that I leave to keep you out of trouble rather than willingly."

"Noted," she smiled, taking a pace back into the room.

"Wait," I said, holding tight her fingers and drawing her closer again. "Do you truly sleep naked?"

"As naked as the day I came into this world," she replied with a smile, pushing up onto her toes to plant a kiss on my cheek.

I swallowed, releasing her fingers as my arm slid around her waist automatically. "Alexis," I whispered. Her lips were so close when I turned my head to hers. Her chin lifted in response.

"I believe *now* would be a prudent time to leave," Agrias' voice was forceful.

I immediately took my arm from Alexis, spinning around to face the king. My eyes met his only briefly before I dropped my head and upper body in a bow. "Apologies, King Agrias. Please, do not punish the princess."

"Return to your room. Do not visit Alexis again."

"Father," Alexis began, her hand on the small of my back as she came to stand beside me.

"I believed we had an agreement," Agrias cut over her, his eyes on my face when I raised them to his.

"We did. We do," I stammered. I turned back to Alexis, taking her hand in both of mine. "Be safe," I said quietly.

"And you," she whispered, giving me a small smile.

I returned it and took my hands from hers. I nodded to Agrias, making my way from the chamber and through the garden to my room, the courtyard thankfully devoid of anyone else this late. I opened my door, taking a last glance back to the royal suites, but finding no one still there.

The knowledge of how deeply I desired Alexis, lusted after her, wished to both protect and care for her for as long as I could was overwhelmingly clear. As was the truth of what I would do if she encouraged and laid hands on me. If she had allowed me to kiss her just now … oh I knew I wanted her with nothing short of desperation.

22

"Have you seen her? Is she well? Is she safe?"

"She is fine," Father replied with a chuckle. "She asked the same of you."

"She did?" I asked, the smile lighting my lips automatically.

I had thought of Alexis more than often since the night at her door; the night I had almost kissed her. I had found myself daydreaming about conversations we would have, the way she would answer, her entire face lighting up when she spoke. I wished to see her smile, to have her smile at me, for her hand to rest on my arm and her fingers to engage mine, warmth rolling from her body to ignite mine when I held her. My desperation at wanting to see her warred with my wish for her to remain safe and keep my word to Agrias.

"Your presence here in Trachis appears to have influence over the princess," Father said.

"How so?"

"She asked Thaddeus to teach her how to use a sword."

"He did not allow it, did he? She could be injured," I frowned.

"He told her he would only teach her if she promised to use one of the wooden ones they practice with. Come, you can see them down on the plain." I hastened to join him at the window. "I believed you would want to see such a display, so I asked him to take her out there."

"I only watch to ensure he does not allow her injury," I insisted, though I suspected my father knew I spoke with no truth. "Why can I not go to the balcony to watch?"

"Melanthios observes from there, apparently interested to see what his intended is capable of."

I grunted, my good mood faltering with the reminder of who Alexis would soon belong to if we could not find a way to prevent it. "Does Agrias have word from Moeris yet?" I asked.

"They have organized to meet after the sun has set, I am certain Agrias shall visit you tomorrow and share any news he has."

"I hope so."

"Alexis did not wish to use practice weapons so Thaddeus handed her his sword; she almost overbalanced with the weight of it," Father laughed.

"I am glad to see she did not appear too proud to agree to the wooden version," I murmured.

"Not as you would be," Father noted, nudging me with his elbow.

"Mmm." We watched Alexis and Thaddeus spar in silence for a few moments, the princess' movements awkward and unskilled, though she attempted to follow the older man's directions. "She drops her shoulder before she goes to parry to the right. A skilled enough opponent would notice and target that weakness in battle," I noted.

"Allow us to hope that she never finds herself in the midst of a battle then," a new voice entered our conversation. Father and I turned, finding Gnosidicus entering my room. "I believe I left you with specific instructions to remain lying on this bed," he said.

"I am not engaging in training, is that not enough for now?"

"No. Come," Gnosidicus insisted, patting the bed.

"Father brought no weapons. Unfortunately," I continued.

"I believe that signals my time to leave. I shall find my way down to the grass and visit our new friends," he said, planting a kiss on my forehead. "I shall give the princess your regards."

I growled, remaining at the window as Gnosidicus seated himself on the chair beside my bed, appearing to settle himself in for another lengthy watch to ensure I did not leave my room.

"Now, where were we? Ah yes, we had just finished discussing Heracles' labors," he smiled.

"I am sick of the stories, Gnosidicus. I need to move, to train, to get out of this damn room!"

"Until I say you are well enough, you shall remain here."

"My shoulder is fine, it barely hurts and you said that I did not reopen it much when I tussled with Melanthios. Please, allow me to leave."

"No," he said firmly. "Now, as I understand it, you and the princess spoke of my father, Nebrus, and what he helped do at Cirrha."

"Your father?" I asked, raising an eyebrow as the old man successfully distracted me from what lay outside the window.

"Yes. He was a healer before me and passed much knowledge down, both for healing and incapacitating one's enemies so I would advise you to lie down and be quiet or I shall ensure you cannot stand upright for the duration of your stay here."

I huffed out a breath, but returned to my bed, stretching out on my side and resting my head on my hand. "Alright, entertain me, Gnosidicus, and make it good because I am just about over all these bedtime stories. If it escaped your notice; I am not a child."

"You pout as though you are a child," he said with a smile.

"Just begin your story, old man," I said, rolling my eyes.

"Very well," he chuckled. "I shall tell you of the great goddess, Artemis. The beautiful daughter of Zeus and twin of Apollo. Goddess of the Hunt, lover of animals, and lone huntress in the sacred grove in the mountains of Taygetos. When she was but a child in Zeus' lap, she asked him for a silver bow and arrow to aid her in mastering the art of hunt. She asked for nymphs to tend her and to be free to protect her chastity, teaching young girls to value the same when they came of age."

"Obviously I missed that day at lessons," I drawled.

Gnosidicus shook his head, laughing as he continued. "She guided the girls for many winters, until a young man named Hippolytus entered her temple. He wished to serve the goddess in the same manner the girls did; vowing to protect his chastity, live only for the hunt and hold sacred all that Artemis did."

"I know of Hippolytus, but why did he wish to live as they did?"

Gnosidicus considered my question before shaking his head. "I do not know, but Artemis welcomed him into her confidence and taught him as she did the others. Hippolytus' stepmother was not pleased for she was very fond of the boy and when he refused her advances, she told her husband – Theseus – that Hippolytus had attempted to rape her. Theseus was furious and had the boy killed."

Not Theseus' finest candlemark, I thought.

"As you may imagine, Artemis was devastated by his death and enlisted the aid of Asclepius, God of Medicine and Healing," Gnosidicus continued.

"What for?" I interrupted, not having heard this part of the tale before.

"Patience does not appear to be your strength this day," Gnosidicus said with a smile. I rolled my eyes again and he continued. "Asclepius had a vial of gorgon blood, with which he had already brought two people back from the Underworld. Artemis asked him to use the blood to return Hippolytus to her, rewarding him with gold so he could build a house with many rooms to treat more patients at once.

"Varying stories abound with what happened after Asclepius returned

Hippolytus to Artemis, but needless to say, Zeus and Hades were not pleased with the power Asclepius held over their realms and Zeus struck Asclepius down with his thunderbolt."

I yawned, laying my head down on my arm rather than my hand. "Your story is not nearly as exciting as the tales of Heracles."

"Ah, but that is because I have not reached the most interesting part," he smiled. "I mentioned earlier that Artemis was twin sister to Apollo, did I not?"

"You did," I confirmed, closing my eyes.

"And you know that Apollo is the God of Light and Healing?"

"Mmm."

"Well, Asclepius was Apollo's son."

I opened one eye. "I am listening."

"When Asclepius was a boy, Apollo had visited him, telling him of something so powerful, so amazing that only he, Artemis and Zeus knew of its existence amongst the other gods." Gnosidicus paused, an excited grin on his lips.

"Well, go on," I encouraged, opening my other eye.

"Apollo had told his son of the five golden hinds that Artemis kept at her side on Mount Taygetos. He told Asclepius that when his time in the mortal realm was done, he would take his place among the gods if he spoke of the hinds to Zeus."

"What was so special about Artemis' hinds and why would Zeus place Asclepius among them if it was his thunderbolt that struck Asclepius down in the first place?"

Gnosidicus leaned closer. "Because it is said that the blood of Artemis' hinds is the only thing able to kill a god. You can imagine that Zeus did not wish for Asclepius to speak of *that* to Hades or any other god, lest they get the idea to use it against the King of the Gods himself and take his throne."

"How is it you know so much about the hinds and what their blood can supposedly do if Asclepius never told anyone but Zeus of what he knew?" I asked, suspicious of the truth of his story.

Gnosidicus smiled and leaned even closer. "Because Asclepius kept his word; never speaking of the hinds to any *immortal*. He told only one person – his own son – and it is through his line that the knowledge was passed, father to son, one after another in a great line of healers until it reached my own ears as a young boy."

"*You* are a descendent of Asclepius?" I asked, a little incredulous.

He smiled widely, sitting back. "I am. Proudly so."

"Perhaps Asclepius or Apollo himself administered this amazing gorgon blood and healed me," I mused. The memory of the voices I had heard after I was injured resurfaced, but I dismissed them – it was more likely that Morpheus had still held me in his realm, for I had never dreamt of anyone who claimed to be my grandmother. I had never wished to know any of my grandparents; I had my father and he had always been enough.

"I admit I wondered the same on more than one occasion as you not only survived the injury, but regained your health so quickly. Besides, Zeus destroyed the gorgon blood many winters ago. I do not know if it ever truly existed, just as I have never been certain that the blood of Artemis' hinds has the power to kill an immortal."

"But it is a nice story," I finished with a smile, his words confirming my own disbelief of what he had just spoken.

He nodded, pulling a himation over me and patting my shoulder. "Rest now and allow Hypnos and Morpheus to guide you in your journey towards Eos' dawn."

I nodded, closing my eyes once again, visions of Artemis and her hinds playing behind my eyelids. Chasing, hunting, drawing her arrow across the fine strand of her bow. Beautiful, brilliant, but as she turned to me, far less chaste than Gnosidicus had described; her features that of Alexis, as she invited me to shed my clothing and join her in the woody copse she called home.

23

I woke to a firm shaking at my shoulder. I opened my eyes, finding King Agrias before me. "What is it? What is wrong?" I asked, instantly alert as I pushed myself up. "Is Alexis in danger?"

He smiled and shook his head. "No, she is well. But I wondered if perhaps you would be up for a little sparring match with me. Gnosidicus reports that your shoulder is well enough; and he feared that even his best concoction would not put you down if he kept you in your room any longer, given what you have already endured here."

"That may be true," I replied with a smile, the adrenaline that flowed through me slowing again.

"Apparently you left this sticking out of someone's stomach," he laughed, handing me my xiphos.

"I remember," I nodded, attaching the belt and sheath for my sword to my waist.

"You have Thaddeus to thank for bringing them back for you, though your father and I agreed that they be kept out of your room whilst you healed, in case you had ideas about using them to escape."

I laughed as Agrias held out my shield and javelin. "I assure you, it would have crossed my mind. You did not bring my cuirass?"

"We shall not require it this morning, but your father still has it. Come, we shall use the field beneath the northern balcony," he said, gathering a sword and shield of his own.

I nodded, following the king from my room and through the walkway leading onto the balcony.

"I must make apologies for the other night. With Alexis," I explained.

The king waved off my words. "There is no need. Alexis told me it was she who sought you out."

"Still, I gave my word and what you sa—"

"Skylar," Agrias said, turning to face me. "I am not angry. Truly." He smiled and gave a curt nod. "Now, come."

There was a ramp at each end of the balcony and we took the closest one, stepping down onto the damp grass at the end of it. I hooked my arm through my shield and weighted my javelin in my palm. It felt good to finally hold both again.

"I have noticed some of your soldiers wear a rope around the middle of their bodies. What is that for?"

"You do not miss much, do you?" Agrias grinned. "It indicates warriors who have not yet made their first kill. It is another of the Macedonian customs I have kept."

"I see," I said with a nod.

Several more spears lay to our right, I lifted a brow when I saw them and Agrias smiled. "I understand the Greek hoplites use their spears for thrusting more so than throwing, though you have mastered the art of both. Today I seek demonstration of your skills at finding mark in a target." He pointed to a row of bundled wheat standing upright about fifteen feet away.

"They are perhaps a little close for me to perform at my best," I told him, returning his grin.

"I know, but it is not only Gnosidicus that wishes you to be free of your secular rooming arrangement. As such, I have not placed them far enough away to tempt fate that you reopen your wound."

I laughed again. "That is appreciated." I took my shield from my arm and set it aside, settling my javelin in my palm and loosely wrapping my thumb and fingers around the smooth wood. I drew it back, the skin at my back stretching without discomfort at the movement. I blew out a deep breath, took two deliberate steps back, planted my feet and concentrated on the target, sending the javelin sailing through the air towards it.

It sliced through the binding that held the middle bundle of wheat together, the stalks fanning out as they met the ground. I smiled, flexing my arm, relieved that finally my wound had healed and I had full use of my body again.

The king cheered, picking up another javelin and handing it to me. I threw that one, and the one after and the one after that until there were none lying on the ground beside us. The sheaves of wheat lay scattered along the field, Agrias clapping in delight when I freed the last from its bindings.

"A drink to the victor," he offered, pouring wine from an amphora I had not noticed when we arrived.

I accepted it, taking a long gulp. "Very pleasing," I commended him. "Father said you were to meet with Moeris, how does he fare with Melanthios?"

"Moeris has done well," Agrias grinned. "Melanthios was only too eager to get him on side when he heard his grievances towards me. Melanthios confided that his brothers and the armies shall arrive within the week."

"Do they know Basileios is dead?" I asked, nodding when the king offered more wine.

"They do. They also believe his killer is still here in Trachis."

"Not untrue, though I suspect you do not refer to Melanthios."

"No. He named you as the one. When he sent his messenger to Andreas, he told his father to ensure his brothers heard that, with only the two of them knowing it is not the true way of it."

"Smart," I conceded. "They shall seek their revenge as one and occupy my weapons while Melanthios and the Epirote and Illyrian armies fight your men."

Agrias nodded and took my skyphos, placing it beside his own and the amphora on the ground. "Speaking of occupying your weapons, I believe it well past time I saw how well you handle yours." I smiled, picking up my shield and drawing my sword. Agrias held his own against mine, parrying and defending the movements I made as we became accustomed to each other.

"You say Melanthios ensured his brothers knew someone else killed Basileios, so I wonder if they cared for him more than you originally thought," I said. "Perhaps, though they are warriors as Melanthios is, they looked up to their eldest sibling."

"I wondered the same, and it appears that there was understanding from the younger men as to why Basileios did not join them on the battlefields – his main task was to father heirs for their family so they could continue to rule the tribe."

I was pleased to find my rhythm returning quickly as our movements became less tentative towards one another. "Basileios was not a *princess*," I frowned. "It appears strange that would be his main role."

"True, though as I mentioned when we first spoke of him, he was considered weaker than his other brothers, so a more feminine role would have been seen as punishment from his father."

I nodded, though it was more to myself than the king. "Has Melanthios spoken then of the reason he gave his brothers for Basileios and Alexis coming to Trachis, why he himself would have been coming here, rather than joining them at Stratos?" I asked, meeting a well-executed attack from Agrias.

"Oh yes. He told them it was because Basileios had finally grown a backbone and wanted to prove himself a true Epirote – just as they were considered to be – by pretending to want to leave Epirus and move to Trachis. Once in the palace, he was to kill me, take my queen as his second wife and make Trachis their vassal.

"With my army under his control, they would join up with the Epirotes and Illyrians and take their battle for lands and power to the Thessalians, before deciding if north or south would be their next target."

"And they believed this?"

"They did," Agrias nodded, holding his hand up. I paused to allow him to catch his breath. "It appears you are not disadvantaged by your recent departure from your weapons," he panted.

"From the moment I first held a sword it was as though I had always known how to use it," I acknowledged. "It would appear our plan to have Moeris turn them against Melanthios shall not work. Basileios' new found boldness would elevate him in their eyes," I added, returning our conversation to its previous path.

"Perhaps, but Melanthios has asked Moeris to meet them at the Melas River when they arrive, so he shall attempt to speak of it then."

"If he cannot convince them to join us, we must be ready to fight, for there shall not be another option."

"Agreed," Agrias nodded, holding his shield and sword up again and inviting me to continue our sparring.

"What of Antigonos? He and Melanthios appeared close when I saw them together at the barracks. Has Melanthios recruited him to his cause also?"

"Moeris says he has acted no differently. They have dined with the former Epirote a number times but there has never been discussion of plans to overthrow my position, or of making Trachis a vassal."

"That is one advantage then," I nodded.

"Indeed. There is another … more disturbing truth that Moeris has learned," Agrias murmured, bringing his sword down on mine as we continued our dance of weapons.

"Oh?" I asked, raising an eyebrow.

"About Alexis."

I held his attack off, holding his gaze as we stood face to face.

"Go on."

"Melanthios has spoken freely of the prize that is to be his. He cares nothing for Alexis; she represents only the power he will have when he makes her his wife. I have known the ways of many men, slavers, barbarians even if you shall allow such a term, but never have I heard them speak of treating a Princess without respect or reverence."

"Most men *I* have known – savages or otherwise – believe the prize of a Princess to be very great," I agreed. "They do not treat her as they do other women. They worship her, treat her with kindness so she shall *want* to lie with or pleasure them how they imagine only she can. Alexis told me she had tended to slaves Melanthios had to his hut on occasion, and that his treatment of her would be worse if she fought him."

"Moeris alluded to the same, and he does not intend to wait until they are wed for it to be so," Agrias frowned. "That is why I want you to now spend time with Alexis."

"And the queen – she is agreeable to it also?"

"She protests otherwise, but she wants our daughter to remain safe and so does not complain too loudly."

"The queen and Alexis have a complicated past," I noted.

The king regarded me silently before nodding. "They do," he finally agreed. "Alexis has spoken to you of it?"

"She has," I nodded.

We continued our attacks and defenses in silence for a while longer before Agrias spoke again. "Do you ever wish for a home to call your own?" he asked.

"You ask questions akin to the princess," I replied.

"And you answer them as your father does; evasively," the king grinned, blocking my sword.

"I–" I began, unable to finish as I caught sight of Alexis making her way from the opposite end of the balcony towards us. She wore a chiton in a shade I knew would match her eyes, the same as she had the first night I met her at the palace. Her hair had been allowed run loose, held back from her face by a thin band of green.

I was so entranced by the vision that I did not register Agrias' attack until it was almost too late. I barely managed to get my shield up in time, the ferocity of his sword sending me stumbling to the ground, my xiphos falling from my grip.

He immediately joined me. "Apologies," he panted.

"I am not injured; I should not have allowed my focus to be taken from you," I said, more embarrassed than hurt.

He turned, seeing Alexis walking towards us. "Ah," he smiled, offering his hand and pulling me to my feet. "Perhaps we have tested your body enough for one day. My daughter wears a most determined look, among other things." I colored ever so slightly at his words. He bent down and picked up my sword, holding his hand out for my shield. "I shall take care of all we have used here. Your weapons shall be returned to your room."

"That is not necessary," I said, unwilling to be separated from them now they had been returned.

"Do not fear, you shall not have need of them this day," he replied, and I heard the grin in his voice as I turned back to watch the princess' approach. I acknowledged his words with a nod, untying my sheath and handing it to him absently, unable to take my eyes from his daughter. He chuckled and made his way towards the wheat as Alexis arrived.

"Hello," she said, her wide grin instantly tripling my heartbeat.

"Princess," I replied, bowing slightly.

24

"You are well?" I asked.

"Very," she replied. "You appear to have fully recovered."

"At last," I agreed.

"Hesper and I are to visit the agora. Father said you would be able to join us if you wished. Do you?"

I could not miss the hopeful edge to her voice. I smiled and nodded. "I do."

"Good. But you cannot wear that," she said, pointing to my sweat-stained tunic.

I put my hands on my hips. "And just what do you suggest instead?" I asked, an eyebrow raised in question.

"I have an idea," she replied, taking my arm and pulling me back in the direction of the palace.

We walked across the grass in companionable silence, Alexis' hand still on my arm, neither of us removing the familiar touch. "Though we have not known each other long, I have found myself missing you much when we are not together," Alexis admitted, looping her arm through mine as we climbed the ramp to the balcony.

"As have I," I told her, placing my hand over hers and squeezing. "I am afraid I have not been a very willing patient for Gnosidicus, who was charged with ensuring I did not leave my room again."

"So I heard," she laughed.

I shrugged. "There was much I wanted to do. Someone I very much wished to see." Alexis blushed and dropped her focus to the marble beneath our feet. "I saw you sparring with Thaddeus yesterday from my window."

"Oh," she murmured. "I hope you did not watch for too long, I am not very good. Thaddeus began to lose patience with me by the end."

"Not long," I smiled. "It takes a lot of practice. You have never picked up a sword before?"

"No, it was not permitted, and I had never considered doing so until recently."

I felt the heat crawling up my own neck and cleared my throat, thankful Alexis had averted her gaze. "You drop your shoulder just before you fend off an attack. Against a skilled opponent that would be used against you. You should raise your shield or sword directly to meet it, do not lower it first."

"You noticed that just from watching me for a short time?" she asked, raising her eyes to mine again.

"I pay attention," I replied simply. "My father taught me to study my enemy and find his weakness, then use it to my advantage."

"You consider me your enemy?" she asked, a frown forming between her eyebrows.

I laughed and reached across, smoothing the gathered skin. "No, it just means I can read people's body language. I pick up on certain things," I replied, realizing the ease with which I had just bestowed the touch. I lowered my arm again.

"Oh," Alexis said, clearly as surprised at the gesture as I was.

"Thaddeus did not tell you of it?" I asked, hoping to quell the heat that had begun to stir in my stomach. She shook her head. "Perhaps he did not wish to discourage you from your attempts. Not everyone has the ability, though most soldiers are trained to look for the signs. It does not happen for me with everything, mainly just in battle. But we are not in such a situation so …" I trailed off, feeling as though I had said too much.

"I do not believe I would want to meet you in battle, you appear a formidable opponent," Alexis mused, a grin lifting the corners of her lips.

"Always," I assured her, returning the smile.

We arrived at her room and she unhooked her arm, opening the door and standing aside to allow me to enter in front of her. Closing it again, she pointed to the blue material draped over the end of her bed.

"I thought perhaps you could wear that," she said. "It is my way of thanking you for your constant aid, though I wish I did not need it so often," she added, blushing a little.

"It is not necessary," I assured her, taking the soft material between my fingers. I drew a breath. It was some of the finest linen I had ever seen. "Besides, I cannot. This is fit for a princess, or someone of noble blood, but not for me. I am not worthy of such garments."

"Well, *this* princess does not agree. If you would allow me to show you how, there would not be anyone at the agora who would believe you were anything other than highly born."

I raised an eyebrow in doubt.

"Trust me?" she asked.

I smiled as I rolled my eyes, helpless to deny her request. "As you wish, Princess."

She smiled, taking the linen and stepping behind me. "If you remove your tunic, I shall dress you," she said quietly.

I reached for the pin at my shoulder, glad she could not see my face as I recalled the last time she had offered the same. How badly I had wished for her to touch me that night. How much more I wanted it now. I pulled the metal from the material, allowing it to fall from my body as I had at the baths.

"This appears far better than the last time I saw it," Alexis murmured, her fingers skittering across my back, her breath close to my shoulder.

I shivered with the unexpected touch, my body instantly hot as desire knotted itself in my stomach. It had not been wise to allow her to dress me. "I have found it to heal better when I am not breaking noses," I managed, closing my eyes as the throb of my heart beat between my thighs.

Warm hands drew the material around me, across my chest and up to my shoulder. It reached to my ankles, the softness tickling the tops of my feet as it settled there. "But other than that you have enjoyed your time here at the palace, with our baths?"

I swallowed. "I have found there is much to enjoy here in Trachis."

I opened my eyes to find Alexis in front of me, the material held firmly in place, though how or with what I did not know, for I still held my pin.

"I shall have to introduce you to our hot springs at Pylae ... Thermopylae," Alexis said, her cheeks tinging with the familiar red as she took the fibula from me.

"Pylae?" I repeated.

She smiled again as she nodded. "It is the old name for the area between the Phoenix River and Alpeni on the Malian Gulf. Those still among our number from the Malian tribe, continue to call it Pylae, though my father encourages us all to refer to Trachis and the area we call our own as far as Locris as Thermopylae; to align ourselves more closely with the neighboring Greeks who refer to it as such."

"The springs are to the south?" She nodded. The springs at *Pylae* must be the ones Father spoke of as we journeyed towards Trachis.

"My mother always referred to the area as Pylae and the springs as Chutri when she wished to annoy my father," Alexis smiled.

"I would enjoy going to them very much," I replied.

She nodded then paused, her voice quiet when she spoke again. "When I return with Melanthios to Epirus, would you consider accompanying me? I would feel safer knowing you were nearby."

I drew in a deep breath. "I would not wish to accompany you," I replied, my voice soft.

Her face fell with her eyes. "Oh, apologies I ..."

I lifted my hand and tilted her chin until our eyes met again. "It is I who owes the apology," I hastened to explain myself. "I only meant that I would not wish to see you harmed, to know that I was close by but could do nothing to stop Melanthios from doing to you what he wanted because you belonged to him. You would be his betrothed; his wife," I said, my words ending in a whisper.

"I would not want for you to see me that way either," she agreed quietly.

I ran my thumb ever so lightly across her chin. We stood, unspeaking, staring at one another, my thumb continuing to caress her, steadily nearing her lips, yet never touching. Her hand found its way to my hip, robbing me of my breath as her fingers made small circles above the bone.

Her gaze held mine, lightly veiled desire swirling in their depths and this time I allowed my thumb to glide over her lips. A small sigh escaped her, her eyelids fluttering shut with the motion. I held my breath, drawing it back the other way. Her hand tightened against my waist and I stepped closer, the heat of her stomach radiating through the linen. I leaned down, her breath warm against my mouth as I brushed my lips over hers.

She did not flinch, nor push me away, but I felt her surprise at the gesture. I allowed the barest of spaces to separate us again, skimming my fingers over her forearm and feeling the skin rise beneath. Alexis drew an unsteady breath as I settled my fingers in the curve of her side, pulling her towards me ever so slightly. Her breasts rose and fell beneath mine, her breath as short as my own.

I kissed her again, her lips parting as I increased the pressure against her mouth. Her hand tightened at my side as I tentatively ran my tongue across her bottom lip, tasting her, enjoying the building need in my blood. Her fingers twisted in the material she had so carefully positioned around me and my body ignited as tinder to a fire.

I slid my hand beneath the hair at the nape of her neck, the skin soft and warm beneath my touch. I slipped my tongue into her mouth, stroking, teasing, and when hers returned my movements, I was desperate that no material separate us any longer. I took my hand from her neck, gliding it down the side of her body, past the gentle curve of her breast, over her hip to her thigh.

Her chest rose and fell quickly again, her hand twisting in my chiton as she separated our lips. "Skylar," she murmured, her eyes reopening.

"Yes?" I asked, desire pulsing through my body.

"Hesper waits for us to join her."

I swallowed, torn from images of her naked flesh writhing below mine. "I … yes," I stammered, unwilling to take my hands from her body. Alexis cleared her throat, her hands also remaining where they were. Her tongue touched the corner of her lips as though she prepared to speak, but she did not. "Alexis," I whispered.

Her eyes found mine again, but she shook her head. "We cannot," she said.

A thousand emotions fought within, disappointment and frustration the most prominent, but I drew my hand from her side and inhaled deeply as I nodded.

"This color favors you as well as I had hoped," she murmured, smoothing the material at my hip again.

"Thank you," I replied as she took my hand and led me from the room.

Hesper met us outside the apartment   she shared with Thaddeus, delicately not mentioning the high color in Alexis' cheeks, though I knew she noticed it when she smiled conspiratorially at me.

"You look different, beautiful," she noted, looping her arm through my right as Alexis already had my left.

"Thank you," I mumbled, uncomfortable in the fine material now that Alexis and I were outside her room. What I would have given for my tunic and cuirass, or indeed to simply return to Alexis' room where there was no one else but the two of us.

We walked towards the main entrance of the palace and I wondered if this could have ever been my life – not living in a palace of course, but the simple friendship of girls my own age to visit the agora or share fine food with. I had not considered it for many winters, but as I walked along listening to Hesper and Alexis speak of what they wanted to look at in town, I realized there was part of me that wished for it, just a little.

"What about you Skylar, what stalls do you want to visit?" Hesper asked.

"I do not know. Is there a metalwork hut or somewhere that sells weapons?" I replied with a shrug.

"We should have guessed," Alexis laughed. She squeezed my arm to her body, just beneath the swell of her breast, and I returned her smile.

"Princess, Hesper, how does this day find you?" my father's familiar tone greeted us.

"Very well, Leandros, and you?"

"Well, thank you. Where are you … Skylar?" he asked, his eyes widening when he realized I stood between the other two. "I … er. Well, you look exquisite," he stuttered.

"I believe we all agree on that," Alexis said with a grin.

I only nodded, dropping my eyes to my feet.

"I shall not keep you from your destination, but may I have a quick word with the princess before you go?"

I looked at my father quizzically, but he would not meet my gaze, holding his arm out for Alexis to take as he moved a few paces away.

"Come, Alexis can catch us up," Hesper suggested, tugging the arm she held as the warmth at my side disappeared.

"But, I …"

"Come on, Alexis shall join us momentarily."

Reluctantly I turned my gaze from Alexis, starting towards the agora and town below with Hesper.

"If you do not have other plans tomorrow night, Alexis is holding a banquet for the women and wishes for you to be there. Has she asked you already?"

"No," I replied, sneaking a look back to the palace.

"Well then, consider this your official invitation. The men have a symposium planned in the west wing, which shall no doubt contain a mixture of heavy drinking, tall stories, supposed military and tactical talk and general debauchery, if it follows the usual procedure."

"I see," I replied, though I was not truly listening; Alexis had emerged from the entranceway.

"Yes, there are often fights and I would not be surprised if the Harpies appeared to carry the victor off on its back," Hesper continued.

"What?" I asked, shaking my head to clear the visions that danced behind my eyes.

"Never mind," she laughed.

Alexis re-joined us, looping her arm back through mine, her fingers resting at my wrist. "Is everything well with my father?" I asked.

"It is," she replied with a satisfied smile.

"Do you intend sharing your words with him with us?"

"No," Alexis replied, her smile widening. "Come, the agora awaits."

25

The marketplace was a large area covering ten blocks in the heart of the town of Trachis. The sun had begun making its way behind Mount Oetaea and a majority of items had been sold, though I knew the stall keepers arrived at dawn in preparation for their day's trading. Their tables were always full to overflowing. Cheese, charcoal, wine, material for clothing, farmers with live pigs, or blankets woven by their wives from the wool they cut from their sheep; almost anything you could wish for could be found in the agora.

"Is there a stall to purchase armor or weapons?" I asked.

"No, There is a small metalwork hut, but they only make minor repairs," Alexis replied. I nodded, but said nothing further, content to allow Alexis and Hesper choose which stall we would stop at or which street we would follow next as they had for the past few candlemarks.

They paused at the perfume stall, neither buying anything, but sampling many. I tested a few items myself, finding one that had elements of similarity to Alexis' and the bath oil she had given me. I considered purchasing it to wear to the banquet the next evening, but with all that had happened before I left the palace, I had not remembered to bring coin with me, though the more I watched, the more I realized coin was not always exchanged during transactions. I decided to return the following morning, alone, to search for the right scent; perhaps I would find the one the princess wore also and surprise her with a gift. I smiled at the idea, composing myself as Alexis put her arm through mine and we continued along the street to the next stall.

"When you were in Athens, did you visit the agora?" she asked.

"Yes, it was bigger than here, but it appears that many of the same goods are sold," I replied.

"What were you doing in Athens?" Hesper asked.

"Meeting the King of Sparta," Alexis supplied with a grin.

"Really?" Hesper enquired, eyes wide.

I smiled at her reaction and nodded. "We were not there to actually meet King Cleomenes, but we ended up aiding him."

"You never got to speak of how you helped him the other night, would you tell us now?" Alexis asked.

I nodded.

"You have heard of Hippias, the tyrant who ruled Athens?" I queried.

"Of course," Alexis replied. "Melanthios speaks often and with admiration of him."

I nodded again. "Well, Father and I were in Athens during the festival of Apaturia."

"What is that?" Hesper interrupted.

"Apologies, I forget you are unfamiliar with their festivals. Apaturia is held in the moon of Pyanepsion and the various clans of Attica meet to discuss their affairs. At a banquet, my father struck up a conversation with Cleomenes. He told us he had attempted to rid Athens of Hippias, but had been unsuccessful."

"If Sparta and Athens are rivals, why would he aid them?" Alexis asked.

"Cleomenes had been told by the Delphic Oracle that he must aid the Athenians; that he was not to return to Sparta until Hippias had been expelled and the people freed from his tyrannical reign." The three of us stopped walking, stepping off to one side to allow other customers to find what they searched for at the stalls. "We spoke until well into the next day and I convinced my father to aid the king in his quest. We met again a few days later to finalize our plans and when the time arrived, Cleomenes and his men pursued Hippias and his supporters to the temple of Athena.

"While Cleomenes besieged Hippias, Father and I took Hippias' family hostage, meeting up at the temple and forcing Hippias to give up the city in exchange for returning his family members safely to him."

"Did he?" Hesper asked.

"Of course," I replied. "People do more than you can imagine to ensure their kin are safe from harm."

"Have you been to other Athenian or Spartan festivals?" Hesper asked.

"Leandros says the Spartans and Athenians do not always celebrate the same festivals, though they worship the same gods," Alexis added. I nodded, not surprised my father had shared that knowledge with her. "You have celebrated festivals in both cities?" she continued before I had the chance to make further reply.

"I have never been to Sparta itself," I answered with a shake of my head. "But, yes there are differences in the celebrations and games held. Often it depends on which gods and goddesses are most important in the individual town or village. I have twice attended the Festival of Sunium in southern Attica. Leaders of Athens' army travel to Sunium then sail in a sacred boat out to the cape."

"Why?" Alexis asked.

"They offer prayers of thanks to Poseidon for his continued protection of them and their men during the summer fighting seasons when they have cause to travel by sea to meet their enemies. It is the least frequent of any festival I know of, held only every fifth winter."

"You were fortunate to be at Sunium both times it was held," Hesper noted.

"Well, our first visit was at the insistence of new friends, but our attendance last autumn was very much planned," I replied. "The sailors certainly know how to hold a festival, I shall say that. Many woke with sore heads and little memory of the revelry of the night before," I added with a grin.

"You?" Alexis asked.

I nodded again. "The sore head, yes, though I remember where I was and how I returned to my lodgings well enough."

"Your father speaks of the various games as well, have you attended any of those?" Hesper asked. I was starting to understand how she and Alexis had grown so close from an early age; both held an eager thirst for knowledge.

"Over the winters I have been fortunate enough to attend each of them; the Nemean games in Nemea, the Pythian games in Delphi, the Isthmian games near Corinth and the Olympic games in Olympia," I replied with a grin. "Though they are not held each winter, competitors from all over Greece attend to great applause and welcome. The games are not as wild as the celebration at Sunium though, for example at the Pythian Games in Delphi they have wonderful music and art, athletic competitions and races in the nearby plain and hills."

Alexis' hand tightened against my arm and she regarded me seriously. "How old were you when you found yourself at Delphi?"

"Almost fourteen winters," I replied as my eyes found hers. She nodded again, sliding her fingers down my arm to rest on my hand. I turned it and she threaded her fingers through mine. I knew she was recalling the story of my time in Anticyra two winters previous to the Pythian Games and I was glad she did not feel the need to share the reason for her question with Hesper. I drew my eyes from Alexis and addressed her friend again.

"At the Nemean Games they run around the stadium, wrestle and race their horses with chariots. I wanted to enter Skotos; I believed he would be fast enough, until I saw them run. The hippodrome afforded them far greater speed than the horses had been able in the hills around Delphi and, though I had had Skotos almost five winters, I was nowhere near competent enough to have raced him in such a manner."

"The Games sound amazing, we do not have the same types of celebrations here as they do in Greece," Hesper said.

"That is a pity for there is much enjoyment to be had." With Alexis' hand still in mine, I offered Hesper my other arm again and we resumed our exploration of the agora.

Hesper and Alexis paused at yet another stall of material and I freed myself from their arms, drifting ahead to find one that sold amphorae of wine. The round man who owned the stall offered me a few skyphoi for free when I smiled at him – perhaps Alexis had spoken true when she assured me I would appear nobly born in the fine linen.

When Hesper and Alexis finally joined me, I had lost count of how many cups of the sweet beverage I had drunk. Alexis rounded the stall and wrapped her arms around the merchant.

He responded with his own embrace, placing a kiss on her cheek. "Greetings, my darling," he said.

"You are well on this day?" she asked.

"I am." Another customer arrived and the stall holder turned to speak to him, Alexis returning to my side.

"And what have you found?" she asked, her hand finding its way to my arm. I held the cup out to her, our fingers brushing as she took it from me and sipped. "Very pleasing," she agreed. I nodded.

She drained the skyphos, her head thrown back, throat gloriously exposed to the winter sun. It would be so easy to lean across and kiss her there, to run my hand from her chin to her chest, and far lower. I was caught in my daydream, with lips parted and breathing shallow, when she turned. I watched the pulse beat at the base of her neck.

"Skylar?"

"Mmm."

Her cheeks darkened under my gaze.

"It appears the warrior did not hear your question," Hesper chuckled, nudging me.

"Apologies, what did you ask?" I added hastily, my body warming further.

"I wondered if you had asked to purchase any of this," Alexis said.

"No, I was only sampling it."

"But you enjoyed its flavor?"

"I did," I nodded.

"Good." She turned her attention back to the merchant who had finished his other transaction, handing back the cup we had finished with. "You have supplied much wine to the woman who saved me, I gather you recognized her?"

"Of course, she is difficult to forget," he replied with a lopsided grin.

"Indeed," Alexis agreed, and I was certain my cheeks darkened further.

He appeared familiar, though I could not place him, nor where I had seen him before. I dismissed the notion, watching as Alexis took a small pouch from somewhere beneath her chiton and emptied coins into her palm.

"Please have twelve amphorae sent to the palace for tomorrow," she asked.

"I shall bring them myself, but you know you do not need to make payment in such a manner to me."

"Of course I do. You need coin to purchase your goods, the offers and bargains we make here do not sway traders from afar," Alexis insisted.

He shook his head, but accepted the coin she pushed into his hand. "Aspasia and I have more than we shall ever need."

"Princess, is that you?" a voice called, interrupting the exchange.

Alexis turned, a smile lighting her face when she saw who called to her.

"Friends from childhood," Hesper whispered to me before joining Alexis in greeting the four women.

I stood in place, uncertain suddenly of what I should do. I wished I still held some wine, but the stall keeper was already in deep conversation with a young man and I could not ask him for another. I fidgeted with the fold of material at my waist.

"Who is your friend?" one of the women asked, breaking from the group. "Did you bring her from Epirus with you?" she added, laying her hand on my arm reminiscent of the way Alexis was wont to do when nearby.

Alexis was immediately at my side, sweeping aside the other woman's hand and taking my own in hers as she replied. "This is Skylar, a new friend. New to Trachis."

"She is tall."

"Pretty," another agreed.

"You are not from here, that is plain to see, where do you call home?" the third asked.

"Does she speak at all?" the last of the group offered with a laugh.

"I speak very well. Yet I could not respond with all of you questioning me at once," I replied, a little sharper than I had intended.

The women did not appear offended, the first speaker laughing loudly at my answer. "She has fire. I imagine she keeps her husband well heeled, as we all wish we could."

"I call no man husband," I informed them stiffly.

"A widower?" one enquired.

"No," I replied firmly.

The four friends exchanged a glance, eyebrows raised, but were afforded no further questions as Hesper spoke. "Allow us to speak of plans for the banquet tomorrow evening," she said, stepping between me and them.

"Oh, yes, you must. It has been so long since we have all been together," one of the women gushed.

They turned their attention to Hesper, and I was grateful to her for the timely diversion. Alexis squeezed my hand and gave me a small smile. I retrieved it from her, discreetly moving a few paces from the group.

"You shall arrive with your husbands and when they are happily entrenched in the andron, you shall make your way to the banqueting hall as usual," Hesper said.

The wine I had drunk swirled in my head, a pleasant sensation for the most part, yet sparking a restless feeling I recognized all too well. I could hear Alexis' voice, the melodic way it dipped and rose as she spoke with her friends.

"We shall meet just before sundown," she said.

In my mind I saw the way my hand had pressed against the curve of her side, the heat that had radiated through the green of her chiton to burn my skin. The way her tongue had run the length of mine, exploring, tasting. Curious, yet certain. I wanted to feel it against mine again, to know every part of her intimately. My throat went dry. I needed more wine. I needed relief. I looked up, drowning in the concerned green depths that met me.

"What is it?" Alexis mouthed.

I shook my head and indicated I was going back to the palace. I turned before she saw the rest of what I wanted to do when I got there.

Her presence heated my side before I was halfway through the agora, the familiar arm looping through mine. "Apologies, I did not mean to be rude to your friends," I murmured.

"Do not apologize, they can be intimidating when you meet them for the first time. They like you though for you did not cower from them."

"It is difficult to cower when you are half a foot taller than people," I smiled.

"True," Alexis agreed, returning my grin.

We walked in comfortable silence back to the entranceway and I paused when we arrived, stifling a yawn. "Do you wish for me to return you to your room?"

"Would you walk me to my room?" Alexis asked at the same time. We both laughed and I indicated she lead the way.

26

Alexis did not rush to have us arrive at her door, and I was more than curious to know if things between us would go further than they had earlier, though I could not imagine how I could approach such a subject.

"I notice many stall holders do not accept coin, you do not have a mint here in Trachis?" I said, attempting to keep my mind from wandering into dangerous territory.

"No. Those who purchase their goods from traders outside our town accept coin, but those who grow, make or rear their own produce prefer a barter system of sorts."

"I see," I murmured, presuming the merchant who sold perfumes would accept the coins I had.

"You said there was a small metalwork hut, but I did not see a metal workshop or armory of any sort, how do your soldiers get weapons?"

"They are crafted in Macedonia. My father oversees their purchase when he holds his assembly in the spring," she replied. "Hesper said she asked you to attend the banquet tomorrow evening. Shall you come?" Alexis asked, a look of genuine eagerness lighting her face as we arrived at her room.

"If you wish for me to be there."

"I do."

"Then I shall attend," I answered, taking my arm from hers and opening the door. I took a discreet look inside before allowing Alexis to enter. She closed it behind us, stepping around me to stand by her bed.

"Today was the nicest day I have had in a long time," she said, smoothing the material of the tunic I had left discarded on the floor many candlemarks earlier.

"It has possibly been the nicest day I have *ever* had," I agreed, wondering who had been inside the princess' room to put it up on the bed.

"Hmm … impatient when healing, determined, stubborn yet loyal; there is much I have learnt about you these past weeks; though I did not realize competitiveness was such a strong trait."

I tilted my head and regarded her as she often did me. "Competitiveness?"

"The nicest day you have *ever* had?" she asked with a smile. "Must you always have the last word on everything?"

"Maybe," I grinned, tucking my hands behind my back and leaning against the closed door. "Though I should think after what I spoke of with Skotos you would realize that when there is something I want, I am always *very* competitive." I was glad she had not included jealousy in her list, though I was certain she had learnt that of me also.

"Some would call that arrogance, or just plain stubbornness."

"True, but a warrior must rely on a little of both to be victorious."

"I shall take your word on that," she said, pausing before she added, "You had much wine at the agora. Are you certain you shall be able to find your way back to your room?"

"I also have an excellent memory," I assured her.

Her eyes were fixed on my lips, flaring my already heated body. Did she know what I saw written on her face? I wanted Alexis to know my secrets, to know of Kuria and what had happened. There was a chance she would deny me, deny us both of what grew between us, but I needed her to know. The darkening of her eyes told me I must speak of it now for I would not be leaving the princess' room without tasting her lips again and I doubted my resolve would hold if she kissed me before I kissed her. I swallowed as she neared, unable to find the words to say anything.

"Do you remember how to take your chiton off?" she challenged, hands on hips, her eyes finding mine again. "If you recall, I did not use your pin to gather the material at your shoulder," she added, taking another step towards me.

"I remember," I agreed hoarsely. I also remembered she told me she could not do more with me; I had wondered earlier if it was because I was a woman or because she had made plans to go to the agora with her friend. It appeared to be the latter.

She took my hands in hers, pulling me from the door and drawing them to her right shoulder. "Perhaps if you see how mine is held together, you shall understand how to take your own off."

My hands trembled and I found myself unusually conflicted; did she seek only to aid me with clothing I was not accustomed to wearing, or was this part of her seduction? I *must* speak of Kuria, yet I did not dare without Alexis confirming she wanted more between us. "I am certain I could work it out myself, it is only material after all," I said quietly. "But should someone else not aid you with your clothing? You are the Princess."

"No. You are here now."

She turned her back to me, keeping one of her hands on mine as she explained how the ends had been tied together beneath a gathering at her shoulder. I freed them from one another and parted the fabric. I skimmed my fingers over the soft skin of her shoulder and back, noting the shiver that ran the length of her spine. "I have never undressed one I did not intend to take to bed."

Alexis drew a sharp breath and I realized I had spoken aloud. She faced me again, her chiton held loosely to her chest, the tops of her breasts exposed. Heat flooded my veins and settled urgently in my stomach, shortening my breath. "I suppose you shall have to share my bed tonight then," she said before I had the chance to take it back.

"Er ... no, Princess. I cannot."

"You can and you shall," she replied firmly, twirling her finger to indicate I should allow her access to the material held together behind me.

I needed to tell her about Kuria. I had to set aside my desire and speak of what I had not with any lover, with anyone at all, since it happened. I turned around obediently.

A breath of air at my feet told me her chiton now lay on the floor. "Alexis ..." She reached up, warm fingertips making quick work of the ties. I closed my eyes, my body humming with desire. "This is not a good idea," I whispered as she ran a finger over the scar at my shoulder blade.

"Why?" she asked, her breath tickling my spine.

I held the linen against my chest as I turned to face her. She stood, exposed, before me. I swallowed loudly, unable to reply as my eyes covered every curve, every rise of her. Her breasts were full, high on her chest. I yearned to reach out, to take the peaked tips between my fingers, to run my tongue over them as I smoothed my hands down her sides and over her stomach. I wanted to press my fingers through the dark hair between her thighs, to feel her, to hear her moan as I entered her, to bring her pleasure time and time again. I returned my eyes to hers, my breath refusing to steady.

She reached out, her fingers finding mine and twining with them as she led me to the bed. "You must be exhausted. You were able to spar for the first time in weeks with my father and then you spent candlemarks walking through the agora with Hesper and me."

"I should ... go," I murmured, unable to share my secret shame with her.

"Stay," she insisted. "My bed is far larger than the one in your room; you shall be more comfortable here. Your body shall thank me tomorrow." Alexis released my hand and pulled back the blanket, sliding beneath it, her head resting on her hand as she waited.

It was a bad idea, a very bad idea. She only wanted me to sleep beside her, but my body screamed for more. If I touched her, if she touched me, I would not stop. I did not want to have to stop; she was all I wanted.

I allowed my chiton to fall, watching Alexis' eyes trace the contours of my body as I had hers. I joined her on the bed, its length easily accommodating my own. Alexis gave me a shy smile and pulled the blanket up.

"Do you have enough room?" she asked.

"Yes," I murmured. "Thank you." We lay, facing one another, for a long moment, our bodies so close I could feel the heat coming from hers. I wanted to forget all that had come before, for us both. I waited for Alexis to reach out and place her hands on me, or tell me she wanted mine on her. But she did not, turning over before I found a way to ask her or to continue what we began earlier.

"Sleep well, Skylar," she whispered.

"And you," I replied weakly.

I lay on my back, my right arm beneath my head as I watched the torch cast shadows across the roof of Alexis' room. I should be grateful she had not placed her hands on me, being with her would only complicate matters. I should return to my own room and calm the desire in my body on the small bed. It would be her I dreamt of, her I saw when I touched myself and found my release, her I would … Alexis' warm length suddenly pressed against my own. I gasped. Her deep breaths told me she was asleep and yet her body had craved touch.

I should leave. I could not stay any longer. I needed to quiet the desperate yearning between my thighs. She did not wish for more between us even though she invited me to share her bed.

I rolled onto my side, wrapping my arm around her. She was warm, her body melding into the curve of mine. It did nothing to calm the raging inside me, yet I was helpless to deny her body the comfort it craved, that my own craved. *I shall stay just a little longer, until it would not wake her if I left* I told myself. I forced my hand to lie motionless on her thigh, to not run my fingers along the smooth skin.

"I have fallen for you, Alexis. It frightens me, but I cannot deny it," I whispered, pressing my lips to the top of her shoulder and eliciting a sigh from the sleeping woman in my arms as she pressed herself against me more firmly. My breath caught. How I wanted to hold her every night in such a way, to know that I would wake with her each morning, to touch her, to make love with her and know that she was mine, that she had chosen only me and that it was allowed. That she would not be harmed for such a choice. It was foolish to even entertain the ideas when she had not spoken of wanting the same, but when I closed my eyes it was all I saw.

I joined Hypnos in his realm before I roused myself to leave the warmth of the bed and body beside me.

27

I quietly closed the door to Alexis' room, not wishing to wake her. She had looked so peaceful, so beautiful, lying there with her soft hair tickling my chest as I breathed in the spicy scent I had come to associate with her. I had caressed the soft skin of her back and beneath the hair at the nape of her neck. Part of me hoped she would wake and allow me to show her how she made me feel, that I could tell her what I must. Yet I feared that she did not wish for anything more than friendship between us and I did not know how I would explain how she came to be in my arms if she woke to find me wrapped around her. It astounded me how she had come to mean so much to me in such a small amount of time.

I had placed a gentle kiss on her shoulder and untangled myself, dressing hastily in my tunic, leaving the chiton on the chair and attempting to push the images of my hands on her soft skin from my mind.

I turned, finding Melina at her doorway, arms crossed, and a deep frown creasing her forehead. I squared my shoulders and met her stare unflinching.

"I told you to stay away from her," she said, keeping her voice low.

I crossed the chamber, allowing my full height to tower above her as I spoke. "I shall not deny the princess my company. What is it that terrifies you so about her spending time with me?"

Melina stepped so close that I could feel her shortened breath against my neck. She slid her hand down my side, gripping my hip and pushing me against the stone wall. She leaned in close, her mouth at my collarbone as she drew in my scent. "You smell of her perfume, but there is nothing else beneath that; she did not allow you to have her the way you wish, did she?"

I did not reply. The queen's fingers stroked my thigh, the gentle caress calling my body to respond.

"I see how you desire her, how you hunger to feel her body against yours," she continued, lowering her lips so they grazed my breast. I closed my eyes, willing the skin not to respond, but of course it did. Melina felt it and smiled up at me, taking my hand and pulling me into the room she and Agrias shared. I possessed strength far superior to hers; I could have broken her grip and remained in the central chamber, but I followed her inside, my body screaming to be touched, to feel flesh covering mine, moving against me.

She pushed me against the door so it shut with a thud, her body meeting mine, lips at my breast before I could stop her. I fisted my hand in her hair, longing for the sweet relief a lover's hands and lips would provide.

"Is it jealousy that causes you to warn me from your daughter?" I managed as her hand skittered towards my inner thigh. I trapped it, gripping her fingers tightly as I captured her eyes again. She smiled up at me.

"Do you wish it was *your* bed I spent the night in?"

She shrugged, her lips leaving my breast, her hand replacing them as she reached up and pulled my head to hers. She drove her tongue into my mouth, firing my body further. My thighs were wet with my desire but when I placed my hand on her cheek I knew I could not allow myself to take her to bed. It was not the Queen of Trachis I wanted to find pleasure with. With the hand I still had tangled in her hair, I pulled her lips from mine and sent her stumbling backwards.

Melina smiled triumphantly, unclasping the gold brooch at her shoulder and dropping her chiton to the floor. "I know what you desire. Come, take it from me," she said, reclining on the bed, her body spread wide, inviting me to feel her, taste her.

"No," I told her.

"You truly wish only for my daughter?"

"Yes."

"You would deny yourself a Queen? Refuse to take the pleasure you want though I offer it willingly?"

"Yes," I panted, balling my hands by my side.

"You do not wish to run your hands across my skin?" she asked, her hands mirroring her words. "You do not wish to touch my breasts, to take them in your mouth? To draw cries from my lips as you plunge my depths?"

I gasped, watching as she touched herself. "No," I insisted, swallowing loudly.

She laughed, enjoying the war that raged within me. "You are stronger than I believed," she continued, her fingers working faster. "But Alexis shall not gift herself to you. If you want her you shall have a battle far greater on your hands than you have ever faced before."

I crossed the room, planting my hands either side of her legs, my face level with hers. "Why?"

Melina smiled, her hands skittering up the inside of my thighs again. "The princess does not *ever* disappoint nor question what her father asks of her, though I have wished it many times."

I gripped her wrists tightly. "Do you wonder at her loyalty to him when he was the only parent who showed concern for her as she grew?" I hissed.

The queen hesitated. "She told you of our past."

"She has shared much with me."

Melina held my gaze, the muscle in her jaw working as she considered her next words. "Though not what you most desire. Why do you not ask it of her?"

I released her and stepped back, my body cooling at last. "I was wrong when I said it was jealousy that caused you to warn me from Alexis. You do not wish for me to be in your bed. Indeed I wonder if you would know what to do if I asked you to bring *me* pleasure." I folded my arms across my chest. "So what is it you want? What do you hope to achieve by confirming my desire for Alexis? You tell me to stay away from her then challenge me to take her to bed."

Melina smiled again, gathering her chiton from the floor. "There is much you do not understand," she said.

I crossed to her, ripping the chiton from her hands and throwing it aside. "Then explain," I demanded, grabbing her arms. She stared me down, but did not answer.

"Melina, what is the meaning of this?" Agrias asked, entering the room.

I dropped my hands, only too aware that the queen stood naked before me. She smoothed her hand between my breasts and down my stomach as she replied.

"Skylar was just leaving."

My eyes went immediately to Agrias'. "King Agrias this is not wh–"

"Leave us," he cut me off, his eyes fixed on his wife. I hesitated. "Go, Skylar," he insisted.

I beat a hasty retreat, closing the door behind me and resting my head against it as I attempted to catch my breath. Would Agrias ask Father and me to leave? Would I be allowed to say goodbye to Alexis? I could not bear to think of leaving her, not this way. What would Melina tell her had happened between us? What would she think of me if she believed her mother's words?

"What did you think you were doing?" Agrias asked quietly.

"I wanted to know how deeply her feelings ran," Melina replied.

"So you attempted to seduce her?"

"Attempted, yes. Succeeded, no. She has eyes only for our daughter."

"If Alexander had lived, would you have interfered in such a manner? Pushed him towards a certain girl of your choosing?"

"Do not bring up my son."

"Why not? You have brought him up every day for over twenty winters and missed out on seeing the precious second child we created. You were always so quick to dismiss her. You allowed me to marry her off, to send her far from here when it was time with no instruction of how her life would be."

"I attempted to teach her, but it was too late then."

"Of course it was, you had ignored her for almost thirteen winters! How did you expect her to react when you finally paid her some attention?"

"You were the one who insisted we spend the time together and it made no difference."

"So *this* is how you intend to encourage her to remain? By daring Skylar to defy you and speak of feelings you hope our daughter shares? You suddenly want Alexis to stay. Why?"

"You do not believe Alexis feels as Skylar does?"

"That is n—"

"Do you not want to see them together? Do you still hope Alexis produces an heir of your line for the throne of Trachis?"

"No, you know that has never mattered to me. Though I have mourned for her losses, just as you have, as I am certain she has herself, if she never has a child of her own, we have other options."

"Thaddeus," Melina supplied.

"Yes. Just as my father named his chosen successor, so have I by naming Thaddeus as mine, and then his eldest son if Alexis is no longer alive when Thaddeus passes on and she has no children of her own."

"When Alexis lost her first two babies, I feared she would suffer to create more, just as I did."

"Which is why we put it in place with Thaddeus and Hesper back then. You cannot interfere between Skylar and Alexis, Melina. If they are ever to be together they must discover it in their own time."

"They do not have *time*, Agrias. Melanthios is insisting their betrothal go ahead within the next moon."

"And I shall make him wait, forever if I am able."

I pushed off the door. If Melina spoke the truth about time being short then I had to tell Alexis what I had kept from her last night. If she spoke of wanting me to take her to bed then I would speak the words I had been too afraid to. It did not appear that the Agrias or Melina would be outraged to find the two of us in bed together. I must steel myself, be as unafraid to speak of my feelings as I was to face an opponent in battle. Tonight. After the banquet.

28

"She has recovered, and it would appear she has deep feelings for the princess, you are prepared to allow her to pursue them rather than making yourself known to her now?"

"Yes. The Epirotes have a fierce reputation, and if her feelings increase she may need our assistance to stand against them. It could be advantageous to us."

"You would test her against the combined Molossian and Illyrian tribes?"

"Perhaps."

"What of the Bessoi boy? Perhaps we should separate them; he fooled us once, he should not be given the chance to do so again."

"Leave him for now. He still has a part to play."

"As you wish, Master."

29

"Would you stand still? You are making me nervous," Father said as I paced. "What is wrong?"

"Nothing," I frowned.

"Skylar," he reached out, halting me. "What is it?"

"I spent the night with Alexis," I admitted.

"Ah," he said with a smile.

"We did not ... I only shared her bed to sleep."

"You did not wish to say goodbye to her this morning?"

"I woke before she did, I did not say goodbye at all."

"And you are worried about seeing her again, that she shall be upset?"

"No. Yes. I do not know. I want to see her but ... I do not know if I should go to the banquet this evening."

"Why?"

"There shall be women there, a lot of them, and I do not know anyone."

"You know Alexis and Hesper," he amended.

"But I have never attended a banquet such as this one, Father. I shall be expected to hold conversations, to speak of customs or heroes I know nothing of. You know the sorts of banquets I have attended; they contained only a small number of women, and were not there for conversation."

He smiled kindly. "Skylar, you are overthinking it."

"No, I am not. Do you know what I did today? I went to the agora and bought material. Nice material, expensive. When have you ever known me to do that?"

"Never," he agreed. "But it does not mean that you cannot. Why did you buy it?" I did not reply. "Skylar?" he pressed.

"Because I wanted to look nice for Alexis," I mumbled.

He smiled again. "You care what she thinks. Alexis understands that you have not lived as she has, as most girls and young women have, yet she wishes you there anyway."

"But ..." I blew out a long breath, attempting to put my thoughts into words. My resolve from early that morning had waned the later the day became. I wanted to be with Alexis, wanted to feel her skin on mine, taste her lips, learn how she enjoyed being touched, what gave her the most pleasure. But Kuria ... The words I would have to speak, the guilt and sadness I still felt for what had happened; I did not know if I could share that with her. Besides, apart from one kiss, that one look that had crossed Alexis' face last night, she had given no indication she wanted to be with me, with a woman at all. "What if I am confusing friendship with something else?" I asked. My father allowed me time to speak. "You know I have not had many friends, our constant moving and secretiveness prevented that."

He nodded, but remained silent.

"But here, it is different. I feel different. *You* are different. You speak of matters with Agrias with a freedom I have never witnessed before. You trust him."

"And you appear to have found one you enjoy spending time with also," he ventured.

It was my turn to nod. "I have found myself speaking of things long since hidden away, thoughts I have never spoken of with anyone but you."

"You have spoken of what happened with Kuria to Alexis?"

"No, I have spoken of much, but not that. Alexis wants to know where I have been, what I have seen and who I am. She does not run because of my differences, she embraces them, finds them fascinating. She wants to hear of it all."

"That is unusual for you, and disconcerting."

I nodded. "The day she brought the honey-sweetened bread she asked if I wished for a husband, a lover."

"How did you respond?"

"I told her I did not want a husband."

"You did not explain further?"

"No."

Father regarded me thoughtfully before he spoke again. "You do not wish for mere friendship with the princess. You wish to take her to your bed," he said carefully.

"I do," I replied. "But perhaps I confuse friendship with believing she wants more; I do not have comparison."

"Are you afraid also that if the two of you spend more time together that it shall end in the same manner as it did with Kuria?"

I shrugged. "I do not believe that Agrias, or even Melina, would harm Alexis, but I cannot say the same of Melanthios. Alexis is set to become his wife and though he has invited many women to his hut, with Alexis I do not believe he would be willing to share."

"That may be the truth my darling, and I still take blame for being absent until the dawn; unable to hear Kuria's screams for aid that night."

"Stamatis was shrewd, he did not wish anyone to know of his crime until it was done. Had you been there I do not believe you would have heard her, just as I did not," I murmured, adding, "Alexis asked me to accompany her back to Epirus when she and Melanthios leave. I told her I could not."

"Why?"

"Because I ... I cannot leave you."

"The true reason, Skylar," he rumbled.

"Because I do not want her to leave with Melanthios at all. If I went with her, I could not stand by and allow him to hurt her. I could not protect Kuria, did not know I had to, so how can I allow Alexis to go with Melanthios knowing that he shall harm her?"

"You could not, I know that."

"Father, what if Alexis only wants me as protection or only speaks kind words to me because I saved her? Twice."

"Do you believe you only care for her because you saved her?"

"No."

"Then perhaps you already have your answer."

"But how can I be certain of it?"

"When you are together, the answer shall be clear, it always is," he paused then continued. "It appears you care for Alexis far deeper than you are willing to admit to me. Than you admit to yourself even," he added, laying his hand on my shoulder.

I knew exactly how much I felt for Alexis but I only shrugged in response.

"Father, would you ... would you tell me of my mother, of how you knew she was the one for you?" I asked, meeting his eyes again.

He blew out a long breath of his own, pulling me over to sit on the bed beside him. "We have never spoken of her in such a manner, you and me," he murmured.

I shook my head. "I have always known it pained you to speak of her, to remember that she did not walk beside you any longer."

He nodded. "You speak the truth, but perhaps I should have, for you."

"You have always been enough for me, Baba, but I find I do not have experience with caring for anyone other than you, for loving anyone as I believe you loved my mother. I wish to understand what it is to feel that way about someone. How I know when it is true and not just a confusion of something else."

He blew out another deep breath. "My darling Skylar, when she is the one for you, there is no doubt in your mind. You cannot imagine a world that does not contain her; her smile, her laugh, the way her hair blows in the breeze, the way she holds your hand or feels wrapped in your arms," he smiled a sad smile and I laid my hand on his arm. "When I met your mother that was how I felt."

"You have never loved another the same way," I observed.

"Not in the same manner, no," he replied. "She was many things, but beautiful and kind above all else. I loved her from the moment I saw her."

"How did you meet?" I asked quietly. "Why did you have to leave your tribe?"

"I was bonded with another when I met Zita; being bonded in Thrace is akin to a betrothal in Greece. I was the first-born child to my parents, and as such was bonded to another first-born – Irina. First-borns were always warriors, expected to take their place as defenders of the tribe and they were also always bonded together, which meant that when we reached twelve winters we left our parents' huts and lived alone in our own. There was no feast, no revelry; one day my father simply came to me and told me which hut Irina and I were to share, that was the end of the discussion.

"The two of us were a good match as far as our leaders were concerned; fierce, ruthless, skilled. But Irina loved another: Theron. Theron was also a first-born warrior, though he protected the Satrae; the priests and priestesses of our tribe. Theron was a good man, a good friend, and I almost lost his friendship when it was time for Irina and me to move into our own hut.

"I cared for Irina, but never loved her, not as Theron did and I did not stand in their way when they wished to celebrate their love. Theron would come to our hut late at night and I would leave them to their whispered conversations and lovemaking, walking for candlemarks beneath the moonlight, watching the sparkling lights overhead as they appeared against the darkness. In the summer I often slept beneath the trees, returning to our home when Eos' dawn lit the horizon, and sending Theron back to his."

"Was Theron not bonded with another?" I asked.

"No. As protector of the Satrae it was not permitted."

"Were you and Irina expected to produce children together?" I asked carefully, wondering for the first time in my life if I had brothers or sisters still in the north.

"Of course and she birthed three, though they belonged to Theron, not me. I fathered no children to the Bessoi tribe."

"Oh," I murmured, finding myself relieved there were no children my father had loved and then had to leave before I was born. "How did you meet my mother?"

"One night I was dozing beneath a large silver birch tree, when she appeared. She told me she had been walking for many days, though from where I do not recall. Her hair was the same shade as yours, long and tangled from the wind that whipped up around us, her eyes bright beneath the new moon. I offered her water and when she thanked me, she smiled a brilliant smile. I instantly lost my heart to her. We made love beneath the moon, but in the morning she was gone and I was not certain she had truly ever existed. But she had, for she waited for me beneath the branches of the birch the following night.

"From that moment on I knew there would be no other for me, I had found the one I was supposed to be with, to love, to protect. Though in the end it was she who protected me, protected you," he drew breath, but continued before I could question him on what he meant. "It was not just her smile that captured me, but her words when she spoke of our future together, the many ways she proved how deeply she cared for me day after day.

"Zita and I had not lived our lives akin to one another, as you and Alexis have not, yet we could not imagine a life that did not contain the other. We did not wish it."

"When did you decide to leave Thrace? Was it when my mother found she was with child, with me?"

"No, it was before that. Only Theron and Irina knew of my Zita, and we often dreamed of leaving the Bessoi; of being with the ones we *wanted* rather than those we *must*. After a fierce battle with the neighboring tribe of the Dentheletae, we disappeared."

"All of you?"

"Yes," Father confirmed with a nod. "Theron, Irina and their children. We ended up in Konitsa, in Epirus, in a region belonging to the Molossians."

"The Molossians? The same ones that Melanthios' family belongs to?"

"No. Andreas and those faithful to him had already broken from the main part of the Molossian tribe and headed a day's travel south to Dodona, claiming it for themselves. Neither Andreas or anyone from that original group appeared interested in finding out if their fellow Molossians still dwelt at Konitsa, and as there were few who were there when we arrived, we quickly took them over.

"Irina and Theron have been joined many winters in Konitsa, raising their children together as they always dreamed without interruption; the fierce Molossian reputation keeping enemies far from their mountainous door."

"And yet you were forced to walk alone, without Zita."

"After a time, yes," Father agreed. "The days we spent together were not nearly as many as I wished for, as I believed we had, but she gave me you, a most precious gift indeed, and one I would not change for anything," he replied, planting a kiss on my head.

I smiled, wrapping an arm around his waist. "You told me we were near Sparta the night Mother birthed me and for a long time I thanked the gods every night for ensuring you did not abandon me beside the road or on a mountaintop as so many Spartan children have been. I asked them to ensure you never did. You kept me, cared for me, loved me and protected me even though I was here instead of my mother. It was my fault she died, I killed her when I entered this world, yet you did not despise me. I shall always be grateful to you for that."

"My darling Skylar, it was not your fault she died. Please do not believe that, for I never have. You were the part of Zita I got to keep, the part of her that lived on outside my heart. I would have never allowed you to be taken from me, to be raised by anyone else or left to die because I could not have both you and her."

I nodded, thankful to finally speak the words I had kept from him for so many winters. "Where was my mother from if not your tribe? Who were her people?"

Father drew a deep breath. "That is perhaps a story for another day; it draws late. Go. Ready yourself for the banquet. Impress your Princess."

I gave him a shy smile. "She is not *my* Princess."

"Perhaps one day she shall be. Take your cues from her. If she wishes to be with you, she shall show you. Do not fear the unknown for sometimes it is where the most joy is to be found."

I stood, wrapping my arms around him and hugging him tightly. "Thank you for speaking of my mother, I know it causes you pain to think of her."

He smiled and kissed my cheek again. "Do not keep the princess waiting," was his only reply.

30

I counted out the number of paces it took me to cover the length and width of the palace again; the counting a particularly good distraction as I drew level with the royal suites across the courtyard. It was one hundred-and-five podes from the walkway to the balcony on the north-east side of the palace to the walkway beside the farthest banqueting hall of the andron on the west; sixty-six podes from the andron to the baths.

I had spoken to Hesper when I returned from the agora early that morning, asking her to aid me to ready myself for the banquet, but I could not bring myself to knock at her door. Guests filtered in through the open palace doors; the women turning left and making their way to the south-east wing banqueting hall, the men cutting through the garden, occasionally nodding to me before they entered the andron. Finally I blew out a long breath and squared my shoulders, striding purposefully across the yard.

"I wondered if you had changed your mind about tonight," Hesper said, allowing me entry to her apartment.

"Apologies," I replied, closing the door behind me.

"Come, we shall begin with your clothing." I nodded. "Alexis was here earlier, she believed the material you left was for me and I did not correct her."

"Was she fond of the color?"

"Very, she mentioned it would be a pretty color on you."

"I only hope I have chosen correctly," I murmured.

"I believe we both know you have," she said with a smile. "Take your

152

tunic off." I did as directed, dropping the material onto her bed. My heartbeat increased only with thoughts of the evening ahead as opposed to the knowledge that I stood naked in front of another woman. Hesper did not hesitate and admire my body or run her eyes over my muscular curves; she simply draped the linen around me and secured it at my shoulder with practiced efficiency. "You are going to much trouble for Alexis. I see that you care for her."

"I do, very much."

"She thinks highly of you also," Hesper said, returning to stand in front of me. "She is definitely going to notice you in this," she added, standing back to admire her handiwork. I smoothed my hands over my sides and hips, sending up a silent prayer that I would find the courage to speak of all I still kept from Alexis when the time came. "Sit, I shall fix your hair."

"I usually just pull it back and hold it with a piece of material," I admitted taking the chair she indicated.

"Not tonight," she said with a smile.

A highly polished rectangle of bronze leant against the wall, its base resting on the table behind a number of pyxides, simple yet elegant hair clasps, an amphora and two skyphoi.

"Your sons slumber already?" I asked, noting the toys strewn across the many klinai in the room.

"Hopefully, though they spend the night with my parents in town so there is the chance they are still awake," she smiled. Hesper drew her hands through the dark mass at my head, freeing the snarls she found. I closed my eyes as she worked, opening them again when she put her hand on my shoulder. "All done," she informed me.

I looked into the bronze before me. Hesper had braided my hair around my forehead, the end held in place with the rest of my hair by a clip at the back of my neck. "I am barely recognizable."

"You look beautiful, it suits you."

"Thank you."

"Shall we go?" I took a deep breath and nodded. "You need not be nervous, there shall be questions and you shall be a source of fascination to some, but I am certain Alexis shall stay close to aid you should you need it. Though from what I understand you are rarely in need of assistance," she smiled, squeezing my arm.

"Thank you," I said again, returning her grin.

The banqueting hall was already filled with the bodies and laughter of many women. Alexis stood with a group on the far side of the room. She faced the doorway, though she did not notice Hesper and me as we entered. I took a kantharos of wine from the nearest table, sipping at it as I watched her.

"I must speak with someone," Hesper said. "You see Alexis?"

I nodded, but made no move to go to her. Hesper moved off and I drank in the sight of the princess; she wore a vivid purple chiton, her hair held back in a design similar to mine, though the brown strands were plaited down her back where mine lay loose. Her cheeks held a slightly pink hue and she held a kantharos of wine in her left hand. I was struck once again by the favorable elegance of the clothing that hugged her body. I recalled the curve of her waist, the rise of her breasts as she had stood naked before me.

Her hand often found its way to her companions' arms and jealousy flared inside me each time it did. I could have crossed to her so her hands found their way onto mine – as I knew they would – but I enjoyed watching the easy way she laughed and spoke with those around her.

"Well, hello again," a voice said beside me. I turned, finding the woman who had first spoken to me at the agora. She smiled widely, resting her hand atop my arm, fingers cool on my skin.

"Hello," I replied.

"Apologies we did not have the opportunity to speak more yesterday, I am Voleta."

"Skylar," I replied.

"I must tell you, I find myself extremely curious about you, as did my husband when I spoke of you to him." She stroked my arm as she spoke.

"I am not one to be curious about," I assured her.

I did not miss the frank appraisal she made of my body and, whilst normally such attention at banquets I attended would lead in only one direction, tonight I did not wish for it to be so. At least not with her. Voleta dragged her nails up the inside of my forearm, her fingers brushing my breast as she pressed her body the length of mine. She looked up, her eyes finding mine again.

"Perhaps you would join us in our room this evening; late, when the moon is high. We enjoy the company of many women, many men in our bed. You would be a most welcome addition, and highly sought after, I assure you."

Her thumb traced the underside of my breast. "Apologies, but I have a prior engagement," I said, attempting to discreetly remove myself from the heat of her body, and her wandering hands. Her brow furrowed at my rejection and I wondered if it was wise to displease her; especially without knowledge of who, or how powerful, she and her husband may be. I gave her a smile, running my finger from her shoulder to her elbow, her lower body pressing against me as I did so. "Perhaps another time," I told her. "For the offer and your words please me much."

The smile returned to her lips and she nodded. "Hesper and Alexis knows where we can be found, should you change your mind," she said, her hand sliding down my side and over the curve of my bottom. "It would be a shame to have you so close and be unable to touch such fine features." She pressed her lips to my shoulder.

I dipped my head in acknowledgement. "Until then," I told her, having no intention of seeking her out for such pursuits.

Voleta squeezed my flesh, her teeth crushing her bottom lip as she pressed herself against me again, a deep groan escaping her lips. "I hope you shall not disappoint me," she purred, gracing me with another seductive grin as she left my side.

I exhaled deeply, moving to the far edge of the room, murmuring polite greetings to several women who nodded in my direction. Voleta stood with Melina, who raised her brows in my direction when our eyes met. Thankfully she made no move to come and speak with me, turning back to their conversation.

I leaned against the wall, watching as Hesper arrived at Alexis' side, heads bending together in consultation. When Hesper pulled back, Alexis' eyes scanned the room, widening when they settled on mine. Her mouth fell open before she regained her composure. She smiled and held her hand up in acknowledgement. I returned her grin, and her wave, enjoying her reaction. She kept her eyes on me, but turned her head to speak to those she stood with, stepping away from the group to make her way over.

"Ladies, I present for your entertainment the famed poet, Lasus," Melina announced, halting Alexis' progress towards me. Reluctantly I drew my eyes from the princess' and settled them on the named man. He smiled beneath his dark beard, bowing in Melina's direction as she moved to stand with a group of older women.

"I thank you for the introduction, Queen Melina," he said. "I come to you this evening from the great city of Athens, to share with you poems from another infamous poet, Sappho." Several of the women in the room nodded in approval, voices rising as they spoke excitedly to one another. I returned my eyes to Alexis, having heard many of Sappho's words and wondering which poem Lasus would choose to tell. "One can only imagine that Sappho knew many beautiful women on her island of Lesbos, some friends, many of them lovers. I see you also have many beauties here," he said, circling the room and bowing before Alexis when he found her amongst the other women. "So it is only fitting that I read for you one of Sappho's most favored works."

Lasus continued to pace through the crowd, pausing in front of me and smiling briefly before drawing me forward to stand beside him. I colored instantly at the attention, but did not attempt to return to my place in case more of a fuss was made. "Whilst I cannot say for certain that the exact conversation ever took place between the poet and the Goddess of

BELINDA HARRISON

Love, Aphrodite, I have always wanted to believe it did; that the great goddess gave council to a woman who wrote some of the most beautiful love poems I have ever had privilege to perform." I found Alexis' eyes within the throng, feeling as though I turned the shade of my dress when she smiled at me. "The poem I have chosen is Sappho's *Prayer to Aphrodite*, and it begins in this manner:" Lasus said, finally releasing my hand.

"On your splendid throne Immortal Aphrodite,
enchanting daughter of Zeus,
I implore you, do not crush my heart
with pain, lady of beauty
but come, as you came before
when you heard my voice from afar,
and left your father's golden house,
sweet birds on beating wings
brought you forth
from Olympos down to the darkened earth
where soon you arrived. Dear one,
your immortal face did smile
as you asked what suffering I felt
and why I called you,
what I most wished for.
"What does your heart most deeply desire?
Whose love do you most seek? Who,
dear Sappho wrongs you?
If now she flees, soon she shall pursue.
If she refuses gifts, soon she shall gift them.
If she does not yet love, soon she shall love,
no longer unwilling."
Come now and release me
from my anguish. Grant
me my heart's deepest desire.
Forever stand beside me as my ally."

31

Lasus ended his poem and the room erupted in applause, though my hands remained at my side. Sappho's words repeated themselves in my mind and I stepped back as Hesper and the other women crowded around him.

I was too warm. I placed my cup on the nearest table and turned, leaving the banquet hall. I stepped out into the cooler air of the courtyard, my breath refusing to come. *If now she flees, soon she shall pursue, if she refuses gifts, soon she shall gift them, if she does not yet love, soon she shall love, no longer unwillingly.* It was as if he had spoken directly to me, as if Sappho spoke directly to me, advising me that what I most sought with Alexis I could have. It was within my reach if only I believed it to be so.

"Skylar, are you ill?" the words were softly spoken but a warm hand pressed against the exposed skin at the small of my back.

I swallowed and turned to face the green emeralds I knew would hold my heart forever. "No," I replied, taking Alexis' hand in my own.

Her brow furrowed ever so slightly. "Did you not enjoy the poet's words?"

"I enjoyed his words very much, they gave me much to consider," I replied, my thumb caressing the soft skin of her fingers. "Could we go to your room and speak further?"

"Of course."

I kept her hand in mine as we made the short walk to the central chamber and into her room beyond. I would tell her of my feelings and then I would tell her of Kuria.

"We have our own version of the Goddess of Love in Macedonia, she is known as Zeirene," Alexis murmured, taking her hand from mine to close the door behind us.

"You worship so few of the Greek gods, are the rest Macedonian equivalents?" I asked as she returned to stand before me.

"Some, though we are influenced by the Thracians, the Balkans and the Paeonians also. You could say we are quite inclusive," she replied with a smile.

"I see," I breathed, unable to add anything further as her eyes travelled the length of my body.

"You look beautiful tonight."

"As do you," I whispered.

"Tell me what Sappho's poem gave you to consider," she said, her eyes finding their way back to mine.

"They spoke to me of you."

"Me?" she asked, a shy smile lighting her lips.

"More than you can imagine," I replied, drawing a finger down her cheek and following the line of her jaw to her chin.

"He is here at my request, I wanted to hear words of the gods and goddesses you grew up learning of and worshipping. I asked him here for you."

"I do not know how I could repay you for such a kindness," I murmured, stepping closer so that barely a breath separated our bodies.

"There is one way."

"And what is that?" I managed, my heart feeling as though it would burst from my chest.

"Reconsider accompanying me to Epirus when I leave." I inhaled sharply, the answer not what I had imagined, nor wished, to hear from her. Her hands were at my waist, holding me tightly as she spoke again. "Please Skylar, I beg it of you. Come with me."

"I cannot."

She opened her mouth to speak, but I pressed my fingers over her lips. "I do not intend to allow you to return to Epirus with Melanthios."

"Why?"

"Because you do not deserve to be treated as he would treat you."

"Is that the only reason?" she asked, raising one hand to rest on my arm. I swallowed, shaking my head. "Do you care for me?"

"I do, Princess, and I … I want more," I said quietly.

She hesitated, searching my face for the answer she sought. "You wish for more between us?"

I slid my hands down as far as her hips, drawing her against me and holding her stare. "Yes. Very much." I leant down, claiming her lips. My

158

tongue caressed her, tasted her, as it had the day before and I groaned when her own tentatively returned the movements. When we parted my breath was short and desire pulsed through every inch of me. "I want to be more than just a friend to you, for you to be more than that to me. I … I want what the poem spoke of."

"Oh," Alexis breathed, dropping her eyes from mine. "Skylar, I … I cannot, I do not …" she trailed off, shaking her head. The breath left my body, but not in the pleasurable way it did whenever I found myself within reach of her. Disappointment and regret gripped me instead. I had spoken words she did not want to hear, shared feelings she did not understand or mirror. "I …" Alexis began again, again unable to finish.

I watched the crease of her brow, how she opened her mouth, yet found no words to speak. What I had feared most was true – she only wanted my protection from Melanthios, she did not desire my touch, my love. She did not return my feelings. "No. Say nothing further," I told her with a shake of my head; I could not bear to hear her speak the words. "I must go."

I dropped my hands from her body as her own left mine. I backed away until I found the handle of the door. I turned and lifted it as she spoke again.

"Wait. Please. Do you need aid removing your chiton?"

I paused, squeezing my eyes shut before facing her again. I could not allow her hands near me, not when I so desperately wished for them to touch me in a way I now knew they never would. "No. Thank you. Goodnight, Princess." I pulled open the door, walking through without a backward glance.

It appeared Melina had spoken with truth; Alexis would not disappoint Agrias, she would honor her commitment to become Melanthios' even though she feared him, even though she knew what he would do to her.

I started across the courtyard. I sought relief, I needed to take pleasure from one who would freely give it, who would not reject my advances as Alexis had. I paused, briefly considering returning to the banquet hall and finding Voleta, but it was not her I wished for either. The raucous laughter of the banquet in the andron drifted out into the night and I headed in that direction instead. Women sat in the laps of men, their bodies barely hidden beneath material as they plied them with wine and food.

My father reclined on a couch by the door and, after much gesticulating on my behalf he rose, stumbling his way towards me. "Sky, love, how is your evening?" he asked, a lopsided grin on his face.

"I need someone," I told him, keeping my voice low.

"Who?" he asked, looking around.

I rolled my eyes, infuriated by his inebriated state. "A woman," I hissed.

"Ah," he said, smiling as he understood. "Go to your room, I know who to send."

"Thank you. Hurry."

He smiled again before returning inside, signaling someone I could not see.

I hastily made my way to my room, pushing open the door and sweeping aside the tunic and himation that lay on the bed. I had been a fool to believe Alexis felt the same way about me. We had kissed yesterday, that was true, but she had been clear after that; she did not want anything more. She was a Princess and I was no one, I was worthy only to protect her, not to love her. My body simultaneously ached at the knowledge and flared at the thought of her body pressed against mine as she had slept. The backs of her thighs against mine, my breasts hard either side of her spine. I drew my hand down my chest and over my stomach.

A knock sounded and I flew across the room. A woman with hair the color of Alexis' stood on the other side. I took her by the wrist, dragging her inside as I slammed the door shut. She smiled, though it was not the smile of someone shy; it was predatory. She knew what I needed, why she had been sent for and she grabbed me by the hair, pulling me against her body as she kissed me.

I kissed her back, hard, my tongue demanding entry to her mouth. She allowed me to possess her, my fingers dragging her short chiton up, searching desperately for skin, for warmth, for a wetness that would match my own. I wished for her hands and her mouth to touch me in all the places I desired it of Alexis. I would have the princess, if only in my mind.

Without breaking our contact the slave girl freed me of the fabric that held me, dragging it down to squeeze my breasts. I moaned, pushing my hips into her. Her mouth left mine and she pushed me backwards until my thighs met the bed.

She followed, her mouth trailing her hands as she drew them down my body. I closed my eyes, imagining it was Alexis' fingers against me, her lips at my neck, my breasts, and the apex of my thighs. When the slave girl entered me I drove my teeth into my bottom lip. She slid her fingers in and out, pushing me towards the release I so desired, her mouth meeting my heated center moments later.

I whimpered, holding her to me as I moved on her. A cool breeze wrapped around my legs, my eyes flying open at the soft 'no' from the doorway.

"Alexis!" I gasped, my insides quivering around the fingers inside me as I met her horrified stare. I pushed away the head of the slave girl, her fingers sliding roughly free. "Wait!" I cried as Alexis turned and fled.

I picked up the himation from the floor, wrapping it around me as I went after her. I ran through the courtyard garden, jumping several small bushes in my haste to catch Alexis before she entered her room and locked me out.

I caught up to her in the central chamber, stepping around her to block her path to her room. "Please, allow me to explain."

"You do not owe me an explanation," she said, refusing to meet my eyes.

"Alexis, please, it was no–"

"Do not say it was not as it appeared, for we both know that would be a lie. How could you *do* this?" she asked, angry eyes meeting mine again.

"I ... I did not ..." I struggled for an answer.

"I understand desires of the flesh, better perhaps than you may believe, but I do not understand your behavior tonight," she said, her voice breaking.

"Alexis, wait, please," I began again, reaching for her hand. "I did not mean to hurt you, indeed I did not realize it would."

Her mouth gaped open again, but she closed it quickly, ensuring her arm was out of my reach. She wrapped both across her chest, her face hard when she spoke again. "Leave now, Skylar. There are no more words to be spoken between us."

I dropped my hand, the ache in my chest returning, more painful than ever. I stepped aside, allowing Alexis to enter her room and close the door, the locking device dropping into place with a thud. I trudged back across the courtyard to my room.

The slave girl had waited. "Leave," I told her, holding open the door.

"You do not wish to finish?" she asked with what I was certain was supposed to be an inviting grin. I shook my head. She frowned, but readjusted her chiton and made her way past me. "If you wish to find me again I have a place in town," she said, sliding her hand down my side.

"Just leave," I said, slapping her hand away.

"If that is what you desire," she replied, stomping back towards the andron.

I slammed the door shut and flopped down onto the small bed. Alexis had no right to be upset with me; I had told her I wished for more between us and she told me she did not. *But I do not understand your behavior tonight.* That was what she had said. She referred to the pairing of two women, obviously, but why had she allowed me to kiss her if the thought disgusted her so? She had kept her arm through mine, her fingers between mine, almost the entire time we had been at the agora. Was such touching common between female friends? Had I simply mistaken it for deeper affection? Hesper had held my other arm for much of the time, yet I did not think of it in the same manner. Was it merely because I did not have the same feelings, the same desire, for Hesper as I did for Alexis?

My eyes found the bottle of perfume I had bought for Alexis when I was at the agora earlier; it appeared it would go to waste now. I had made such a mess of everything. I did not know how to begin repairing it; if I even *could* repair it.

32

Sweat dripped from my brow as I fended off the attack from Moeris, his sword clashing against mine. He may have sixteen winters on me, but his body showed no sign of age and he pushed me hard. I welcomed the challenge, reveling in the opportunity to train with the soldiers for the first time since arriving in Trachis.

I allowed the constant challenge of identifying and finding ways to exploit my opponent's weakness to fill my head, rather than visions of a future with Alexis that could never be. I wished I could take comfort in knowing that at least if we were not together, she would be safe from harm by those who were as appalled by the idea of two women together as she was. But her rejection cut me too deeply and she was still intended for Melanthios, whose cruelty I was certain would continue for too many winters.

"Next!" Moeris shouted. Thaddeus moved into position opposite me.

We nodded to each other, raising our swords and beginning to battle one another. "Hesper is well?" I asked.

"She is," he acknowledged.

"And the princess?"

"As well as can be expected, given that the two of you have not spoken these past three days." I only grunted, ducking his swinging sword. "Skylar," he hesitated then continued, "Just as in battle you must sometimes be bold and make the first move, so too it is with love. You may be exposed and vulnerable, but without boldness there can be no greatness."

His sword met mine with a metallic ring. "You assume I love her," I said, pushing him away with my weapon.

"Do you deny it?" he asked, blocking my advance.

"It is of no consequence being that she does not share the sentiment."

"Next!" Moeris yelled again and Thaddeus moved to my right, partnering with my father as a young man named Brygos arrived to challenge me.

Brygos was far less accomplished than Thaddeus, his movements raw and clumsy and it was not long before he found himself in the dirt at my feet, pulling tight at the rope he wore around his middle so it did not fall off.

I had waited at the baths for Alexis two nights in a row after the banquet, but she did not come.

I landed a blow against Brygos' shield. He stumbled backwards, tripping over his sandals and finding the ground with a puff of dust. I offered my hand, pulling him to his feet and waiting for his next attempt at attack.

I wished Alexis would yell or accuse me of disappointing or disgusting her. I wanted her to explain her actions, and why she did not return my affections as I had believed she did. But more than that I wished she would tell me she still wanted us to be friends, for I found that if nothing else, I still wanted to be that to her. I also still hoped she would allow me to free her from the union with Melanthios.

Brygos landed on his backside again. I did not offer him my hand as he got to his feet.

I understood she was angry with me, but did she not have questions? Did she not want to ask me – to understand – why I was with the slave? When I kissed Alexis, she had kissed me back so her revulsion when she saw me with the girl made no sense.

Brygos found the dirt again.

Did Alexis kiss me only to find out the depth of my feelings, just as her mother had? Did she allow our kiss only to experiment? Did she truly not feel more for me as I had believed and wanted?

I defended Brygos' wild swing, my foot finding his stomach. He dropped to his knees, gasping as the dust blew up around him.

I grabbed him, attempting to pull him to his feet but he collapsed to the ground again. "Get up!" I yelled.

I raised my sword, bringing it down against his shield as he struggled to regain his breath. He scrambled backwards as I advanced, holding his shield up to ward off my attack.

A hand grabbed my wrist. "Enough!" Moeris insisted. "The poor boy still learns his craft; go easy on him."

"If he should find himself in battle, the enemy would not go easy on him," I countered, ripping my hand from his grip.

"Brygos, train with Thaddeus. Leandros perhaps a quiet word is required." Brygos jumped to his feet, relieved at being spared my company as my father approached.

"Come," he said, steering me away from the other soldiers by the elbow.

"I do not need speaking to," I replied, snatching my elbow from him. "I am not a child."

"You are acting as one," he murmured as we walked towards the doorway and out onto the plain. "What is it? Why did you attack Brygos?"

"It is nothing."

"Skylar, I am not blind, I know something has happened." I remained silent. "The day of the banquet we spoke of much. Your questions of the relationship your mother and I shared told me what you did not. You clearly have deep feelings for Alexis. I have to assume you did not broach them with her, for if you had you would not have asked for the slave girl. There would have been no need. Do you feel guilty for being with another when you care so much for her?"

"Alexis does not share my feelings," I said, keeping my voice low.

"What? Are you certain? Perhaps you misunderstood."

"There was no misunderstanding. Not about that at least," I replied, slipping my sword into the sheath at my thigh.

"What do you mean?"

"I told her I wanted more between us and she made it clear she did not. As I thought, she only wants me to accompany her to Epirus for protection."

"But she ... No, I cannot believe it," he said with a shake of his head.

"It is the truth. She saw me with the slave girl and fled. I went after her and she told me she did not understand what she saw me doing. She does not prefer women, not as I always have. There is no future for us."

"You want to leave Trachis and allow Agrias to deal with Melanthios and the other tribes alone then?"

"No, I ..." I began. It was not as if I had not considered the option, but it hurt that Father would be so quick to ask it of me. "You would leave so easily if I said I wanted to?" I asked.

"The real question is do *you* want to stay? Do you not wish to attempt to repair things between you and Alexis? You began to have a friendship with her, if nothing else, you must still wish for that?"

I hesitated, wondering how he could possibly know it was indeed what I still wanted. "I ... I do not know if it is possible. She refuses to speak with me," I finally replied.

"If you care for her at all, you must attempt it," he said, laying his hand on my shoulder. "Tonight is the women's celebration in town. Agrias asked for you to accompany Alexis in case Melanthios decides to find her. Explain your actions, perhaps she shall surprise you."

"I doubt it," I muttered.

"But you shall keep her safe should she find herself in need of it?"

"Of course," I replied with a nod.

"Good."

*

I stood outside Alexis' door, my hand clenching and unclenching at my side. It was ridiculous to be nervous. I had to think of my accompaniment of Alexis as duty only. I needed to see her safely into town and back to the palace. I could do it. I had done it numerous times before for those in my care. Of course it had been easier then – I had not been in love with any of them. I drew a deep breath and squared my shoulders, rapping my knuckles against the wood.

"Come."

I pushed open the door to find Alexis sitting at the small table, combing the end of her long, brown hair. She turned and when her eyes found mine, she jumped ever so slightly, putting the implement aside. The green of her eyes shone in the torch light, as did her chiton which was a deep red, similar to the color I had worn the night of the banquet. Her hair framed her face, long braids keeping it from her eyes and meeting at the nape of her neck where the ends sat softly after her attentions.

"Princess," I said with a bow.

"I was expecting Hesper," she murmured, her face unreadable.

"Apologies. Your father sent me to collect you. I am to escort you into town," I replied keeping my voice neutral. Professional. Respectful. As I had always been to those under my charge.

She rose from the chair, the long chiton trailing her. I watched her gather it at her thighs, pulling it up slightly to push her feet into her sandals. When she turned to me again I saw how the material sat over her body; favoring her with that gentle elegance. I drew a sharp breath, my stomach clenching with the beauty she possessed. She met my gaze, her cheeks coloring under my stare. I dropped my eyes to my feet so as not to make her uncomfortable, nor see how much I still desired her.

"You look beautiful."

"And you have your weapons back. That must please you."

"Yes, though I have enjoyed aspects of their absence," I agreed, raising my eyes back to her. "I … I have missed your company these past days."

"My company has not been worth missing."

I swallowed, wishing I could take back everything she saw so we could return to our easy banter. "I would not agree with such a statement," I said quietly, taking a step towards her. "Alexis, can w–?"

"We should leave, I do not wish to be late arriving," she cut over me, smoothing her chiton.

I bowed my head, my hand on the pommel of my sword. "As you wish, Princess." I opened the door, stepping aside when she neared and closing it behind us. The familiar scent of her perfume drifted behind her and I could not help drawing it in; its fragrance both a comfort and a piercing reminder that I had ruined what was between us. "Shall there be poetry this evening?" I asked, joining her again.

"No. This is my grandmother's gathering. There shall not be such frivolities."

"Oh." I wanted to ask Alexis about her grandmother, but her determined strides as we made our way out of the central chamber, told me she would not give me any answers.

Melina and Hesper stood at the entrance to the palace, Thaddeus to accompany the older woman, and another soldier I did not know, Hesper. Father and Agrias were in the andron, the soldiers and I allowed to join them when our duties were complete. I nodded to the men and we made our way through the grand entrance, across the east balcony and down into the town of Trachis itself. I took up position at the back of the group, the soldiers in front knowing the way and leading the women through the streets.

The stall holders of the agora were still set up as we passed through the main blocks and I mentioned it aloud. It was the queen who replied to my observation. "They remain in the hopes of extra business due to the gathering," she said.

"I see," I murmured.

We reached the stall keeper who had given me the skyphoi of wine the day I had accompanied Alexis to the agora. He embraced both Melina and Alexis, looking twice in my direction when he saw me following, before recognition crossed his face and he raised his hand in greeting. I inclined my head in return and we soon passed by.

The leading soldiers stopped at the open door of a large home; its elaborate portico reminding me of Cleisthenes' house in Athens. I shook my head to dismiss the memories of the slave girl I had enjoyed there and followed the three women inside. The soldiers were to remain outside, and dutifully took up position either side of the entrance.

33

We had been at the celebration for almost two candlemarks; the conversations I had overheard were uninteresting or related to people or immortals I had never heard of. I trailed Alexis as she moved about the room speaking to old friends and acquaintances, her frequent laughter cutting at me rather than pleasing me. Her hands remained far from my own and she did not introduce me to anyone nor invite me to share stories or include me in the banter – an obvious change from our day at the agora. I was introduced only briefly to Aspasia; Melina's mother and hostess of the banquet, and it was by the queen herself. I wished to remain and exchange words with her, but Alexis had crossed the room and I dutifully followed her instead.

Alexis ignored me for the most part, addressing me only when she wanted food or another kantharos of wine. I complied without complaint, hoping to win favor with her, but my constant closeness appeared to cause her annoyance and her treatment became less courteous than I had come to expect, inciting my own ire. I did not help my cause any when, on several occasions, I was not paying attention as Alexis moved to another group and she bumped into me.

When her head crashed against my bronze cuirass for a fourth time, she rubbed at it angrily, turning on me with a deep frown creasing her forehead.

"Why must you remain so close? I am in no danger here. Make yourself useful and fetch me a fresh kantharos of wine. This one is empty."

"Perhaps you have had enough," I shot back, desperate to return to the palace and be done with the festivities of the evening.

"You dare question my wishes?"

"I am not a slave you can order around, *Princess*."

"No, I expect it is you who is used to having slaves do whatever you wish."

My jaw clenched tightly, back teeth grinding together. I grabbed her forearm and leaned in close. "I understand you are angry with me but do not treat me with disrespect or you shall find out just how commanding I can be," I snarled.

"You understand nothing. Release me immediately, you cause a scene."

I raised my eyes, finding that a few of the women had turned their attention to us. I took my hand from Alexis and straightened again. "I did not seek this assignment, but your father entrusted me to see you here and back to the palace safely and I shall not disappoint him as I clearly disappoint you." Alexis said nothing. "Perhaps it is time I observed you from the opposite side of the room."

"Good idea," she agreed, moving off in Hesper's direction.

Fuming, I spun on my heel and made my way to the far wall, keeping Alexis in sight easily with my height. I crossed my arms over my chest, leaning against the wall as I frowned. Alexis' conversation with Hesper was animated and more than once both of them looked in my direction. It appeared Hesper attempted to calm Alexis, though she was not having much success.

A sudden presence at my side drew my attention, but I did not take my eyes from Alexis and Hesper until the familiar voice spoke. "Skylar, I am so pleased to see you join us here." Voleta moved closer, running her hand down my upper arm and resting it on my topmost forearm. "You cut a striking figure in your armor. Even more delicious than the chiton you wore to the banquet." My hands balled into fists. Voleta was the last person I wanted to encounter, for though I could not have Alexis as I wished, neither did I want the attentions of the other woman. "I am disappointed. You have not sought us out as I offered."

"No, I have not," I agreed. "I have been rather occupied since we last spoke."

Voleta found what I had been focused on and raised her eyebrows. "I did not realize Alexis had such appetites. You are fortunate to have such a beauty to lie with."

"She does not," I assured her.

"Then why have you not come to visit us?"

"I have returned to training with the soldiers. When I reach my room each evening I am sweat-stained and tired," I replied simply.

"I imagine you would be in need of a warm bath and hands to knead sore muscles. I would have gladly provided both." Voleta's hand found its way beneath the base of my cuirass and I willed myself not to squirm beneath her touch.

I swallowed, looking up to find Alexis watching Voleta and I with an almost murderous stare. I met it, the muscle in my jaw working. I told myself Alexis was not allowed be upset if I found affections with another when she did not want to be with me and contemplated allowing Voleta's hand to reach its intended destination as she slid it lower. Instead I uncrossed my arms, releasing the fists I had made and covering Voleta's hand, halting its progress.

"I imagine you are a woman of many talents, Voleta, but I am not in need of them at this time," I told her, my eyes never leaving Alexis' face.

Alexis inclined her head towards Hesper again, and I did not need to be any closer to know she spoke with venom. Hesper's surprise was evident when she too looked in my direction.

Alexis started for the door. "The princess takes her leave and as I attend her this evening, I too must depart," I said, returning Voleta's hand to her side and going after Alexis.

Alexis stomped through the courtyard and out into the street. I followed, passing several women gathered near the entrance to the home and nodding in greeting to them. Alexis stopped at none of the stalls she passed, lifting her chiton slightly off the ground to quicken her pace.

"You are ready to return to the palace?" I asked, my larger strides allowing me to catch her up quickly.

"You seek my childhood friend for affections also?" she asked angrily.

"No."

"She is beautiful and belongs to another so obviously is perfect for you," she added, still pacing quickly through the street.

Alexis' words cut me deeply and I reached out, grabbing her arm to halt her progress. "Is that what you think of me? That I am attracted only to those who call someone else their own?" She shrugged. "Unbelievable," I muttered, releasing her as I began to pace. "I never encouraged Voleta, nor gave her cause to seek me out for more than conversation. In return I did not go to her, though she offered me a place in her bed. Instead ... instead I spoke of my feelings for you." Alexis sucked in an audible breath, but I pressed on. "I spoke words you did not wish to hear, spoke of feelings you do not have. I offended you and ruined the only friendship I have had in more winters than I can count. I am sorry I even spoke o–"

"No!" the cry rang out through the streets. A dark figure dropped to the ground not far from us and I pulled my sword from its sheath, my other sweeping Alexis behind me. Three shadows headed in our direction and I pushed Alexis into a dark doorway, waiting.

As they neared, arguing, I stepped from the shadows, felling the first with a fist to the stomach. He dropped to his knees, unable to catch a full breath. The second attempted a punch which I ducked, delivering him to his friend's side in the same manner. The third held the handle of a broken dagger and came at me. I avoided his wild thrust forward and he threw the weapon aside, drawing a sword from its holder instead.

He was obviously the instigator of the attack, larger than the other two and more proficient with weapons, but none of them could have been more than fourteen winters old. I allowed him his attempts to injure or disarm me, denying him of both when I kicked the sword out of his hand. He charged forward and I laid him out cold with the end of my sword.

"Get up," I demanded of the other two.

"Please, we did not mean f–"

"I said get up." They got to their feet, eyes wide with fear as I gathered myself up to my full height. "Pick up your friend and come with me." They looked at one another. "Do not make me repeat myself," I warned, pointing my sword at each.

They nodded and hustled to grab an arm each. They followed me, dragging the third of their party between them.

"Alexis," I called. She emerged from the doorway and I led her and the boys to the gasping man on the ground.

I re-sheathed my sword and took three long lengths of material from a nearby stall. "Put him down and turn around," I ordered.

The boys dropped the arms they held, their eyes meeting again. I saw their intentions before they made the move. I shook my head, giving them a two stride head start before going after them. I caught each by the dark himatia they wore and slammed them together, their heads cracking against the other and knocking them out. I caught them around their waists and hauled them back to where Alexis was kneeling beside their victim.

I dumped them on the ground next to their friend, tying their wrists and ankles together before joining Alexis and the man – who I now realized was the wine stall holder. The commotion had brought others out into the street, though no one approached us. A crude dagger protruded from the stall holder's side, dark blood staining his chiton. I frowned at the amount of blood he had lost. He would need to be sewn back up, but it was also a good sign he had his eyes open and was speaking quietly to Alexis.

"Do not attempt speech, it shall only weaken you, Grandfather. I shall send for her," Alexis told him, addressing a young woman in the gathering crowd. "Aspasia is holding a banquet at her home, tell her to come quickly."

Grandfather? Of course – it was why he had appeared so familiar when I first met him; he shared the same mouth and chin as Melina and Alexis.

"Someone fetch Gnosidicus," I added. For a moment no one moved. "Now!" I demanded.

"I know where he is, I shall go," a young man said, taking off.

"I need thread and a needle as well," I called.

"I have both," an older woman replied.

Alexis moved aside to allow me room. "What is your name?" I asked her grandfather.

"Ophelos," he replied. I nodded and opened the rip in Ophelos' chiton, inspecting his wound. The end of the dagger was not in too far, but it was crudely created and chipped along its length. I needed to remove it.

"They are mere children," Alexis noted, having crossed to the boys who had caused the injury.

"Mercenaries in training I suspect," I grunted. "Though they shall have nothing to show for their actions tonight except sore heads and dented pride."

The crowd around us parted at the sound of footsteps. Aspasia and Melina rushed through the gathering. They dropped to their knees, Aspasia immediately cradling Ophelos' head in her lap and pressing her lips to his forehead.

"My darling," she whispered.

"They attempted to rob me of my best wine," Ophelos gasped, taking her hand. "But do not fear, the warrior appears to know what she is doing. All shall be well."

Melina took her father's hand, stroking his fingers, and when her eyes found mine I gave her a nod.

I gripped the end of the blade, meeting Ophelos' gaze as I spoke. "This is going to hurt," I told him. He nodded in reply and I silently counted to three before pulling it from the jagged skin. He cried out, Aspasia wrapping her arms around him protectively. Blood spilled from the wound and I placed my hand against it, praying the old woman returned quickly with the needle and thread. "Alexis, come here."

Ophelos moaned, though I could tell he was doing his best to keep quiet. Alexis knelt beside me, her mother shuffling sideways to accommodate her.

"Take my himation and wrap it across your chest."

"I am not cold."

"It is not for warmth."

"I do no—"

"Take it."

"I do not need it."

"Gods. Must you argue with me on this point also?" I grabbed Melina's hand and pressed it to Ophelos' wound. "Remain where you are," I demanded, planting my hand firmly on Alexis' shoulder when she attempted to rise. I wrapped the himation around her shoulders, fastening it at her back rather than the front, ensuring her chiton was covered, but leaving her arms free. "If I tell you to take my himation, I expect you to do so," I added, returning to the injured man before us. Alexis did not reply, but left the cloak in place as I replaced Melina's hand with my own.

The old woman arrived with the needle and thread I had asked for, along with a large amphora of wine. She handed the wine to Melina, who offered it to Ophelos. He took a long drink, his eyes on the bone implement I held.

"Do what you must," he said, his voice wavering ever so slightly.

I nodded and tied the fine thread around one end of the needle before ripping a wider hole in his chiton. "Aspasia, Melina, speak with Ophelos of happy moments you have shared. Your most precious days together."

"Why?" Aspasia asked.

"It shall aid me in what I must do," I replied.

Both women nodded, Aspasia bending her head to her husband's ear and Melina re-settling herself beside Ophelos' head.

"You need to keep the top half of his body still," I told Alexis. "I have no herbs to take away his pain and we cannot wait until Gnosidicus arrives."

"You have done this before?" she asked, meeting my eyes.

"Many times," I replied with a nod. "But it does not make it any easier."

She put her hands on Ophelos' arms as I knelt on his thighs. I took a steadying breath before driving the bone through one side of the skin, threading it through the other edge of the stab wound and pulling it taut. Ophelos screamed, his wife sobbing as she held him and I saw Alexis' eyes glistening as well, though she did not allow him to move. She pushed against his arms as he struggled to get free, flecks of blood hitting us both. I continued as quickly as I could, though Ophelos passed out before I was done; the shock of it all too much for his body.

I tied off the ends and slid the knot from the needle as Gnosidicus arrived. "You have a good eye, and work nimbly," he noted, looking over the wound when Alexis moved aside.

"He did not have time to wait, but he would benefit from your further care," I replied, standing.

Gnosidicus nodded, getting to his feet as well, his eyes settling on Alexis. "You appear to be confused at how to wear such a long himation, Princess."

"She attended the banquet tonight and wears a beautiful chiton. It would not do to have it ruined," I replied before Alexis had the chance.

"Ah," Gnosidicus said, nodding once more.

At the mention of the garment, Alexis reached around, taking out the pin and handing it back to me.

I took it and settled it around my shoulders. "Do you require aid to move him?" I asked, indicating the slumbering man.

"We shall assist," other stall holders offered, shuffling forward. "We should have helped when the boys first approached."

"Intentions are not always obvious at first," I noted, allowing them to lift up their friend.

"There are more than enough hands here, take Alexis back to the palace," Melina said.

"I should accompany you to Grandfather's house," Alexis countered.

"There is nothing you can do tonight. You may visit in the morning."

Alexis opened her mouth as though she was going to refute her mother's insistence, but closed it again after only a moment's hesitation. Moeris and the young soldier named Brygos arrived and gathered the young men from the ground.

"Thaddeus," Moeris supplied when I raised a questioning eyebrow. "We shall deal with these three. It is not the first time they have attempted to steal," he added.

"Perhaps another reminder to choose their future paths wisely is in order," I offered. Moeris nodded in return.

Gnosidicus indicated the way he wished for the merchants to go and offered his arm to me. "Your aid here tonight is appreciated."

"Of course," I replied, taking his outstretched limb.

"You saved his life, as you did our granddaughter," Aspasia added. "We shall not forget your kindness."

"We shall not," Melina agreed.

34

"Are you ready to return to the palace?" I asked Alexis when her mother and grandparents had gone, along with the crowd that had gathered.

Alexis suddenly grabbed at her stomach, bending in half before she could reply and relieving herself of the wine she had consumed.

"Alexis," I murmured, instantly at her side. I rested my hand on her shoulder, noting the flecks of liquid that splashed up onto her chiton.

"No. I am fine," she insisted, shaking off my hand. "Return me to my room. Please."

"As you wish," I replied, my hand going to the pommel of my sword once again. We walked in silence the entire way. I wanted to return to the conversation Alexis and I had begun before her grandfather had been stabbed, but we reached her room before I found the right words to do so.

I opened the door, taking a look inside before allowing her to enter. She walked in, keeping her gaze from me as she turned to shut the door. "Alexis," I murmured.

She raised her eyes to mine but shook her head. "Goodnight, Skylar."

I put my hand up to halt the door, but it was too late; she had already closed it and I heard her bring the locking device down into place. I stood a long while with my hand against the wood, but did not speak again. Finally I turned and made my way out of the central chamber, returning to my room with a heavy heart and blood stained cuirass and tunic.

Two figures stood outside my room. My hand went to the sword at my side automatically, relaxing when I realized it was only my father and King Agrias. An amphora of wine sat on the ground between them and each had a kantharos in hand. Their quiet words reached me as I neared and I was not surprised to hear what they spoke of; given their fast friendship this past moon.

"I had to leave more than my family behind in Thrace," Father said with a nod.

"I can imagine. You needed to appear of Greek origin to ensure you and your Zita were safe as you travelled?"

"Yes," Father nodded again. "There was the clothing and shield of course, but also the ways and customs I had grown with."

"Your height must have been a hindrance."

"Some, though as the winters passed it became an asset."

"What of your hair – it is of such a light color, it gives you away as a northerner."

"True, but I kept it under strips of material until it, just as my size, no longer became important."

The king's face lit up when he caught sight of me. "You return early, do you intend to shed your armor and return to my daughter? You were able to speak with her?"

"No," I frowned, pushing open my door and entering.

The older men followed. I slid the pin from the hinge and lifted the cuirass over my head, crossing to the small clay basin and wetting the cloth that lay over its side.

"You did not clean Skylar's armor before returning it to her?" Agrias asked.

"I did. What happened?" Father frowned.

"Ran across some trouble in town," I replied.

"But Alexis was not injured?"

"No." I cleaned the blood from the bronze and set it aside, reaching for the brooch of my tunic and unclasping it.

"Perhaps we should leave," Agrias said.

"As it pleases you," I replied with a shrug, dropping the tunic to the floor and settling a clean one about my body. "Alexis remains unharmed and is back in her room as promised. Melina's father was attacked by some boys."

"Ophelos? Did someone target my wife's father? Melanthios was with us, but do you believe he was responsible for the attack?" Agrias asked, his body turned slightly from me.

"No. I believe it was simply a case of poor choices being made by a few young men. Do not be concerned, Gnosidicus arrived and shall ensure Ophelos is well again soon. Aspasia was also there and shall remain at her husband's side."

"What of the banquet?" my father asked.

"I presume it has ended, but I did not return after the commotion in the street. Why are the two of you not in attendance at your own celebration?" I asked, taking my bloodied tunic and submerging it in the clay basin.

"The drinking and revelry continue, but I wished to ask your father about his time in Thrace."

"And I did not want an audience for such answers," Father replied.

"Hmm," I grunted, scrubbing the ends of my tunic together.

"May I ask, do you recall much of your old language, Leandros?"

"Some," Father acknowledged. "Just as your Macedonians do, the Thracians dress differently to the southern Greeks. We wore tunics, and intricately patterned cloaks, which were known as zeira. In my youth I wore a cap made from the scalp of a fox; it was called an alopekis and my boots, made from fawnskin, were called embades."

"Wonderful," the king said and I heard the smile in his voice. "What weapons did you favor?"

"I had a crescent shaped shield, though our designs were on the inside rather than the outward face. I also carried two javelins. Others in my tribe favored clubs, which are useful for knocking the heads off the spears of enemies. Single and double sided axes, bows, daggers or short swords, as well as long swords were also favored. The short swords were called akinakes."

The blood stubbornly remained on my tunic and the easy chatter between my father and Agrias was beginning to get on my nerves. "Perhaps you could find somewhere else to continue your conversation," I grumbled. I wrung the material out and slapped it over the back of the chair, spraying droplets of water over the two men.

"Skylar," Father growled.

"No, no, I should really go and check on Ophelos," Agrias said, raising his kantharos in my direction in farewell. "Until the morning."

"Until the morning," Father agreed with a nod. When Agrias had closed the door behind himself, Father poured me a skyphos of wine. I drained it in one mouthful and handed it back for a refill. He raised his eyebrows, but filled it again, holding it out as he spoke. "I gather you were not able to repair things with Alexis."

"No," I replied, taking the wine and sitting heavily in the chair.

"I have never seen you act this way before. You care very deeply for her."

"It is not important for she does not share the feeling."

"Are you certain?"

"Yes. I kissed her the day we went to the agora, though I believe for her it was only experiment. Or perhaps she too was caught up in the moment we were sharing – forgetting momentarily that I too was a woman."

"You kissed her?" my father repeated. I nodded my reply. "You spoke of spending the night with her, of sleeping beside her. Was it the kiss that caused you to remain?"

"No. I believed much to be between us before she invited me to stay, though obviously I was mistaken."

"Tell me what it was that first drew you to her, what caused you to believe she felt as you do."

"For what purpose?" I snapped, taking another sip of wine.

"Perhaps I can assist," he shrugged.

I drained the cup again, placing the empty vessel on the nearby table. "I am tired. I have no wish to speak of Alexis and the useless feelings I possess for her any more this evening."

"Skylar."

I shook my head. "No, Father. Please. I cannot."

He held my gaze for a long moment before nodding curtly and holding his arms open for me. I stood and crossed to him, allowing his larger frame to enfold me. "Perhaps tomorrow shall see Alexis speak with you as you wish."

"Perhaps," I replied, though I could not imagine what would cause it to be so. He released me and left my room, closing the door behind as I sat on my bed, closing my eyes as the words Alexis and I exchanged earlier replayed in my mind.

*

I spent the following day with the soldiers again, returning to my room as the sun made its descent behind the mountains. My body ached and dust stuck to my face, hair and arms where sweat had gathered. I wished for nothing but the taste of sweet wine and a warm bath to soothe me inside and out.

I gathered a clean tunic and a large amphora of wine, making my way to the baths, pleased to find I had both rooms to myself. When the water was sufficiently warmed and in the oval tub, I disrobed and immersed myself in its heat. The thoughts and images I had managed to keep at bay as I trained during the day resurfaced with ferocity. Alexis' face loomed large in my mind, the feel of her lips against mine, her tongue tangling with my own. Her words to me the night before about Voleta. Melanthios' treatment of her in that very room. The way her eyes had traced my body as I stood naked before her in her apartment.

I frowned as the last drops of wine hit my tongue, wishing I had brought two amphorae with me. I stepped out of the bath, wrapping my tunic around me haphazardly and stumbling towards the door, my head pleasantly spinning. As I cleared the outer door of the bathing area I looked up. Alexis emerged from the central chamber. She caught my eye and I paused, leaning against the wall as I took in the sight of her in a simple chiton, hair piled high atop her head, the nape of her neck exposed. I was taken back to the night in her room when I slipped my hand beneath her hair, drawing her body to mine as I kissed her. I could feel the heat of her skin beneath my hand and my body ignited with the memory.

Alexis drew a himation around her shoulders and turned, hurrying to Hesper's apartment. I pushed off the marble and followed. She entered, the door closing solidly behind her before I arrived. I knocked, my hands clenching and unclenching as I waited. If I could just explain. If only Alexis would tell me why she had returned my kiss. Perhaps she would tell me she had been mistaken to drive me away and felt as I did.

The door opened a crack and Hesper appeared. "I must speak with Alexis," I said, pleased my words did not come out as blurred as my head.

"She does not wish to speak with you."

"Please, Hesper, allow me to enter."

"No. You must give her time."

"I have given her time, now she must hear what I have to say," I replied, my voice rising with each word.

"It has not been long enough," Hesper said, closing the door.

"Wait," I insisted, halting the door's progress with my hand and stepping halfway into the room.

Thaddeus arrived behind his wife. Hesper ducked beneath his arm and he placed a hand in the middle of my chest, pushing me back out of the apartment. "Enough, Skylar. Not tonight."

"There are words that must be spoken between Alexis and me."

"Not tonight," he repeated. "I shall escort you back to your room, for I doubt you can get there on your own."

"I do not need your assistance," I shouted, knocking his hand away. "I am more than capable of returning there alone."

"Then go, for your presence here is not welcome," he murmured, closing the door on further protests or attempts at conversation.

I stood, blinking, at the wood in front of me before slamming my palm against it; the sound echoing around the empty courtyard. I could easily burst into the room – Thaddeus would certainly not be expecting the action. I rolled my shoulders and took a step back in preparation for the attack. The sudden image of Alexis' fearful gaze when Melanthios took hold of her in the bathing area gave me pause and I did not rush forward. I did not want Alexis to fear me as she did Melanthios.

I blew out a deep breath, taking several paces back until the cold marble statue of Artemis in the courtyard halted my progress. I slid to the ground, my eyes firmly fixed on Thaddeus and Hesper's door as I waited for Alexis to re-emerge.

*

I woke to find the moon high and bright overhead, many of the torches around the palace now dim or extinguished. My body – and my head – protested as I pushed off the cold statue and got to my feet. I crossed to Hesper's door, pressing my ear to the wood and straining to hear anything from inside. Nothing.

I turned and made my way to Alexis' room instead, knocking quietly and calling her name. I waited several moments, but there was no reply. I tried to open it, but it was locked from the inside. I knocked and waited again, but Alexis made no sound. Eventually I returned to my own room, head throbbing in time with my heart.

35

"She is separated from the girl. It does not appear she shall join her in Epirus. Why do we not test her? She has proven her body is recovered, you see the fire within her – her pain, her anger. Now is the time to do it; give her something to focus her energies on. She would welcome the challenge."

"No."

"What is it you wait for, Master? You have never deliberated so, why this time?" the woman pressed him.

"You speak with boldness, Child. You question me relentlessly. Do you wish for your time here to be done?" he asked; voice soft and dangerous.

"Of course not. Apologies. I just ... I do not understand why you wait. You have always tested our line within a moon of them becoming nineteen winters, yet with her that time passed moons ago. Did her injury, her mortal blood, require you to wait longer?"

"No. I have always known when those in the line were ready, when the correct time was to test them. It was a specific moon, a specific immortal age they had to reach, but this one, my Chosen One; she is not ready. Not yet. True, she has fire and passion. She hurts. But she would be reckless and unfocused, unwilling to be who I need her to. She does not have enough to lose."

The woman nodded. "The girls in our line were taught to want, to believe they were who and what had been predicted so long ago, to train and learn all they could. The only thing they had to lose was the knowledge they were not who you wished for them to be; but that was incentive enough."

"Yes. But she knows none of that; there is much she must learn, much the Bessoi boy has not told her. I thought he may tell her when she asked about her mother, when she spoke of her feelings for the princess, but even then he kept it from her. He appears to believe that she has escaped the line, escaped *us*; you hear him speak of the future, of remaining in one place." The man smiled a wicked smile. "But she shall soon learn the truth and know just who she is, and he shall be powerless to stop it, to stop us."

"You have a plan?"

"Of course, but there is much that must occur first, and only when it does shall we appear to her and tell her of her true past." He smiled wider, disappearing in a flash of light.

36

My head throbbed as I swung my legs over the side of my bed and I paused as my stomach rolled dangerously. I clamped my mouth shut, swallowing down the taste of wine and waiting for the feeling to pass. I raised my eyes, finding the small amphora of perfume I had purchased for Alexis at the agora. It appeared to mock me as it sat on the table beside the door; a reminder of what I could not have, of who I was not worthy to call my friend, and certainly not my lover. It spoke of my weaknesses, rather than the many strengths I had always prided myself on. I stood quickly, closing my eyes momentarily against the spinning of my head and crossed to the table, snatching the bottle up.

I strode across the courtyard to the central chamber. Alexis may not wish to speak to me, but I had bought the perfume for her; she should have it. End of discussion. As I reached the chamber, Alexis and Hesper emerged from Alexis' room.

Hesper saw me first. "Skylar," she said, as surprised to find me standing there as I was to see them suddenly appearing.

"Hesper," I replied with a nod, my eyes going immediately to Alexis. The princess' brow was furrowed, and deepened when she caught sight of me.

Hesper paused, but Alexis continued towards the entrance of the palace. "Wait," I insisted, reaching out to grab Alexis' wrist. She kept it from my reach and the stormy look on her face made me falter. I dropped my hand, offering the amphora to her with my other instead. "This is for you," I told her.

She dropped her eyes briefly to my hand before continuing towards the entrance of the palace. "Come on, Hesper," she added when she realized Hesper hesitated.

"Apologies," Hesper whispered. "She is hurting."

"Take this for her. I want her to have it," I insisted, holding the perfume out.

"Of course," Hesper nodded, taking it and moving off again.

I watched them make their way to the banquet hall and – I was certain – the kitchen beyond. I had held Alexis against me in the pantry there, her sweet scent clinging to my hair and tunic afterwards, her lips tantalizingly close in the dimness. I drew in a painful breath and when they had disappeared into the hall, I returned to my room to gather my weapons and cuirass. Clearly I could not make up for what I had done and the small token of the perfume was not nearly enough of an apology. I took the walkway to the northern balcony and plain beyond, unleashing my anger and feelings of inadequacy on a large tree that stood by the Melas River.

37

"Hesper is well?" I asked.

"She is," Thaddeus acknowledged.

"And the princess?"

"As well as could be expected given that the two of you still do not speak." We had had the same exchange the past few days, me wishing to ask him more, he wanting to offer more; neither of us doing so. "She accepted your gift," Thaddeus said, surprising me. "It is the aroma she favors. Hesper knew she appreciated it, though she did not speak specific words."

"She has not thought to come find me and mention it."

"Perhaps she wanted to but was afraid you would treat her as you did the tree," he grinned. It had been Thaddeus my father had sent to fetch me late in the afternoon, the soldier unafraid to offer his weapon and skills to challenge me in place of the inanimate object I had assaulted for the best part of half a day.

"Perhaps," I conceded, a grin tugging at my lips.

He began a forward thrust and I brought my shield up to defend it. "Perhaps you are both too stubborn for your own good," he remarked.

I had not truly expected Alexis to come and thank me for the perfume, but neither had she returned it, and that was just as frustrating. If only she had attempted to bring it back, I would have another chance to explain, and to apologize. I ignored his remark and raised my sword, bringing it down onto his shield with a deafening clang. Thaddeus stumbled, his foot catching in the mud beneath our feet; earning him a sandal full of the think goo.

He righted himself with a laugh and shook it out. "She does care deeply for you. You would not consider speaking of your feelings with her again?"

"For what purpose? I cannot change her mind, cannot make her love me, despite your insistence I should attempt it."

"So you *do* love her?" he smirked.

I paused, regarding him. "If I was a man, Thaddeus, if I had the means to claim her as my own it would be simpler. Perhaps having her love me in return would not be important if I had other things to offer. If I possessed more than Melanthios, it would be easy for Agrias to say it was me Alexis must spend her future with. But I have nothing. I have no lands, no army to merge with Agrias' or to have at his disposal should he require it. I cannot offer any sort of strategic alliance such as the one that was formed when Alexis was betrothed to Basileios. So why would I pursue her?"

"Skylar," my father murmured, arriving beside us.

I lowered my weapons.

"Thaddeus," he acknowledged with a nod.

"Leandros."

"You speak of your feelings towards Alexis?" Father asked.

I shrugged. "I was making the point that all I had to offer Alexis was my love, and that it is not enough."

My father's mouth hung open momentarily, but he quickly composed himself. "All I had to offer your mother was my love. When I agreed to leave Thrace with her, we had nothing but one another."

"It was easier for you – Zita loved you in return. That is not the case with Alexis and me."

"All relationships have challenges, but if you love someone enough you can face those challenges together. You can be together."

"How? The two of you speak as though you do not know Alexis has already rejected my advances. It cannot be between the two of us. I have to live with that knowledge from now on."

"That is not all you shall have to live with knowing, and I must say, I am surprised your anger is not hotter. You have not told her?" Father asked.

"I was atte–"

"Tell me what?" I cut Thaddeus off.

"Melanthios' brothers and men from the Illyrian tribes of the Taulantii and Dassaretii arrived in Trachis this morning. They are preparing to fight if …"

"If Alexis does not go through with our betrothal tomorrow evening," a familiar voice said. I jumped, Father, Thaddeus and I turning as one to find Melanthios leaning against a tree, smirking. He drew his sword from its holder and spun it around his hand.

"What did you say?" I snarled.

"To protect her parents and the people of Trachis from war, Alexis has agreed to become Melanthios' wife," Father replied before Melanthios had the chance.

"What? Alexis would never agree to that," I insisted.

"She would and she has," Melanthios said, setting himself to face off against us. "She understands her father's army is no match for mine. Agrias has agreed to become a vassal to me. Not that he has a choice if he wants his precious daughter to remain here at the palace. I cannot decide if I should call myself Prince of Thermopylae, or King of Thermopylae. Which do you believe suits me better?"

I gripped the handle of my xiphos tightly. "You do not deserve to be either. I shall ensure it is never so," I growled.

"You may have been Alexis' hero once or twice, but she no longer holds you in such esteem," Melanthios laughed, twirling his sword again. "But I *am* surprised to learn that she rejected your advances. She was with you so often as you recovered, I was certain you had already taken what you wanted from her. I would have."

"Skylar," Father murmured. "Thaddeus, fetch Moeris," he added in the same undertone.

"You are far stronger than she, you could have simply taken her, demanded that she pleasure you when and how you desired as payment for saving her from my advances at the baths ... Or perhaps you know you are not worthy of her. You are nothing but a mere peasant, a wild thing that roams free without home to call your own, and she is a Princess." I spat at his feet. "See? Wild," Melanthios laughed.

Father put a warning hand on my shoulder. "Ignore his words, Skylar."

"You are less than nothing to her. You cannot put a child inside her. You cannot give her father an heir to the throne of Trachis. You are worthless and Alexis knows it."

I screamed, launching myself at him, our swords meeting loudly. He rebuffed me; far stronger than he had been the night we fought at the baths, but then so was I. He pushed off, quickly swinging his sword at my head. I ducked, backing up a step.

"I shall enjoy breaking her. My brother was too soft; he did not understand that the only way to make a woman obey is through pain. Through pain they all learn to do what they are told without hesitation, complaint or defiance," he grinned. "I wonder how long it shall take; a week, a moon? Perhaps she shall surprise me and I can visit her with my tools every night for a winter before she bends to my will."

I yelled again, rushing him. Our swords clashed, our faces level, breath puffing against one another's cheek. He held my gaze but I brought my foot up, slamming it down sharply above his knee. He dropped to the ground, clutching at it as his sword fell from his hand. He looked up at me, laughing.

"I shall take to her without hesitation to ensure my child grows inside her. When she has given me sons, I shall kill her, along with her parents. Then I shall send one of my children back to Epirus to rule in my place, while the other remains here to rule alongside me."

"No!" I yelled, bringing the end of my sword down hard at his temple. He hit the ground with a thud. I kicked him where he lay, turning him onto his back as I raised my sword. I gripped it between my palms, facing the blade at his exposed chest. "You shall never touch her," I told his unconscious body.

"Skylar, no!" Father cried, his hand preventing me from driving my weapon into the flesh beneath it. "Stay your weapon."

"Why? You heard what he intends for her, for them. I can change their fate here, today."

Father pushed me backwards and I stumbled. "It is *not* the way."

"I shall do whatever I must to protect her. I would kill to have it be so," I argued.

"No. Go to Alexis. Tell her what Melanthios said. Ensure she explicitly understands what she would be agreeing to if she betroths him. I am certain you can convince her it is a mistake. She cares for you – remind her why that is, allow her to know not only your strength, but your fears as well."

"I cannot allow Alexis to belong to him, no matter what she says, or if she tells me she can never love me in return."

"Good, then go, Thaddeus and I shall take care of Melanthios."

I drew a deep breath, warring internally with allowing Melanthios to live, and my need to speak to Alexis. Finally I nodded and, sheathing my sword, I raced towards the palace, barely clearing the walkway near the baths when I met Agrias.

"Skylar, there you are, I must tell yo–"

"I know," I cut him off.

"I am sorry, she told me not to deny Melanthios of her any longer. I thought, at first, it was part of a plan the two of you had, but I understand you still have not spoken since you … spoke of your feelings for her. She told me what happened the night of the banquet. She said she no longer cared what happened to her."

"Where is she?" I asked, my blood heating for a number of reasons.

"She and Hesper left for the hot springs candlemarks ago."

"I shall not allow her to become Melanthios' wife. I give you my word."

"Thank the gods. I have not seen her so resigned to her fate since she was to leave for Epirus with Basileios all those winters ago," he paused then asked, "How much do you love my daughter, Skylar?"

"More than I ever knew was possible," I replied.

He nodded, laying his hand on my arm. "Then convince her she does not have to go through with it. You and I can ensure it never comes to pass. If she shall listen to anyone it is you."

"I hope so," I replied, squeezing his hand briefly.

"Do you know your way to the springs?" I shook my head. "It is not difficult, travel south to south-west for five stadia and cross the river you come to – it shall be the Asopos. Another twenty-six stadia shall see you at the Phoenix, which is small and runs meekly, though with a slight red hue. The hot springs are barely thirteen stadia after that, I am certain you shall have no trouble finding them and if you take Skotos, it should take you less than a candlemark to reach her."

"Thank you," I nodded, heading for the stables as he murmured 'good luck'.

38

From the outset, Skotos sensed my need to arrive at whatever destination I had in mind faster than I had ever asked it of him before. He galloped from the palace without hesitation, both of us breathing hard. Thought after thought raced through my head, bouncing between anger and fear for what Alexis would endure at Melanthios' hands if I could not convince her to reconsider. My anger also found her; anger that she would allow herself such treatment. I could only assume that she did so as punishment for having another woman attracted to her. I was not foolish enough to believe I was the first, though perhaps I was the only one who had ever acted on what I felt.

I pulled on the reins, slowing Skotos and sliding from his back when I saw the two horses and Hesper. I strode forward, noting that Alexis was not with her friend.

"Skylar," Hesper said, looking up in surprise as I approached.

"Where is she?" I asked.

"At the springs. But she is still angry with you, she shall not be pleased to see you," she replied, taking the nearest horse's reins.

"I do not care if she is pleased to see me, I must speak with her."

"You have learnt of Melanthios."

My eyes narrowed as I stared her down. "How long have you known?"

She looked away. "A day or so."

"And you did not think to mention it, to have Thaddeus speak of it to me?" I hissed. I clenched my jaw and shook my head, speaking again before she could answer. "Take both horses back to the palace; I shall bring the princess back when she has heard what I have to say."

"You hurt her more than you imagine."

I paused, taken back by her words. "So this is how she has decided to punish me?" I asked quietly.

"Perhaps," Hesper shrugged, jumping up onto her horse and giving Calla a tug to follow. "I do not wish this for her either, but she is stubborn and hurting, tread carefully or we may both lose her," she advised.

I stared after Hesper, allowing her words to wash over me, to calm me. I must control my anger. I must convince Alexis to allow me to change her destiny. I swallowed and drew a deep breath, squaring my shoulders and making my way through the trees to the spring beyond.

Acrid steam hovered in the air above the gently bubbling pool as I approached; the water clear and deep. A waterfall fed the spring from the mountain above and a narrow, much shallower creek flowed off from the main pool, the mist accompanying it through the trees to give the entire area a secretive, secluded feel. A small altar stood to one side of the water, nearest the waterfall, though from this distance I could not make out to whom it was dedicated.

The mist parted and I saw her; her back to me as she stood neck-deep in the water. She held her arms out either side of her body, sweeping them back and forth across the surface. I inhaled deeply, taking in the soft skin of her back, the way she had swept her hair up off her neck and pinned it high on her head, the curve of her sides and hips beneath the rippling water.

I exhaled slowly though my heart clattered beneath my chest. If I was to convince her to speak with me she could not feel at a disadvantage. I slipped my cuirass and tunic from my body, dropping them beside Alexis' yellow chiton, and entered the water. The heat momentarily took my breath away and when my feet touched the soft sand at the bottom I was immersed up to my breasts.

"Why do you return, Hesper? You must not keep Thaddeus waiting," Alexis said, keeping her back to me. "One must never keep their betrothed waiting," she added in a voice barely above a whisper.

"Hesper has gone."

She turned, clearly not expecting to find me behind her. "What are you doing here?" she asked, a frown marring her forehead.

"I must speak with you."

"We have nothing to discuss."

"There is much to discuss," I corrected, taking a step closer.

She shook her head, wading towards the bank. I crossed in two strides, blocking her path and reached out to take her hand. She drew it away hurriedly. "Do. Not," she warned.

I withdrew, holding my hands up out of the water to show I would stay where I was. "You cannot leave unless I take you, Hesper took Calla back to the palace along with her own horse."

"Hesper is supposed to side with me, not you," she muttered, folding her arms across her chest. "Speak of what you came to then," she said, avoiding my eyes and bared body in the water.

"You have agreed to be betrothed to Melanthios," I began, my voice unsteady. "Father says it is to prevent war for your people, but there must be another reason."

"My reasons do not concern you."

"But they *do* concern me. I know what he intends to do to you; how he shall treat you. You cannot agree, I beg of you not to."

"What do you care? You have your slave girls, yo–"

"I was only with her because I could not have *you*," I shouted, my fist splashing through the top of the water. I clenched my jaw shut, closing my eyes briefly to calm myself, exhaling a long breath before I spoke again. "Alexis, you know I care for you. Even though we … do not feel the same. I would never wish to see harm come to you, you must know that." She kept her eyes from mine so I pressed on. "We have known each other so briefly, yet we have shared much. You spoke of past hurt; memories and feelings that had long been held inside, never spoken aloud. You entrusted those to me and I kept them safe, wishing to take your pain and carry it as my own, to ensure you walk your future without their burden."

"I did not ask it of you."

"No, but I hold them all the same. If you allow yourself to be betrothed to Melanthios I cannot protect you. I cannot stop him from causing you pain far greater than you have already endured in this life." I wanted to reach out, to lift her chin so our eyes met but I remained in place. "He shall break not only your body, but your spirit. He shall take the light from your eyes and you shall no longer resemble the beautiful, sweet woman you are."

"Then it shall be as it would have had you never arrived in the valley," she murmured.

I drew a sharp breath, her words cutting me. She *could not* resign herself to the terrible fate that awaited her.

I inhaled deeply, choosing my next words carefully. "Alexis, I have seen many ways that men and women derive both pleasure and pain from one another. You spoke of slaves you had tended after Melanthios engaged them for the night and it sickens me to imagine what tools he has at his disposal for use with you. He speaks with great pride that he has claimed the prize of a princess to do whatever he wants with." I closed my eyes, voice trembling when I continued. "The night of the banquet I told you I wished for more, that I wanted to love you as Sappho's poem suggested. I understand you do not feel the same and though it hurts me far greater than you shall ever know, I accept that and I shall not speak of it again whilst we find ourselves together. But I beg of you, do *not* allow Melanthios to claim you. I could not bear to think of him torturing you until you submitted to him. It is not what you deserve."

"But that is the way I feel," Alexis whispered.

I opened my eyes, frowning, as Alexis' eyes finally met mine. "That you deserve to be tortured? How can you believe such a lie?" I asked, water splashing about me again as I threw my arms up. "Do my feelings for you disgust you so much that you would allow Melanthios to do whatever he wanted to you? Would you truly allow him to mark your skin, your soul? Would you allow him to put a child inside you and then kill you? He would not be gentle. He would not treat you with kindness because you gave him sons. By the time you did so, you would be gone, if not in body, then in spirit. He would have won, are you prepared to allow him to have such power over you?" My chest heaved as I attempted to pull in a full breath but Alexis simply held my gaze.

"Your words did not disgust me," she said after a long moment of silence.

"Then *why*?"

She hesitated again. "You have been with many women – the way you were with the slave girl?" she finally asked.

"Yes," I confirmed with a frown.

"Was it ... difficult to find women willing to be with you when you wanted it?"

"Not often, no," I replied, my frown deepening as I attempted to understand her sudden line of questioning.

"But you have always preferred the attentions of a woman rather than a man?"

"Yes. But you do not answer my question." She nodded, but it appeared to be more to herself than to me. "Alexis, answer me," I demanded. "Shall you deny Melanthios of yourself and allow me to do what I must to ensure it, or do you intend to allow him to own you and damage you? To extinguish all the goodness inside you, everything that makes you who you are, everything that made me fall in love with you?" my voice rose as I spoke, the final words tumbling out before I could stop them.

Her mouth fell open but she closed it again quickly, lowering her eyes to the water as her chest rose and fell in quick succession. "Patience is certainly not your strength at times," she mused, one corner of her lips lifting.

"I have no patience when I deem the answer to be important," I told her, my frown fixed firmly in place.

She took a tentative step forward. "You wanted to take me to bed the night of the banquet. You wished for me to tell you I wanted the same," she said, lifting her eyes again.

"Yes," I replied cautiously, my breath catching when she laid her hand on my arm.

"And when you believed that I did not wish for it, you found another, correct?"

"You said you did not wish for it," I amended.

"No, you *assumed* that was what I was attempting to say," she said, denying me her eyes again. She ran her hand down my arm and over my fingers, sliding her own between them, the feeling mirrored along my spine. "I did not hesitate because I did not want to be with you ... I hesitated because I was afraid I did not know what to do. I was scared when you spoke the words I so deeply wanted to hear. You were so certain of them, of how you felt. The depth of your feelings for me was frightening. To hear you speak of it now still is."

My brow smoothed again and when her green eyes found mine, heat and longing swirled within them. The sweet smell of her perfume invaded my senses and I drew it in as though it contained the very air I needed to exist. I swallowed, unable to say anything, raising my thumb to brush it across her lips. She had wanted me that night. Did I dare hope she still did now?

"When you asked me to undress you, to spend the night in your bed after the day at the agora, it took all my restraint not to touch you, but you did not make it easy."

"We shared our first kiss that day," she smiled. "I was afraid to do more, but perhaps I pushed you a little; I wanted to know how deeply you cared for me."

"You are devious, Princess," I said, a smile finally finding my own lips. The knot that had formed in my stomach since Melanthios first spoke finally disappeared, replaced by a warmth I could not deny nor censor.

"Well I did have the poet organized for the following night. I had heard Sappho's words before and when I thought of you, they resonated in my mind," she admitted, drawing a deep breath before she spoke again. "You say you still care for me, but do you still desire me?"

"Oh yes, very much. No other woman has sparked my desire or my imagination as much as you."

"So if I asked it of you, you would show me how you feel?" she asked, color rising in her cheeks as she spoke.

"Are you asking it of me now?" I held my breath as I awaited her answer, my eyes drawn to her lips.

"Yes."

39

I felt the tremor through our entwined fingers when she replied and I took mine, finding the soft skin at her hip and drawing her close. Her lips parted with a soft gasp as flesh met flesh and the heat in my stomach turned instantly to fire, the warm spring water tepid compared to her skin on mine. "Alexis," I whispered, covering her lips.

She opened her mouth, inviting me, teasing me when her tongue met mine. I deepened our kiss, my tongue making its own exploration as my hands began theirs. Gliding my hands over her ribs I felt the swell of her breasts, tracing the undersides with my fingers. She leaned into the touch. I drew my tongue along hers again before moving my lips to her jaw and down her neck, my teeth grazing the heated skin.

"I have never wanted anyone as much as I want you. From the moment I saw you after I woke I wanted to know you, to kiss you," I whispered. I took her breasts in my hands, increasing the pressure. Her nipples hardened against my palms and I rolled them between my fingers as they grew.

Alexis groaned, tangling her hand in my hair and pressing herself against me. She pushed up onto her tiptoes, raising her breasts from the water and directing me towards them. I gladly took the flesh between my lips, my tongue flicking the first hardened peak. Desire beat in my stomach and between my thighs; unrelenting, hard, fierce. It clouded my thoughts, threatening to devour me before I could tell Alexis all I must.

I rose so my eyes were level with hers once again, laying my hand on her cheek. "I am sorry I asked for the slave girl, I did not mean to hurt you. I do not ever want to hurt you. Promise me you shall not betroth Melanthios. Do not punish yourself, do not punish me by allowing him to touch you. "

She laid her hand over mine, drawing it to her lips and kissing my palm. "I shall not, I give you my word."

"I should never have been with her. I did not wish for another's lips on mine. I did not want her, she was but a substitute, someone I *could* have, when the one I most desired appeared to be beyond my reach," my chest heaved with my words, but I continued. "When she touched me, when she kissed me, it was your mouth I felt on me, your hands that caressed my body."

"I was ... jealous. Hurt that you were with another when I wanted so badly for you to be with me; that is why I went to your room. When you left mine I did not know what to do, but I knew I wanted you to touch me and I have never wanted that with any woman before," she said, her fingers at my jaw.

"I ruined everything."

"Hush. Speak no more of it for we are together now," she murmured, returning my hand to her breast as I kissed her again.

My blood boiled as she pressed into me again, but I knew there was still more I must tell her. "Alexi–"

"No," she said against my lips. "No more words now. Please." Desperation laced her words and I nodded. If she chose not to be with me after I told her of Kuria, at least we would have had this moment, though for me I knew it would be far from enough.

"I want to touch you ... everywhere. I want to love you as you have never been loved, treat you as you have never been treated," I whispered, resting my brow against hers.

"Please," she almost pleaded. "Show me how you feel."

"For you I would do anything, my princess."

She drew her fingers across my lips. "Love me."

I claimed her lips and lifted her out of the water, wading towards the bank as she wrapped her legs around me. Without breaking our contact I pulled my discarded tunic closer to the edge, lowering Alexis until the length of her body flattened the material. I remained submerged in the water standing between her thighs as with knees bent, she rested her feet against the bank, her soles half in and half out of the spring. I slid my hand from her thigh, up over her stomach and back to her breast, her back lifting when I reached it. I lowered my head, placing gentle kisses on her stomach. I drew my tongue over her ribs, removing my hand from her breast and replacing it with my lips, my tongue in turn flicking and caressing her flesh. Alexis moaned beneath me, pressing her heated center against my stomach and sliding her hand around the back of my neck.

"Skylar," she murmured.

I pressed into her harder. Desire wet me, my body throbbed. I knew I should go slowly, that I should not rush; Alexis had never been with a woman before and I wanted her to feel my love for her, my desire, my passion. I wanted her to savor every second, to feel the building need inside. I wished to draw the cries from her lips, to be inside her and feel her body tighten around me when I tipped her over that glorious edge. But the hand that gripped desperately at my neck told me she needed me now and I was helpless to deny her, as I had been from the first moment we met. She moaned again, writhing hard against the flesh of my stomach. I did not want it over too soon, but I felt her slick wetness against me and I knew she would not last much longer, that she yearned for me as I had for her for so many nights.

I parted our bodies, her hips still moving rhythmically, begging for touch, for relief. I pulled myself from the water to lie beside her. I skittered my fingers along the inside of her thigh, the soft flesh prickling where I touched her before reclaiming her lips as I cupped tender flesh. I was certain my heart would burst from my chest when she groaned again, her hips lifting to increase the contact. My fingers ran the length of her and I mirrored the movements with my tongue in her mouth. Her hand found my hip and she pulled me against her thigh. I whimpered, knowing that I wanted to satisfy her first, and that I was perilously close to finding my end if she continued to touch me as she was. I entered her slowly. She gripped my hip harder and I could not resist moving against her, filling her when she pressed down onto me. I drew my finger out before quickly re-entering, stroking her as she quivered.

I broke our kiss, wanting to watch, to see the moment she lost herself around me. Eyes closed, pink tinging her cheeks, lips parted, body lifting and lowering as she drew ever closer.

"You are so beautiful," I whispered as I drove my finger deeper, harder.

She opened her eyes, capturing mine as she gripped my wrist and held me inside. "Skylar," she panted. "I am ..."

She could not speak the words as her body tightened around me. I had never seen anyone as beautiful as her. I knew I would never want anyone but her to warm my bed. Her eyes fluttered shut again as her hips bucked, shudders of pleasure lifting her from the ground. She cried out my name, her nails digging into me as she pushed me in deeper, enveloping me in her heat and allowing me to share the totality of her climax.

I felt the beginnings of my own release as her thigh dragged across my inflamed skin, but I would not allow it. Not yet. I concentrated only on holding her tightly as her body convulsed in the aftermath and she sagged back to the ground, loosening her hold on my hand. I withdrew from her, resting my hand atop her stomach where I could feel the furious beating of her heart.

"Skylar," she murmured again. "That was ... you ... I did not know."

I smiled and kissed her gently. "You deserve nothing less," I said sincerely, tucking an escaped strand of hair behind her ear.

She smiled shyly and rolled onto her side, smoothing her hand down my chest to my stomach. "I want to ... touch you. I want to make you feel as you made me, but I do not know how."

I closed my eyes, swallowing loudly as her fingers made small circles at my hip. "I shall guide you, though your touch does much to me already." I opened my eyes again, smiling at the deepening pink at her cheeks. I laid my hand against her neck, drawing her lips to mine.

Her hand journeyed tentatively along my side, finding my breast and squeezing it. I closed my eyes as she trailed kisses across my collarbone and at the hollow of my neck. She slid her hand down my stomach and over my thigh, drawing her fingers back up the inside. I gasped when she reached the top and pushed her fingers through my engorged flesh.

"You are so wet," she murmured.

I opened my eyes, smiling at the wonder on her face. "It is you that has made me so," I replied, reaching down to pull her thigh between my own.

"I am afraid I shall not be able to bring you the pleasure you wish," she said, her hand working tentatively between my legs.

"You need not be afraid of that, what you are doing is ... perfect," I assured her. I took her hand and, with my fingers over hers, I pushed her lower, guiding her inside. We both gasped as she entered me, my nipples aching for touch as she imitated what I had done to her. I threw my head back, reveling in the sensations she created. She pressed her lips to my neck, her tongue caressing the pulsing beat she found there. I groaned and moved faster as I felt my ending near.

I drew her head to my nipple and she took it eagerly, her teeth grazing the raised flesh and heating my blood beyond its limits. I grabbed her thigh, increasing the tempo of my movements as the first wave of pleasure crashed through my stomach.

"Alexis," I breathed, exquisite relief rolling through me as I succumbed to her. With her hand still between my thighs, she kissed me, her tongue matching her hand's movements, elongating the ripples of ecstasy that raged within me. My back arched, my breath refusing to be drawn. I separated our lips, pushing down hard onto her as I felt another burst of desire ignite inside.

"You are incredible," I managed as the second wave gripped me, stronger than the first. My insides stiffened and then exploded. I cried out, holding her body against mine until finally the shudders racking my body quieted and she withdrew her fingers.

Breathing hard, I rolled onto my back, drawing her with me, her body covering mine, unwilling for our bodies to be separated. I needed her. I loved her, of that I was certain. I did not ever want to be without her, I could not.

Alexis kissed my chest, laying her head above my heart. I held her, my fingers drawing lazy patterns across the skin of her back. So many words I wished to speak, yet I feared that it was too soon, too much. The depth of my love, my need for her scared me as much as it enveloped me. As certain as I was that I had found the one who completed me, who was meant for me, she was not mine to have. Not yet.

"What we just did complicates matters," I said quietly. "I sought you out today only to convince you not to become Melanthios', I did not expect that we wou–"

"You believe it was a mistake?" Alexis asked and I saw the fear cross her face as she attempted to remove herself from my embrace.

I smoothed a hand the length of her spine, holding her in place when I reached the small of her back. With my other I tilted her chin, ensuring she met my gaze as I replied. "No. That is the farthest thought from my mind." I kissed her again. "Melanthios cannot have you," I told her.

"Oh," she breathed. "I do not wish to be his."

"Then I shall free you from him, from his family."

She only nodded, resting her chin on my chest, her eyes on mine. I drew my finger down her cheek and across her lips, raising my head and kissing her again. We spent many moments exploring, caressing one another, no words needing to be spoken. Her hands glided down my sides, igniting the smoldering fire in my belly again.

"How is it that I can feel so much for you? I want you so badly to touch me, to keep touching me, to never stop," she whispered.

I smiled; her thoughts mirrored my own. "I want you now and then again later, and tomorrow, and for all our days. I want you to be mine forever," I added, unable to keep the words from slipping out.

She smiled shyly, her eyes finally dropping from mine, but she raised them again when she spoke. "Have you not known that I have always been yours? Since the day you saved me in the Spercheios Valley you have held my heart."

I smiled again and kissed her. Rustling bushes caught my ear and I broke our kiss, laying my finger against Alexis' lips when she began her question. Adrenaline of a different kind rushed through my veins and I reached for my sword, turning my head to the direction of the sound.

My body stilled and I searched the trees to our right for the cause. I could see nothing. The branches of the closest tree moved again.

Something was there, or someone. Was it Melanthios? Had he woken and followed me? The movement in the trees increased as Alexis untangled herself from my embrace. I would not allow him near her. I gripped my xiphos tightly in my hand, rolling onto my side and jumping to my feet in preparation for whoever emerged.

Branches snapped, though they were not at ground level; almost my head height. I frowned, casting a quick glance at Alexis. She stood behind me, my tunic held at her chest, her brow also creased. "Behind the altar," I directed. When she was safely hidden behind the marble, I returned my eyes to the trees and stepped forward. I set myself in a defensive position, though I was certain the sight of my nakedness would give whoever headed our way pause, and I would have time to act before they did. The leaves shook again, harder now, the branches parting. Skotos sauntered through, munching on a branch he had obviously pulled from the nearest tree.

I exhaled with a laugh, lowering my sword and dropping it to the ground. "Skotos," I muttered, relieved at the sight of my faithful steed. "You frightened us."

I took the reins at his neck, looping them over one of the branches and pulling them tight so he could not wander off. I turned back to find Alexis leaning against the altar rather than hiding behind it. I saw now it was dedicated to the great hero, Heracles.

"Did your father commission the altar?" I asked.

Alexis looked down at the marble briefly before raising her eyes back to mine. "No. It was the Dorians who once lived here, before they migrated to the Peloponnese."

"Do your people sacrifice to him?" I asked.

Alexis dropped the tunic from her body. "How eager are you to continue this conversation?" she asked, a twitch of a grin lifting her lips.

She offered herself to me, no longer the shy, scared girl she had been the night of the banquet, the day of the agora; now a woman who intended to allow herself her greatest desires, to learn, to touch without fear. To love.

My eyes travelled over her naked flesh, tongue wetting my lips as I imagined my hands, my mouth possessing her, drawing sighs and moans in equal measure, showing her the depth of my feelings just as she had asked of me. "Not very," I managed, meeting her eyes again and returning her grin.

"Do you see something you prefer?" she asked, her smile becoming a smirk.

"Indeed," I replied, crossing to her.

My lips crushed hers. With hands, with tongue, I took her again to the point of her desire, lifting her higher than she had ever been, blown away by her beauty as she called my name. I became hers completely with every passing moment.

40

We sat atop Skotos on our way back to the palace, the sun having dipped behind the mountains to our left some time before. Alexis and I had spent the rest of the afternoon alternating between the bank and the hot springs, laughing and splashing and holding one another until the sun began to set. I had reluctantly pulled her to her feet, knowing we had to return to the palace so I could face the consequences of what I had done; both felling Melanthios and my intention to claim the woman that was to be his for my own.

I had told Alexis of my scuffle with him, and what he had spoken of that drove me to find her, but I had not found the words to tell her of Kuria. I knew I must, for as we neared Trachis, Kuria came to mind with uncomfortable regularity and I believed it to be in warning.

I attempted to push the dark thoughts from my mind, and could not help but smile as I tightened my arms around Alexis. She wanted to be *mine*. She had spoken the words and they warmed me though the winter night was cool. Her long chiton was gathered at the tops of her thighs and I recalled how she had become shy again when I had pushed it up so she could sit with her legs either side of Skotos' back for our return to Trachis. She suggested I had spent so much time learning of Spartan women that I had forgotten their frequent thigh baring was not as accepted in the rest of Greece. I had not taken offence at her words, but promised that as we neared Trachis I would walk beside Skotos and she could sit astride him with her chiton covering her legs.

Of course settled in behind her as I was afforded me many advantages; for one my hands could rest at her waist, or more invitingly, on her thighs, though I had not placed them there for fear she would cover herself again. Her spicy scent, which was now mixed with the smell of the hot springs, filled my nostrils and I rested my chin on her shoulder. I placed a gentle kiss on the exposed skin of her neck, feeling the slight thrill that ran down her spine. She pressed herself back against me and I slid my hands to her hips, tightening my grip.

"I love you," I murmured at her ear.

I felt her draw breath, half-turning her body and placing her hand on my cheek, drawing my lips to hers. "I love you," she replied when we parted.

I smiled as my heart soared and my stomach tightened. I kissed her again, allowing my hands to slide beneath her chiton and trail along the inside of her thigh. She sighed when I drew my thumb along the heated skin between them.

"Skylar," she whispered.

"Yes, Princess?" I asked with a lazy grin as I found her lips again. She groaned as I entered her once again. She pulled Skotos to a stop, halting my movements with one hand and holding me firmly by the chin, forcing me to look at her as she spoke.

"I want you so badly it hurts, but we cannot, not here. What if Melanthios has woken and sees us? He shall be angry enough when he learns I do not intend to return to Epirus with him ..."

Kuria's bloodied face flashed before me. I could only imagine the cruelty Melanthios would inflict on Alexis given the chance. "You speak the truth," I nodded, stilling my hands and withdrawing them as my blood heated suddenly with fear rather than desire. I slid from Skotos' back, immediately yearning for the warmth of Alexis in my arms. She swung her legs so they faced me and I aided her in resettling her chiton.

"Thank you," she nodded.

We reached Trachis and the stables soon after and I put Skotos in his pen, ensuring he had food and fresh water before lowering the length of wood that would keep him in place. I turned, finding Alexis before me.

"Oh, apologies," I murmured attempting to step around her.

She smiled and reached out, her hand smoothing the fabric at my stomach. "Do you rush to leave?" she asked, her fingertips drawing lazy circles around my navel and dipping lower with each stroke.

My blood instantly warmed and my hand found her hip, but my brows drew together ever so slightly. "Should we not find somewhere more private before we are together again?" She ran her hand down my thigh, lifting my tunic and slipping her fingers beneath, drawing them back up with teasing slowness. "Melanthios could still look for us … here," I groaned, instantly wet, my breath shallow as she paused just below where I most wanted her touch.

"Do you have patience enough to wait?" she smirked.

"Gods," I gasped. "No. But we … we should not."

I struggled to speak as her hands worked expertly. I gripped her hips tightly, pulling her against me as I turned, placing her against a wooden pole. Her hand was still between us, fingers stroking me as I kissed her.

Kuria's face flashed before me again and I pulled back suddenly. I squeezed my eyes shut, willing the memories to disappear. We were too exposed; anyone could walk in and catch us. The fear of that knowledge warred with the arousal that beat the entire length of my body.

"Surrender to me, Skylar," Alexis kissed my neck, the curve of my collarbone.

I could not. It was too dangerous. "Alexis, wait," I pleaded, my hand finding its way to her head.

She looked up at me, the black within the green larger than I had ever seen them before. "I have waited for you forever, for how you made me feel, what you made me want. I did not know how lost I was before you arrived in Trachis," she said, her fingers tracing my lips. "You love me so completely. You are unafraid to speak the words. You showed me the depth of that love when I asked it of you. Allow me now to show you how deeply I love you in return. How your words settle within my chest and create fire and warmth, filling me with wants and desires such as I have never imagined. I want you. Now."

"I want you," I told her, pressing against her fingers.

She shook her head. "My turn first," she smiled, the pulse at her throat beating rapidly.

I had my sword, I had my fists. I would protect her, forever. "As you wish, Princess," I conceded, helpless as always to deny her.

She pulled my head to hers, our lips meeting roughly, fevered. She ran her tongue along my lower lip and I groaned, balling my hand in the material at her waist and pressing my body against hers. I gripped the pole behind her, needing something solid to hold firm as I lost myself to what she did to me. Alexis moved inside me relentlessly until I believed I could take no more, she must have felt the tremors begin for she slowed, withdrawing altogether and breaking our kiss.

"Alexis, sweetheart, I need you," I pleaded, the endearment falling from my mouth effortlessly.

She smiled; her hand on my cheek. "I know."

I allowed her to turn me until it was *my* back against the pole. She placed another gentle kiss on my lips and lowered herself to her knees. I held my breath as she looked up at me, her hands lifting my tunic, eyes drifting to what lay beneath.

"Alexis … " I began, the continuation of my words halted when she pressed her head forward, her tongue darting out to taste me. "Gods," I whispered, placing my hand at the back of her head to guide her. The burning desire began with her measured thrusts. It appeared that she had not only enjoyed the pleasure I had brought her earlier, but recalled how and where I used my tongue. "Do not stop, please," I implored.

My legs weakened as she continued her divine assault and the heat of desire within rose to a towering flame begging to be released. I held her to me, my vision dim, all noise and life outside the two of us disappearing. Her mouth, her tongue, her hands at my thighs, the sensation she created between them. I climaxed with ferocity, my hips bucking wildly as she drew wave after wave of pleasure from my body, her fingers digging into my flesh as I called her name.

My chest heaved with the enormity of my release, of the fear I had held inside these past winters. I had never been with someone I truly cared for, had never expected to. It was too dangerous, too scary, too … much. I felt the tears well in my eyes and leant my head back against the pole, untangling my hand from Alexis' hair.

"Skylar, what is it? Did I do something wrong? Did I hurt you?" she asked, rising quickly to stand before me again.

I shook my head, opening my eyes and placing my hand on her waist. "No. You are perfect," I assured her. "Just perfect."

"Then why are you crying?" she asked, wiping the tears from my cheeks.

"I … I have never felt this way before, no one has ever touched me as deep inside as you touch me."

"I believed it was *I* who was attempting to show you how much I feel for you," she smiled.

"Oh you did, believe me, I felt you everywhere. But I fear for what it shall mean for you."

"I do not understand," she frowned.

I drew her to me and kissed her, wishing the action could convey everything I felt, everything I wanted to tell her about Kuria and what had happened. When we parted I leaned my forehead against hers. "There was someone; a woman, three winters ago."

"Wait," Alexis said, softening her words by laying her hand on my arm. "Not here. Allow us now to return to the palace." I hesitated then nodded, following her from the stables.

We entered the palace via the walkway beside the south-eastern banqueting hall as Agrias emerged from the Throne Room. His brows were drawn together, separating when he caught sight of us.

"Thank the gods you are safe, I was worried," he said, holding a hand out to both of us as he neared.

"We are well, Father. I assure you," Alexis replied with a smile, taking his fingers in hers as I did the same. He looked between the two of us, but I remained quiet, wishing only to return to Alexis' room and surrender the last of my secrets to her – to allow her to know what it had meant for someone to be with me.

"So it would appear," he said, his gaze settling on me. "Melanthios woke earlier, behaving as a Minotaur with a thorn stuck in its paw." I nodded, my lips lifting slightly as I recognized my father's favored saying coming from the king.

"He remains at the barracks though, does he not?" I asked.

"As far as I am aware," Agrias nodded. "But you would do well to keep out of his sight tonight. Both of you," he added, turning his gaze on Alexis.

"We shall. I have no intention of allowing Skylar to leave my room before the dawn greets us tomorrow, longer even perhaps." Agrias raised his eyebrows at her words and I felt the blush creep up my neck.

"I shall keep her safe," I assured him.

"I know," he grinned, resting his hand on my arm and giving me a light squeeze. "If I do not see you before, I shall expect you in the Throne Room when the sun reaches its highest point."

"Until then," I agreed with a nod.

"I shall inform Leandros of your safe return," Agrias said, turning and making his way to the north wing of the palace.

"Thank you."

Alexis looped her arm through mine and raised her eyebrows in question. I nodded and we headed for her room.

41

Alexis closed the door to her room, ensuring the wooden piece was firmly in place before she turned to face me. I stood barely a foot from her, yet I dared not reach out; certain if I did I would keep the words within and enjoy nothing but the feel of her body against mine instead.

"I ... er ..."

Alexis crossed the room, brushing her hand over mine and indicating I join her on the end of the bed. I followed, seating myself beside her, hands pressed tight together in my lap.

"You spoke of a woman," she prompted, her own hands remaining beside her.

"Yes. Kuria," I nodded, my voice sounding too loud. I cleared my throat, inhaling a large breath and releasing it slowly.

"Take your time," Alexis said, the tips of her fingers touching the top of my hand momentarily before moving away again.

"Three winters ago, Father and I found ourselves at Corinth. We were only passing through on our way to the Peloponnese; we had not been called upon for aid or assistance. We were at the home of a man named Stamatis and his wife, Kuria. After we had shared a meal with them, they invited us to stay the night, for Father to join Stamatis at a banquet at another home nearby. We had been travelling for several days and the offer of a warm bed was far more appealing to my father and me than another night on the hard ground. Father and Stamatis withdrew to the men's area of the home to prepare themselves and Kuria sent me to bathe, joining me

206

later and pampering me with fine oils and perfume."

I swallowed loudly, uncertain I could, or should, share everything with Alexis; we had shared much intimacy these past candlemarks, but it had been our own, not mine with another lover. I cleared my throat again.

"Father and I had spent the previous four winters travelling around Attica and the Peloponnese, retracing the steps of heroes and aiding farmers and fishermen against their enemies. I had seen the pain of people losing their homes and livelihoods and wives devastated by the loss of their husbands through battle. But I was removed from it; I could not truly understand how they felt because I had not experienced such a loss. Neither had I experienced the pleasures of another's flesh against my own. I had never used my hands to bring someone pleasure rather than pain or death. I wondered at it, wanted to experience such things, but the opportunity had never arisen. Not until we stopped in Corinth."

I paused again, raising my eyes to Alexis' face. I could not read what was on it, but I saw she held questions back. She gave me a tight smile and I returned my eyes to my hands as I continued.

"Kuria and I shared much wine and she spoke in detail of her life, of where she had been before she and Stamatis were betrothed. She asked much of me, but I did not give her the answers, wanting instead to hear of what she spoke, for I could not deny that her words excited my body. When she invited me to her bed, I did not deny her, welcoming all she offered to teach me. She showed me the pleasures of a woman's caress, of her kiss, how to bring ultimate pleasure to another, and to one's self."

I paused again, my cheeks heating as I recalled the way I had allowed Kuria to own me, and then possessed her in return. At first my movements had been clumsy, but with her gentle instruction I had soon learnt what felt the most pleasurable, and when attentions needed only to be fleeting.

"When Stamatis came to her room candlemarks later, I was still in Kuria's embrace, having fallen asleep there – the effects of physical exertion and too much wine. He roused us both, his intentions for joining his wife plainly obvious as he stood naked before us. I did not wish to join them in their coupling, nor did he want me there. He ordered me to leave but Kuria held tight to my arm, telling Stamatis that she did not wish for him to lay with her that night; that she wished only for me."

I drew breath, recalling the anger and hatred for me in Stamatis' eyes when Kuria had spoken the words. He had run his eyes the length of my body, taking in my well-developed breasts and the short hair between my thighs.

"Stamatis dragged me out the door and slammed it in my face, putting the timber locking device in place. I shivered in the cool night air, but I did not leave, not immediately. I listened to their words, softly spoken, voices calm, not raised in anger as I had expected. I wondered if perhaps Kuria had spoken the words only to excite Stamatis, for she had told me of games lovers often played to thrill one another.

"He told Kuria that she belonged to him now, that he had not taken her from Aphrodite's temple so she could continue her ways beneath his roof. She apologized, giving him her word that she would pleasure only him until her days in this world were done. He told her to lie on the bed, but there was no malice in his voice and I knew she had done as he asked when a moment later he drew a sigh from her lips.

"He asked her what it was that she so favored about my affections, was it my mouth on hers, soft where his was bearded, or was it not her mouth that I had commanded? I had left then, without hearing her reply; I did not wish to. She had taught me much, but she belonged to Stamatis and Father and I would leave in the morning, me far wiser than I had been when we arrived.

"I returned to my room and slept soundly, woken at first light by a scream. I jumped from the bed, head still buzzing from the wine, my body stiff and sore in ways it had never been before. I found Kuria's slave standing in the courtyard, her piercing shrieks filling not only the space around us, but my entire being when I saw Kuria's body lying at her feet."

I paused, swallowing loudly. The sick feeling of that morning returned to my stomach.

"He killed her?" Alexis asked quietly, reaching out to take my hand in both of hers.

"He tortured her. He ..." I could not continue.

"Tell me, please, do not be afraid."

"I cannot," I whispered. "You should not hear the words."

Alexis brought my knuckles to her lips, kissing each in turn. She placed her hand on my cheek, turning my face to hers. I closed my eyes, allowing the tears to fall as the long held guilt settled in my stomach. "It is time you allowed me to take *your* pain; to hold it safe within, as you did for me," she said. "Speak of it so I may."

I kept my eyes closed, the images of Kuria remaining as I gripped Alexis' hand tightly, speaking words I had never expected to share with another, that I had never *wanted* to speak aloud before I met Alexis.

"Stamatis had maimed every inch of her. He had slashed deeply into her stomach and along her hipbones. Her breasts, arms and legs were jaggedly torn where he had hacked them off, the worst at her neck where he had taken off her head. He spared no part of her."

Alexis gasped and I opened my eyes, finding tears sliding down her own cheeks. My heart clenched to see my sadness, my mistake, mirrored on her face.

"Apologies, I should not ..."

She shook her head, placing a finger over my lips to silence me. "No.

Speak of it all. What happened then?"

"I was ill, the red of the wine mixing with the blood on the ground until I could not tell which was Kuria's and which I had contributed. Stamatis appeared, holding Kuria's head by her hair. Holding it up as though it were a prize. He laughed, throwing it towards me, her face as bloody and sliced up as the rest of her. I wanted to kill him, to chop his limbs from his body as he had Kuria's, to drive my sword into his stomach deep enough to draw blood, but not deep enough to kill him quickly. I wanted him to suffer."

"And did you take your revenge?"

I shook my head. "No, it was my father's blade that ended his life. Though I wished desperately for it to be mine, he would not allow it."

Both of us were quiet a long moment, my hand still clasped between Alexis', her thumb rubbing across my fingers. "Is that why you feared so greatly for me becoming Melanthios' wife?"

"Yes," I replied, closing my eyes again. "His intentions would not have been punishment for wanting me in your bed, but he would have been cruel. You would have suffered at your husband's hands as Kuria suffered at hers. And once again, I would have been powerless to stop him."

I swallowed, opening my eyes when I felt Alexis' fingers at my cheeks, wiping the tears that had fallen. I covered one of her hands, pressing it to my skin as I spoke. "I cannot begin to explain how much I love you Alexis, how it is even possible so soon. But I could not bear for you to be hurt so."

"Skylar," she whispered. "Do not fear it. You shall protect me from Melanthios as you have since we met. I am yours. Always. He shall not part us."

I drew her palm to my lips, kissing it as I nodded. "I shall always keep you safe, I give you my word."

She smiled and stood, drawing me to my feet as she wrapped her arms around my waist. I held her tightly, her palms massaging my back and sides, soothing me. "Thank you for telling me of Kuria." I only nodded in reply. Alexis loosened her grip and drew away, taking the pin from her hair and allowing it to flow freely over her shoulders and down her back. "Would you come to bed with me now? Just to sleep," she hastened to add. "I think after the day, and the people we have spoken to and spoken of, we could both use it."

I gave her a tight grin as I pushed my fingers through her hair. "I can think of nothing I want more," I replied.

Alexis grinned shyly and reached for the brooch at her shoulder, taking it from her chiton and allowing it to drop to the floor. "May I?" she inquired, reaching out for mine.

I nodded and she freed the tunic from my body, dropping both accessories onto the discarded clothing and taking my hand as she led me to her bed. Alexis pulled back the covers, crawling beneath them and drawing my body close when I joined her. She settled my head at her shoulder, pressing her lips to my forehead as her fingers traced the contours of my nose, cheek and chin. I had not sought comfort in anyone's arms since I was a child, but lying wrapped in Alexis' embrace felt right. I felt as though I was home.

"Were you afraid to seek the arms of women for intimacy and pleasure after what happened to Kuria? Did you wish to experience a male lover?" Alexis asked after a few moments.

"For a long while after Kuria I sought no one. I was too afraid of the consequences."

"But then?" she prodded.

I drew in a deep breath before I replied. "But then I only sought out women, *specific* women for company; ones who belonged to no man, no husband. They meant nothing to me, I did not seek them out for the promise of more, only to satisfy a hunger in my blood; to calm the restless desires within. I used them to release an explosion of feeling, to extinguish the adrenaline that came with the heat of battle, of knowing I had faced death and beaten it for another day.

"Even before Kuria I knew I was attracted to women. And after that … I believed that a woman lover would not harm me, would give me what I needed without question or jealousy. I had seen what the hands of men could do in battle and in anger and I did not want them to touch me in the same way as Kuria had. I could not imagine them being gentle or kind, though I have since met many men whom I am certain could bring pleasure to a woman if she so desired it."

"But you never wanted it from them?"

"No."

"My words the night of the celebration … when I accused you of caring only for women who belonged to another, they hurt you. That is why you were so angry with me."

"Yes," I murmured.

"I am sorry."

I only nodded in reply, silent a few more moments before I broke the quiet again. "Until you, until today, I have never taken anyone to bed I truly cared about. You touched a part of me I had put away, believing that such an honor would never be mine; that as punishment for what happened with Kuria I would never experience it."

"Oh," Alexis murmured. "I believe it is *I* who should feel honored."

"I would not have wished to feel this way for anyone else."

Alexis continued to administer the long strokes at my face, her fingertips gentle, soothing my open wounds as opposed to igniting and exciting me as her caresses had done earlier. I blew out a deep breath, laying my arm across her stomach and my thigh over both of hers, reveling in the sweet contact. "Sleep now," she crooned, her lips at my hair.

I closed my eyes, allowing her love to fill me, to touch me deep within and close the parts that lay open and bleeding. Her hand at my hair guided me towards Hypnos' realm and I did not resist, falling into a restful slumber surrounded by Alexis and the depth of my love for her.

42

I woke to find my head still at Alexis' shoulder, her chest rising and falling in gentle rhythm. Her fingers lightly caressed my forearm which remained across her stomach and I drank in the feel of her skin beneath mine and the tender ministrations at my arm. Gentle rain fell against the tiled roof above us and I wished Alexis and I could remain locked inside her room forever; silent, together, needing nothing and no one else. Unfortunately, I knew the clouds overhead made it difficult to tell how late the day was and I suspected we would need to leave to meet Agrias before long.

Our conversation from the night before burned in my mind and though I was relieved I had spoken of Kuria to Alexis, part of me was afraid for how it would be between us this morning. I had been vulnerable and exposed. I had bared my deepest hurt, my greatest guilt. I had allowed Alexis to see my tears and my fear. She had encouraged me to open up the darkest part of myself.

I turned and pressed my lips to her chest, smiling as her heartbeat quickened and a swift whisper of desire called to me.

"Good morning," Alexis murmured.

I found her fingers and twined them with mine as I replied. "Good morning."

"How do you feel?"

"Perhaps that is a question better answered by you," I replied, pressing my lips to her skin again.

She took her hand from mine, tilting my chin until our eyes met. She raised her eyebrows, her face serious. I inhaled deeply as I attempted to put my thoughts into words. Her heartbeat raced beneath my ear as she waited for my reply and I smoothed my hand up her body, resting it between her breasts. Blowing out the long breath I held, I allowed the words to tumble out.

"I feel embarrassed, calm, relieved, fearful. I am uncomfortable that last night I was not the strong, proud warrior you have known so far. I want to be that for you, always. To be here protecting you, loving you unconditionally and without fear, ensuring you are never treated with anything other than kindness."

"You do not believe you can do that now I know of Kuria and what happened to her?"

"I am … afraid that perhaps you shall not *want* me to. I wanted you to know about her, about my past, but I have worried you would not care for me as much if you knew."

"That is why you resisted me in the stables … at first," she said, her cheeks tinging.

I smiled, running a finger along her jaw. "When it comes to you, I find I have trouble denying you anything, Princess. But yes, when you … when we … when I felt you so deeply within my heart, I knew I owed it to you to tell you how one woman had been treated because of her actions with me, no matter how afraid I was of turning you away." I drew her hand to my chest, flattening it beneath mine. "I am embarrassed by the tears I shed, for being afraid at all, when in all else I do not fear. I worry you shall not believe me worthy enough for you because I showed you weakness last night," I admitted, swallowing loudly before continuing. "But I cannot live without you Alexis; I would not ever wish to do so." My words ended in a whisper, the bloom of love I felt for the woman beside me threatening to drown me.

"Skylar," she whispered, her fingers tightening against me. "I shall never leave you." She smiled, leaning down to brush her lips against mine. "For all your strength and skill with weapons, it was your words and your heart I first fell in love with. You spoke with passion and purpose for why you fight for those who cannot. You did not speak of fighting because you enjoyed the blood on your hands. You truly care for others. You cared for *me*, protected me though you did not know me. You love me now with that same intensity, you know no other way.

"I feel safe with you, loved more than I ever knew was possible. Your pain and vulnerability, the side of yourself you shared with me last night, what happened with Kuria, none of those things turn me from you, if anything they draw me even closer. If it is reassurance you require then I shall speak the words; you have all of me. Always. I am yours, no one shall change that. If it is strength you need when you feel you have none of your own then I shall give you mine. Take it, feel me within and know the truth of it. I fear nothing when I know you are near."

I closed my eyes, my heart swelling again as I felt Alexis roll onto her side and press her body the length of mine. Her hand stroked my back and I placed one of mine at her hip.

"Alexis," I whispered, finding her lips.

She drew me against her body as her tongue flicked across my lips. "Feel me," she said into my mouth.

"I do, everywhere," I replied. Hot arousal burned me when she pressed her abdomen against mine and I felt no pain, no fear. There was only Alexis. "Sweetheart ... I want you. I need you."

She cupped my chin and I opened my eyes, drowning in the green that met them. "I am here," she assured me.

"I want to touch you. May I?"

"Oh please," she groaned, opening her thighs and pressing my hand between them. "I love you Skylar, always."

My breath caught, the look of undisguised desire on her face inflaming my blood. "Alexis," I whispered again.

I pressed into her, watching her lips part as she took me in. She kissed me, slow, unhurried, her hand caressing my hip then my stomach before moving lower. My skin tightened as I felt the fire ignite between my thighs. "Come with me," she whispered. I groaned and accepted her, riding the crest with her, drawing cries from each other's lips as we fell over the edge of need, of desire, of love; together. As we celebrated *us*.

A knock interrupted us a short time later, and Alexis complained as I took my arm from beneath her. I picked up my tunic, holding it against my chest as I padded to the door. I removed the wooden lock and opened it a few inches. Hesper stood on the other side, eyes widening when they met mine.

"Skylar ... I, er, I wanted to ensure Alexis arrived back safely after ... you met with her," she stumbled.

"She is safe," I replied.

"Though annoyed to have been disturbed," Alexis called.

Hesper grinned in reply. "Have the two of you eaten this morning?"

"No," I replied.

"I shall prepare something for you then."

"Honey-sweetened bread?" I asked hopefully.

"Of course," she nodded. She turned to leave, hesitating momentarily before speaking again. "I am glad you are here today. Alexis is fortunate to have found you," she whispered.

"It is I who is the fortunate one," I assured her.

She smiled again and left as I shut the door, taking the tunic from my chest. I turned back to the bed, meeting the two bright green orbs that shone from Alexis' face.

I paused, watching as she took in her silent appraisal of me. "Enjoying the view?" I asked, placing my hands on my hips.

"Always," she replied.

She held her hands out and I crossed the room, taking them as I sat opposite her on the bed. "Hesper is very fond of you."

"And I of her, though I was hurt she did not tell me of your decision to become Melanthios'. Thaddeus also kept it from me, though I had sparred with him for days."

"I asked them not to speak of it. I … I did not want you to know until it was too late and we were gone," she said, dropping her eyes from me.

I lifted her chin again. "You did not truly believe I would allow it to stand?"

"No, but I did not want you or Leandros hurt attempting to keep me here."

"I would have gone after you, if for no other reason than to apologize for the distance I caused between us," I said, tracing her lip with my thumb.

"I am thankful you came to find me at the hot springs, that we were alone to speak of what we had not dared before."

"And to enjoy where that led us," I added with a smile. Her cheeks colored again and I placed a gentle kiss on her lips, drawing a breath before I spoke again. "Once Melanthios is dealt with and you are no longer bound to the Molossians, would your wish be to remain in Trachis, with your family and Hesper? I understand you are not close with Melina but, if you could, is it what you desire?"

Alexis considered the question for a long moment. "Is it what *you* would wish for? To remain in one place for the remainder of your days if I asked it of you?" she replied instead.

It was my turn to hesitate. *Was I prepared to give up all I was accustomed to?* I already knew the answer.

"If you asked it of me, I would stay. My shield and sword would belong to Trachis, to Thermopylae. I would fight for no other again." I took her hand, laying it on my chest so she could feel the pulsing beat beneath. "I would make Trachis my home, with you. My heart, along with my sword, is yours."

"You would not miss the places you would see, the people you have not yet met … the women?" she added quietly.

"I have found all I could ever wish for here," I told her, slipping my hand beneath her hair and kissing her again.

43

A furious pounding at the door interrupted us once more and I hastened to pull my tunic to my chest as I opened it again. I had barely lifted the wooden locking device from its place when Agrias pushed his way in, followed by Melina, my father and Thaddeus.

"What is wrong?" Alexis asked, ensuring the blanket covered her as she reached for a fresh chiton.

"Melanthios is no longer at the barracks," Agrias replied.

"His men have been waiting by the Melas River for his orders, but he must have joined them for they are moving forward in readiness to attack," Thaddeus added.

"Moeris was unable to convince Melanthios' brothers he was the one who killed Basil—" Agrias began.

"The two of you are together ... as lovers?" the queen cut over her husband. "Do our soldiers need to fight to free Alexis from the Molossian tribe once and for all?"

Alexis slipped from the bed and joined me by the door, aiding me to settle my tunic properly. "Yes," I nodded. "I want to be with Alexis for as long as my days are in this world." My blood heated as I spoke the words, my earlier concerns gone, replaced with familiar certainty and determination. I knew what Melanthios was capable of and I would not allow him to use his tools on Alexis; or anyone else ever again if the gods saw fit to grant me such a wish.

"We can discuss that later, for now, we must get you and your family to safety, and deal with the approaching warriors," Father said, addressing Agrias.

"Agreed," the king nodded. "Thaddeus shall take us. The kitchen has two exits but both can be locked from the inside, it shall be the best place. The two of you should go and prepare our soldiers at the barracks. Moeris shall remain with Melanthios' men to continue his ruse, though he shall turn on them as soon as he has the opportunity."

"Allow me to go after Melanthios instead," I insisted.

"No. I need you with the main army; I need the best when they face them." I hesitated a moment, my jaw clenching, but eventually nodded.

"Collect your weapons and allow us to go," Father said to me.

I turned to Alexis, lifting our entwined fingers to my lips. "We shall not be separated for long, I give you my word."

She pushed up onto her toes and kissed me fiercely, her tongue darting into my mouth, her hand at my neck drawing me closer. After only a moment's hesitation, I returned her fevered actions, my fingers gripping her hip, the heat of the skin beneath her green chiton igniting a ball of desire in my stomach. Nothing outside Alexis' lips, her body existed; the feel of her beneath my hand, her intoxicating scent imprinting itself not only in my mind but around my heart. I held her firmly against me as she fisted her hand at my waist. My blood turned to liquid fire, my breath shallowing dangerously when she groaned and pressed herself against my thigh. My father cleared his throat behind us, rudely reminding me that Alexis and I were not alone, and that there was much to be done before it could be so again.

I fought the haze of lust and love that surrounded me as I loosened my grip on her. "You wear the chiton I most favor on you, but I shall enjoy removing it from your body when I return," I told her quietly.

"Then I pray our separation is brief," she whispered, her lips at my neck. "I love you. Be safe."

"And you," I replied, trailing my finger along her jaw. "I love you too."

She smiled and I kissed her again, though it was far more chaste than our previous one. I inhaled deeply, my eyes remaining on Alexis as I attempted to steady my furiously beating heart.

"Ensure they remain safe," I ordered, my eyes lifting to Thaddeus' as he led my princess and her parents from the room. He nodded in return and I scooped up my shield and sword, Father handing me my cuirass as I followed him to the barracks.

*

In the pouring rain we had met the Illyrians on the plains outside the palace. They wore no armor except bronze greaves on their shins and thick helmets; their faces exposed between the side pieces over their ears. They drove chariots and proudly held spears; some wooden, some metal. Others fired their bows as soon as they found range, more carried axes, some only sharpened on one side, others on both. For closer combat they relied on their short, single-edged curved swords, wielding all with skill and ferocity. Many of Agrias' men were felled with the first wave.

My hands and shield would have been thick with their blood if not for the constant deluge that washed them clean. Visibility was already reduced to little more than the range of my weapons and with the sky darkening overhead, I wondered if Agrias or the enemy would call a cease until the morning. With no emergence of the moon or the ability to light torches to guide us in our battle, it would be too easy to remove one of our own from this world instead of an enemy.

I dispatched another attacker, turning at the sound of my name. Through the driving rain I saw Moeris unsteadily making his way towards me, Thaddeus slumped against his side. I kept my shield up as I headed for them, holding it above the three of us as a bowman took aim. Thaddeus crumpled to the ground, blood from a deep cut on his forehead trickled down the left side of his face, his eyes unfocused as he searched my face. The enemy loosed his arrow but it bounced off my shield and fell uselessly to the ground beside us.

"What happened? Where is Alexis?" I asked.

Thaddeus shook his head weakly, struggling to reply. "I … I am sorry, Skylar she … Melanthios. He has Alexis."

Blood rushed in my ears, momentarily blocking out the sounds of battle behind us. "No," I murmured.

Moeris fended off another arrow, and jumped up to deal with the attacker.

"I am so sorry. He broke down the door to the kitchen, another of his men blocking our exit through the other," Thaddeus continued.

"No!" I said again, balling my hand into a fist.

"Melanthios said he saw you and Alexis yesterday."

"Saw us?" I asked, shaking my head. "Where? What does …" I trailed off. The stables? The hot springs? Going into Alexis' room last night? Oh gods, no. I swallowed around the lump in my throat, a movement catching my eye. I bolted to my feet and met the axe of a soldier, slicing my blade across his throat before I knelt and addressed Thaddeus again. "Did he say where he was taking her?"

"No," Thaddeus replied, his eyes getting wide. "Look out!" he cried.

I turned to find a second warrior almost upon us. I got to my feet again, stumbling slightly as I attempted to get my shield in place to protect my stomach from the deadly point of the spear. As iron met bronze, the warrior gave a cry, the end of a sword suddenly protruding from his belly.

Father pushed the dead soldier forward, extracting his weapon and joining me in aiding Thaddeus to his feet as he attempted to stand. "What has happened?" Father asked.

"Melanthios has Alexis," Moeris panted, arriving beside us once again.

I rounded on him, pinning him in place with my stare as I spoke. "You have spent much time with Melanthios recently, pretended to be loyal to him rather than Agrias, tell me it is not how you truly feel. Swear you did not aid him to take her."

"It is not. I did not, I swear to you. I am loyal to Trachis. Always. I would not put Alexis in harm's way. I learnt from another soldier where Agrias and his family were only after Melanthios had taken Alexis. I raced to find the king and queen and ensure they were unharmed before coming to find you. I knew you would want to go after him immediately."

"He speaks with truth," Thaddeus confirmed. "He showed nothing but loyalty and care when he came to the kitchen."

I held Moeris' gaze a long moment, but saw no hint of lie behind his words. I nodded once and turned my attention back to Thaddeus. "Can you fight beside us?"

"Hades himself could not stop me," he replied.

"Good," I nodded. "They cannot have got far." I had promised Alexis no harm would come to her while I was near, and now it was time I proved my words. I may not have always been able to save every man, woman or child caught in a war, but Alexis was *my* responsibility and I would show her why her father had asked me to come in the first place. Cutting down enemy soldiers as we ran, the four of us raced to the stables, sheathing our swords and leaving behind our shields as we collected our horses.

*

We dragged our steeds behind us, the muddy ground beneath our feet making it far too dangerous to attempt riding, though I detested the slow pace we kept.

"If Melanthios said he saw us together yesterday, there could only be a few places," I said. "Being that we did not find him at the palace or the stables, it has to be the hot springs."

The wind that accompanied the rain chilled my exposed arms and legs, my light tunic and bronze cuirass not nearly enough. We had left in such a hurry that I did not think to collect either a chlamys or himation; my thoughts only with Alexis, as they were now.

"His brothers shall be with him, he would want them close by to hear his army has been victorious," Moeris said.

I only nodded in reply. What had Melanthios already done to Alexis? I shuddered as I imagined his hands on her body. He had spoken of his knowledge of our union for only one reason – to warn me that he would not allow it to go unpunished. Alexis had said that she had been mine from that first moment in the Spercheios Valley, and it was true for me too – from the moment her sweet perfume had invaded my senses, she had owned me. No other woman had ever stirred my blood or created that deep aching need in my soul and I had allowed that to draw me to her, to pursue her for more, though I knew I should not. And now torture and pain would befall her because I had taken her to bed.

"I should have kept watch over Melanthios at the barracks after you felled him," my father growled.

"No, the responsibility was mine. I should have gone to him last night when Alexis agreed to end their betrothal," I replied. "Instead I was selfish and allowed myself to partake of pleasure with her rather than plan the attack against him."

"It does no good to place blame with anyone for what is done," Moeris counselled.

"Though it was not what you wanted, Leandros, you understand now there is no other way to free Alexis from Melanthios than by killing him?" Thaddeus asked.

"I do," Father nodded. "We must find Alexis and free her of Melanthios and his brothers for good."

"Agreed. We shall find her and all shall be well," Thaddeus nodded, placing his hand on my shoulder.

"I hope it is so," I replied.

What weapons would Melanthios fashion from the trees and mountains around him? Would he whip her with a thin reed as though she were nothing more than a slave or would he take pleasure in seeing her soft skin bruised and dark from thicker branches? Kuria's white skin flashed before me; the long, angry slashes across her stomach, the deep stab wounds at her chest. I closed my eyes tight against their onslaught, but they did not diminish, increasing in ferocity as I tasted vomit and wine at the back of my throat. How would Alexis forgive me if Melanthios did something similar to her? How would I forgive myself?

My thoughts were interrupted as we reached a large temple, my breath lost in a rush when I saw the simple yellow chiton crumpled at the doorway. I took my sword from its sheath as I approached – Father, Moeris and Thaddeus mirroring the action. I bent down and picked up the material; a large slash severed it in half, but there was no blood. It was the chiton Alexis had worn at the hot springs. Melanthios knew I would search for her, he knew I would recognize it. He wanted me to find them, invited me to. I took up his invitation gladly. "They are at the hot springs," I murmured, certain of my words.

A cry from the building had me raising my weapon as the door to the temple flew open and a stream of soldiers raced to engage us. Though I was already exhausted from the day's fighting, I met them with ferocity, slicing and felling them without hesitation. The three men accompanying me did the same and we were through the first wave before my father cried out over the sounds of battle.

"Skylar, go! Find Alexis. We shall deal with the rest of these soldiers and follow you when it is done."

I only nodded in reply, re-sheathing my sword and jumping onto Skotos, turning him east and digging my heels into his belly. The hot springs were private, secluded and far from where Alexis' screams would be heard. I squeezed my eyes shut as hot tears stung. I refused to allow them to fall. I focused instead on what I would do to Melanthios if he had indeed touched Alexis. I had not been able to take revenge on Stamatis for Kuria, but I would ensure that Melanthios felt every slice, every blow from my weapons. He would suffer at my hand and I would ensure he never harmed anyone again.

44

My tunic was plastered as close to my thighs as my hair was to my face. I struggled to keep my grip on Skotos' mane. His steps had become slow and he stumbled over invisible rocks and divots as I slid dangerously to one side of his back.

Haunting pictures played through my mind; Melanthios driving himself roughly inside Alexis, his blades cutting deep into her flesh. A taunting voice told me I would not find Alexis before Melanthios tortured her – it did not take more than a few moments to inflict the damage I was imagining. The sound of her screams filled my head, over and over again. She called my name, pleaded for me to help her. How many warriors would stand between the two of us? I would fight them all, but while they occupied my weapons, Melanthios would be free to do his worst.

The rain continued its assault against my skin, mixing itself with the hot tears that burned my cheeks. Melanthios would not worship Alexis or love her, he would not protect her above all others. He would rather see her harmed than loved. I would never, I *could* never, raise my hand to her in a way other than to offer comfort or bestow caress. The soft skin of her stomach and thighs, the gentle curve of her waist, her lips against mine; all would be lost to me, forever.

My chest constricted. I could not catch my breath. I slipped from Skotos' back, landing heavily in a muddy puddle, cold water splashing up my thighs as my knees found the ground. I retched. I sobbed; the noises drawn from me with such force that I could not draw full breath between gasps.

Until Kuria was killed I had never felt helpless; not even in Anticyra when I watched the mercenary and his men cut down women and children indiscriminately. I had felt anger towards them, but not helplessness. In Corinth I had not known Kuria was in danger. If I had, I would not have allowed myself slumber whilst she endured terrible cruelties in my name. I vowed that I would never find myself helpless again, that no one I came across would feel that way.

I *had* to find her. Life would not be worth living if Alexis was not in it beside me. When my mother was taken from my father, he was strong. For me. He pushed aside his grief and his anger and carried on. He protected me, loved me, ensuring I had all I needed to grow. I did not have the same; I had no child to see the light of Alexis' smile mirrored back at me, no child to hide my pain from so they did not wish for a mother they could never know. I could not be as strong as he was. Without Alexis I would be broken … Helplessness and despair consumed me. I fell forward, exhausted. I could not fail her.

Skotos reached down to nuzzle my face. I raised my hand and patted his nose, pushing myself to my feet and drawing a deep breath. I climbed onto his back and kicked him forward with renewed determination. A sliver of the fear that I was too late fluttered unwelcome in my stomach.

"I am coming for you, Alexis," I murmured.

I would not lose her. I would fight Melanthios, and as many soldiers as I had to, for what Alexis and I already had and for a future I did not want to walk without her. I only had to hope she would forgive me for whatever she had suffered at Melanthios' hands before I got there.

Wanting to arrive at the hot springs unannounced, I slid from Skotos' back and tied him beneath a tree. I drew my sword and travelled the last distance by foot, scaling the tree I had left Skotos beneath during my last visit to the springs, and surveying the camp beside the water. A large tent dominated the area between the trees and the spring. Two men stood guard at the door, their eyes focused on the scrub where I was hidden, swords in hand, another at their waists. Neither held their shields; they were propped against the side of the thick material, though in easy reach should they require them. A third man bathed in the water, his weapons discarded on the bank, though he too kept his eyes on the bushland around him.

Their uniforms matched what Melanthios had worn the day Father and I came upon him in the Spercheios Valley. I studied their faces; pointed chins, dark hair that lay low on their brows, cheeks and arms sporting raised scars from battle, eyes closer together than most above thick noses. The similarities they bore to each other and to Melanthios named them as kin; Melanthios and Basileios' brothers.

I could not see Melanthios or Alexis anywhere, which meant they must be inside the tent. There appeared to be no other warriors, Molossian or Illyrian, and I nodded to myself. Three, or four if Melanthios joined his brothers, against one were odds I considered favorable, though I did not intend to engage them all at once if I could help it.

I returned to the ground, planning my attack. The man at the spring would be the easiest to dispose of first; he held no weapons and was hidden from the sight of the others by the tent. I made my way through the thick foliage to my right until I reached the spring. Water fell from the mountain above, crashing onto several submerged rocks as it rushed away to the main pool. I followed the stream through the trees until they began to thin again. The man was still facing the trees on the opposite bank, his sword, spear and clothing not three feet from me beside the altar to Heracles. I stepped between the branches, my foot finding an errant twig as I did so. The wood snapped beneath my sandal. I did not have time to drop behind the marble structure before the man spun around, his eyes wide as he realized I stood above his weapons.

Before he had the chance to open his mouth and alert his brothers, I bent down, picking up his spear and launching it in one movement. He managed only a strangled cry of surprise as the metal tip impaled him. He clutched uselessly at the shaft sticking from his neck, falling backwards moments later, his blood turning the water of the spring red as his life drained from him.

A shout from the tent drew my attention and I picked up the dead man's sword at my feet as I sought cover behind the altar. I peeked around the side. One of the two guards posted outside pulled open the large flap of leather and made his way in. In the flickering light that burned inside, I had the briefest glimpse of Alexis. Arms and legs spread wide, bound against two thick poles. Naked. Fear struck at my core and my blood heated as I gripped the sword in my hand tighter. I censored thoughts of what Melanthios may have done to her as she stood in such a vulnerable position, focusing instead on the guard who remained by the door. He appeared to be the same age or perhaps a winter older than me, his muscular frame and the scars on his body indicating he had seen many battles. His eyes scanned the tree line with practiced attention, but he was nowhere near ready to attack should the need arise. He turned as his brother re-joined him.

"Melanthios seeks word from Trachis. Return and confirm the Illyrians have been victorious."

"Send Xylon instead. Melanthios may grow tired of the princess and wish for me to take over from him. My body hardens thinking of how it would feel to be inside her," the younger boy smiled, rubbing himself as he spoke.

"As you well know, Marcario, Melanthios does not often share his prizes with us. But as second oldest, it would be *me*, not you, who would have the opportunity."

"You wish, Cleon. Melanthios favors me over you, eager to teach me not only the ways of battle, but of women as well."

"I do not find myself lacking for women, as you well know. Now, leave and bring word from Trachis lest you find my sword cutting off what you are so proud of," Cleon said, the tip of his sword at Marcario's groin.

"You are just jealous that I possess a larger asset with which to bring pleasure, or pain, to those I wish," Marcario laughed, but he turned and left the clearing.

I retreated into the trees behind me and cut a path diagonal to his. I slowed when I heard him ahead of me, squeezing the sword in my palm as I regained my breath. Marcario stood with his back to me, one arm braced against the trunk of a small tree, the other working beneath his linen body armor. He panted hard, too focused on his intent to hear me arrive behind him. I was two steps from him and still he did not turn. I closed the distance, driving Xylon's sword in through his back and out his stomach, clamping my hand over his mouth to smother his scream.

"You shall never touch her," I whispered into his ear, twisting the sword in deeper. Blood stained the front of Marcario's armor and poured down his legs, pooling at his feet. His body went limp and I dropped him to the ground, placing my foot on his back as I yanked the sword back out.

I rolled him to the side of the track and returned to the clearing, stepping out from between the trees and following Cleon to the spring when he headed in that direction. I had to be fast and I had to be silent. I wanted the element of surprise when I faced Melanthios and if Cleon alerted him to my presence, it could spell greater danger for Alexis.

"Xylon, no!" he whispered, entering the water.

I was upon Cleon in moments, drawing the sword across his throat before he reached the floating body of his brother. I caught him before he slipped beneath the water and dragged him out onto the bank. I hauled Xylon's body ashore as well, leaving the spear in place and dropping his sword silently beside him.

I approached the tent. Melanthios' deep voice rumbled from within and I could just make out his words as I reached the doorway.

"For all your words, your assurances that she would, she does not come for you. She shall not save you this time. You are mine to do with as I please and it is time I gave you something far more permanent to remember me by."

"You shall never put a child inside me, no matter how often you attempt to," Alexis growled.

Melanthios laughed. "Oh there shall be time enough for that. But for now, I shall brand you as a master brands his slave so everyone knows you belong to me. But where shall I place the mark? Not the face, that is too barbaric. Perhaps here, above your heart, so when I am inside you I can see it and know that I won. What do you think?"

"Go to Tartarus," she spat.

He laughed again. "I do enjoy your spirit. But I shall enjoy breaking it even more."

"Skylar shall kill you for touching me," Alexis gasped.

"She clearly finds herself already in Hades' realm. I gave specific instructions to my men to find and kill her first."

I pushed through the flap of the tent, sword drawn, flames of angry heat lighting my body at the scene before me. Alexis' left eye was blackened; a cut at her eyebrow the cause. Purple bruises, in the shape of handprints, covered her thigh and one hip. Four long marks stood dark against the pale skin of her forearm as they had the first time I saw her. Her wrists and ankles were bloodied where the thick ropes holding her bit into her skin. She had fought. She had struggled against the bindings. I could imagine exactly what Melanthios had done to her to make her fight him.

"It appears you still underestimate me, Melanthios, for here I stand alive and well," I growled. "Now get your hands off her before I remove them for you."

45

Melanthios jumped, backing away from Alexis and pulling a length of heated metal from the roaring fire in the middle of the tent. A bloodied length of cloth covered his forearm and he wore the thigh-length linen body armor of his people, his leather greaves and sandals laying haphazardly in the dirt behind him.

"You found my present at the temple then," he grinned.

"The soldiers or the chiton?" I replied, raising my sword and taking a step towards Alexis.

"No closer or I shall have my brothers hold you and make you watch as I drive myself into her again," he warned.

"Your brothers no longer find themselves in this world. Take a look for yourself," I offered. I shrugged and lowered my sword ever so slightly as I stepped aside, pleased the gesture and my words came out strong and calm, though I felt anything but.

Melanthios appeared to consider my offer, his eyes flicking to the door. I took the opportunity to meet Alexis' gaze. She favored me with a tight smile and though I saw pain written on her face, I also found relief. I nodded in reply and returned my attention to Melanthios.

"You lie," he said, bringing the metal up and charging me. I set my feet and met his attack with a strong defense. "I am glad you did not arrive too soon. It gave me time to ... get to know the princess. Intimately. Her flesh is soft and so inviting, as you are well aware," he smirked. I growled and pressed my sword harder against the metal he held. "When I was inside her, she writhed above me. She enjoyed when I filled her and made her body tremble. She sought her end with me – her thoughts no longer with you or what you did to her."

"He speaks no truth, Skylar," Alexis cried. "I wanted him nowhere near me."

"Words may deny, but actions do not," he continued, pressing the end of the metal until it burned hot beside my cheek.

"She shall never be yours," I said, pushing both Melanthios and the heated metal away.

He laughed and took his sword from the table, a weapon in each hand. "She already is," he said, swinging both sword and metal as he attacked.

I fended off his wild movements, wishing I had my shield as well. My xiphos found Melanthios' already injured arm and his grip loosened on his sword as he staggered backwards, allowing the fire between us as we circled it. "Blood loss is a slow way to meet Hades," I murmured.

He lowered the brand to the fire again and transferred his sword to the other hand as he briefly took in the injury. "It does not run deep, I have suffered worse," he replied, indicating the scar at his face and over his chin. "Besides, once I have turned the ground red with your blood, Alexis shall do whatever I ask of her, starting with tending to my injuries."

His hand returned to the metal in the fire as I took a step to my right and he did the same across from me.

"She shall never tend to anything for you. The union you so badly wish for shall never come to pass. And once *your* blood stains the ground here, I shall take Alexis and care for her as you never could."

"As you never would," Alexis agreed.

"You are certain she shall still want you when you could not protect her from me? When I was able to take her away so easily? Perhaps if you are fortunate enough to kill me as you desire, she shall allow you to return her to Trachis, but I doubt she shall ever want for you to share her bed again."

I faltered, his words momentarily getting past all my defenses. I swallowed, my eyes finding Alexis' again.

"I do," she assured me, struggling against the bonds at her wrists.

"She does not want you. She speaks the words you wish to hear only to see us fight. The fighting excites her. Do you not see the raised color in her cheeks? The way her flesh rose when our weapons met? But when she leaves this place it shall be with me, not you."

"Not a chance," I told him.

"Every chance," Melanthios smiled. "She is mine."

He drew the metal from the fire and made for Alexis. I reached her first, raising my sword and denying him the chance to brand her. He pressed down hard, his sword bouncing off my cuirass above my ribs when he attacked with his other hand. He thrust his sword toward me a second time. Anger fired my blood and I pushed upwards against his strength. He dropped his sword, gripping the metal with both hands as I drove him backwards and away from Alexis. I knocked it from his hand. He continued to back up and I followed, stalking him as though he were prey.

"Your time here is done," I assured him. I advanced, bringing my sword down and chopping off one of his hands. He cried out, drawing a dagger from his waist with his other and thrusting it in my direction. I continued towards him, slashing into his thigh. He fell to his knees, grabbing at his leg with his remaining hand as the knife fell from his grip and his blood drained, soaking the ground beneath him.

I drew my sword up, crashing the pommel against his temple. He slumped awkwardly to the ground and I crossed to Alexis, freeing her feet and hands from the ropes. I caught her as she fell forward and tears streamed down her cheeks as she held tight to me.

"Take me away from him. Please," she whispered.

I nodded and re-sheathed my sword, taking the green chiton that matched her eyes from the wooden beam behind her. I settled it around her shoulders and pulled it shut in front. With one arm around her waist and the other beneath her knees I lifted her into my arms as I had in the Spercheios Valley. She laid her head against the cuirass at my chest, her body trembling.

I was not finished with the Molossian; he would pay for what he had done to Alexis, but she would not see me kill him. I would not allow her to witness that side of me or what I had in mind for him.

I pushed through the door of the tent, setting Alexis on the ground and pressing my lips to her hair. "Wait here," I told her.

"I do not believe I could walk even if I wished to," she murmured. I nodded. "You are going to kill him," she said, a statement, not a question.

"Yes," I replied, returning to my feet. "He shall never harm you again."

"Good," she said, dropping her eyes to her hands.

I marched back into the tent, finding Melanthios had woken. He attempted to drag himself to his sword, but the loss of his hand and the wound at his thigh prevented him quick movement. I stalked across the room, picking up his dagger as his eyes found mine. His face was ashen, deep purple bruises painting his cheeks beneath his eyes. I placed my foot on his hand, preventing him from grasping the handle of his sword and crouched down, grabbing his chin and forcing him to meet my eyes.

"The Molossian tribe you belong to may be fierce warriors; you may strike fear into the hearts of the enemy tribes in Epirus, but you bleed and die as easily as any mercenary or soldier I have faced," I said, reaching for his sword. "Your brothers shall claim Alexis no more than you shall. I have ensured that."

I released his chin and dropped my eyes to the stump where his hand had been until so recently. I returned to my feet, throwing Melanthios' sword aside and slipping his dagger into the belt at my waist. Taking him by the arms, I dragged him towards the fire. His eyes grew wide and he thrashed in my grip but I held firm.

"Your brothers found their deaths with barely more than whimpers; you the only one who gave real challenge, though you too have fallen faster than I would have wanted. Allow me to prolong your miserable life a little longer," I growled, pulling his severed limb into the flames.

Melanthios screamed, legs kicking, body bucking beneath me as his flesh sizzled in the heat. I dragged him away again, satisfied that the blood was trapped beneath the skin again, and propped him roughly against the pole he had bound Alexis to.

"You believe you have won, but you have not. I have ruined her for you," Melanthios panted. "She shall never have your touch without thought of me," he smiled defiantly.

I took his dagger from my waist, drawing it down his cheek and splitting open the existing scar. He did not make a sound, but his hand clenched and he pounded it on the ground. I slit the ties on his armor, pulling the linen from his body and tossing it aside. He wore a short tunic beneath and I covered his mouth, jamming the dagger into his stomach and pulling upwards when I felt his blood cover my fingers.

"We are done here, Melanthios. Alexis shall be free of you forever." I drew the dagger out, allowing it to fall to the ground as I rammed my hand into the gaping wound I had created, reveling in the heat of his dying flesh. He cried out but could not raise a defense against me, his body too weak from the blood loss.

With my free hand I grabbed at the short strands of his hair, lifting his face and watching as his eyes rolled up into his head when I reached inside him further; squeezing. His innards, along with his blood, poured from his stomach to coat my hand and arm and I knew it was time to end it.

I drew my hand out of his body and picked up the knife once more. His neck stood exposed, his body barely twitching. His mouth fell open, but no sound came out as I drew the iron across his throat, silencing him forever. I closed my eyes, feeling his blood spray the front of my cuirass and the warmth of it cover my hand as his life ebbed away. "I win," I whispered with a triumphant smile.

I opened my eyes, loosening the hand I had in Melanthios' hair and pushing him away; his body slumping onto its side in the dirt. I stared at the deep red that stained the ground and my hands. My heart beat furiously beneath my chest. I had never killed anyone to have what was theirs – just as I had never felt such satisfaction in killing anyone as I did Melanthios. I hoped I would never feel the same way again, but I knew that if anyone ever attempted to harm Alexis again, I would not hesitate in bringing about their demise.

I had not expected to find love in Trachis but it had found me and if Alexis could forgive me for what I had allowed Melanthios to do to her, then I would do anything I could to keep her by my side. She was everything I needed. Everything I wanted.

I pushed myself to my feet, ripping a long strip from Melanthios' tunic and cleaning the blood from my hands and the front of my cuirass before pushing through the door of the tent.

"Is he dead?" Alexis asked, her eyes finding mine.

I nodded in reply, squatting beside her and taking in the bruises on her face and the cut at her eye. Tentatively I reached out, placing my hand at her cheek, my thumb stroking the soft skin. "We should return to Trachis."

"I am afraid for what we shall find there, or for who is no longer there," she admitted, reaching for my hand.

"I know," I said, wrapping my arm around her waist and drawing her to me instead. I pressed my lips to her hair, her familiar scent masked by another sweat-laden masculine one I recognized. Anger flared in my blood. "You smell of him," I noted when she drew away again. She nodded, casting her gaze downward, color lighting her cheeks. "Wait here," I said, a little sharper than I had intended. She looked fearfully up at me and I drew a calming breath before I replied. "There is something I must do before I take you to the hot springs and rid the trace of him from you."

She nodded and I squeezed her shoulder.

"I shall not be long," I promised. I ducked back into the tent, gathering the himation I had seen on the ground and making my way behind the structure. I dragged Xylon's body on top of Cleon's, covering both with the large cloth. The main pool of the spring was clear again; Xylon's blood no longer coating the surface. The constant addition of the water from the falls had obviously washed it down into the stream that ran away beneath the trees.

46

I returned to Alexis, offering her my hand. She took it, steadier on her feet than she had been when I first released her from the ropes. I led her to the spring, removing my cuirass and placing it on the ground nearby.

"You are hurt," she said, frowning and pointing to my side.

I looked down, finding a tear in my tunic and a dark red stain. I pulled it aside, inspecting the slender line beneath. "It is not deep, the water shall clean it. It does not require any herbs." She nodded and I stripped the tunic from my body as Alexis shed her chiton and stepped into the water.

I joined her, turning her and smoothing my hands across her back, grimacing at the bruises I found there, but remaining silent. I cleaned the soft skin of her arms and shoulders, careful at the bruises above her hip and stomach. Ducking beneath the heated water, I glided my hands down each of her legs, feeling the tremors run through her. I resurfaced in front of her, attending her breasts and the line of her collarbones. I left her neck till last, leaning forward to place a kiss there when I was done, satisfied that the only scent on her was her own, and that of the spring.

Alexis bent her knees and immersed her neck and head, rubbing the water from her eyes as she re-emerged. I reached out, placing my hand at her cheek. She closed her eyes, leaning into it.

"Forgive me," I whispered, swallowing around the lump in my throat. "I spoke words of protection, gave my word that I would not allow him to harm you. You placed trust in me that I would keep you safe as I did at the baths and in the Spercheios Valley and … I failed," I said, my voice cracking.

Alexis covered my hand with hers. "I never doubted you would find me. You did not fail for Melanthios lies dead inside his tent and I am here with you." Her finger traced my bottom lip. "No one shall come between us," she added, stepping closer to brush her lips against mine. "I want you to make love to me. I want to feel you inside me, to heal me and make me forget that he ever touched me."

I hesitated. "I ... we should return to Trachis."

The flicker of a frown crossed her brow and she regarded me intently, her head bent slightly to the side. "You do not wish to be with me?"

My breath caught. "I do. But ..."

"Did Melanthios speak true when he said he had ruined me for you? Am I now damaged in your eyes?" she asked, dropping her gaze.

"No. I ... I just ..."

"If you have to hear me say it then I will. I took no pleasure when he was inside me. I could not stop him; you saw how he held me."

"I know."

"I did not want him to touch me."

"I know," I said again.

"I fought to free myself. When he put his hands on me I felt as though I was being unfaithful to you and that hurt me more than anything else."

"Alexis, stop," I commanded gently. "I know that none of what happened was your fault. I do not hold you accountable for it. It is Melanthios, it is *me*, who is to blame," I assured her, wrapping an arm around her waist. "I am just ... afraid. Afraid that it is too soon. That I shall hurt you."

"You could never hurt me. You are everything I need, everything I could ever want," she replied, placing her hand between my breasts. "Make me forget. Please. I want you to. I *need* you to. Touch me, please," she added, her voice laced with need.

I exhaled. I wanted to give her what she asked, yet I could not bring myself to take her with the abandon I had the last time we met at the springs. She pressed her body the length of mine, sliding her hand to my neck and drawing my lips to hers. She parted them with her tongue, desperate and hungry. My body fired, my hands tightening on her waist but I did not slide them across her skin.

She broke our kiss, her eyes following as her hands roamed. I closed my own, wanting to resist her, but knowing that had always been my weakness with her. She cupped my breasts, squeezing as her breath heated my shoulder and she kissed the point of my collarbone. Her hand glided over my stomach, up my neck and down my arm. She took my hand, placing it between her legs and though we stood in the hot springs, the slickness I found was once again far warmer.

"Love me," she insisted, pushing against my fingers.

"Skylar? Alexis?" my father's voice shouted.

Alexis took a step back, my hand falling from her heated skin. I placed my body between she and the bank as Father arrived, sword drawn and eyes darting around the area.

"Here," I called.

"Thank the gods. Is Alexis with you?"

"Yes," I replied as Alexis stepped out from behind me.

Father immediately dropped his eyes. I crossed to the edge of the water and hauled myself out, picking up Alexis' chiton and holding it out for her.

"I am pleased to … er … see … you again, Princess," Father nodded, keeping his eyes averted.

"As am I," she murmured.

Alexis joined me on the grass and I wrapped the linen around her, fastening it at her shoulder by tying the ends together. "Thank you."

I nodded and bent down to retrieve my own tunic, settling it quickly over my skin as I addressed my father again. "Where are Moeris and Thaddeus?"

"Not far behind."

A sudden breeze swept through the trees and Alexis hugged her arms to her chest. I took a step towards her, pausing when she looked up at me. I could not read what was on her face, but she gave me a nod and I continued towards her, placing my chest against her back and enfolding her in my arms. She shivered again, but drew my hands around her stomach and I reveled in the contact.

"It is time we returned to Trachis. Alexis needs to see Gnosidicus," I said.

"Skylar," Alexis began, turning within the circle of my arms.

"Please Alexis, allow me this request," I insisted, my voice quiet but firm.

She opened her mouth, but closed it a moment later, nodding. "If that is what you need."

I dipped my head and kissed her. "I need you. I need to know that when I touch you, I shall not hurt you," I whispered, resting my forehead against hers. "I want us to be as we were before he took you away."

"I want that too," she replied, both of us turning at a sound from the tree line.

"Leandros, did y–" Moeris broke off as he caught sight of Alexis and me.

"Skylar. Princess, thank the gods." He continued towards us and I released Alexis so he could hug her. He offered his arm to me and I clasped it in response.

"I am glad to find you both here," he nodded.

"You too," I replied.

Thaddeus trampled his way through the trees and joined us by the water, throwing his arms first around Alexis, then me. I blushed with his attentions, and he too appeared momentarily embarrassed at his display, clapping me on the shoulder in a masculine gesture as he released me.

"I knew when it came time you would prove not only to Alexis, but to us all, how much you love her," he grinned.

"Agreed. You have shown you shall take the lives of as many men as needed to ensure our Princess ... your Alexis ... is safe," Moeris added. "We are fortunate to have you here."

"Thank you," I mumbled. "While I take Alexis back to Trachis, would the three of you deal with the bodies?" I asked, pointing to the covered mound nearby.

"Of course," Moeris nodded.

"Do you want me to join you, in case you run across any trouble on the way?" Father asked.

"No," I replied, hoping he would understand how much I needed to see Alexis home safely alone.

He placed a hand on my shoulder and squeezed gently. "Then we shall not be far behind. I shall bring your cuirass," he said.

"Thank you," I replied, covering his fingers with my own. I took Alexis' hand and led her down the path past the tent. "I brought Skotos with me, but would you prefer I carried you back to Trachis? You may find it less ... uncomfortable."

"I can ride, but would you join me on his back – holding me as you did when we left here last time?"

"Of course," I replied. When we reached Skotos, I settled Alexis atop him before joining her, my arms encircling her protectively. I took the reins and pressed my heels against Skotos to encourage him forward.

We travelled in silence until the outline of the palace appeared in the distance. Alexis leaned back, molding her body to mine, her cheek above my heart. "It shall not be long before we reach the town," she noted.

"No," I agreed.

"Before ... before Melanthios' army arrived you said if I asked it of you, you would stay in Trachis. Is that still what you wish to do?" she asked, lifting her chin until our eyes met.

I drew a deep breath, hearing the fear beneath her words. "I want to be wherever you are," I assured her.

"Then remain with me. I do not want to be without you. I cannot," she murmured, resting her hand on my arm.

I took my fingers from Skotos' reins and traced the line of her jaw. "I am yours, Princess. Always." I pressed my lips to hers wishing the gesture could heal her wounds and remove the doubts and fears for what Melanthios had put us through. Her mouth opened, inviting me to taste her and to prove my words beyond a shadow of a doubt. I slid my hand beneath her hair and drew her closer to me, her breath shortening as our tongues met. "Allow us to go home," I said when we eventually parted.

"I have not called Trachis my home for many winters, but when you speak the words I know it shall be so again."

I wanted to reclaim her, body and soul. We both needed it, and when Gnosidicus had checked her over, I would. I smiled. I had found her, she was safe. No one stood between us any longer. Melanthios had sought to put up barriers between us, but he had not destroyed our love. There were still obstacles we must face, but we would do so together, somehow in my heart I knew that and I welcomed the chance.

"I love you so much," Alexis whispered.

"As I love you," I replied, claiming her lips again and ensuring I had the last word. Alexis was my greatest love and I would give her no reason to doubt or fear me. She did not deserve to live in fear of the one she was destined to be with; and her destiny was to be with me. I was hers as she was mine. For all the rest of our days.

47

"Master Ares, your Chosen One's power grows strong; we have all felt it. Is it not time now to go to her?"

"It is time, Dianthe. Gather together your kin and the Valkyrie. Finally I shall speak of my plans. It is time Skylar knew of her Ker history and *all* which has been kept from her."

ABOUT THE AUTHOR

Belinda Harrison was born and raised in a country town in North East Victoria, Australia. She spent some time experiencing 'big city life' in Melbourne and Sydney in her twenties where she held jobs in a packaging company, an online gaming firm, various temp positions and a hair loss treatment center before the lure of the country recalled her.

She joined her family's business in the world of retail plumbing and appliance sales – which is when she started writing the Thermopylae Bound Series before deciding to leave the familiar and join another well respected local firm in the Real Estate sector where she worked in Commercial Property Management.

Belinda then decided it was time for another change and moved across the road to the local newspaper where she looks after Circulation and the Kids' page, writing after hours, and sometimes during lunch.

Belinda holds a Certificate IV in Multimedia, which she has successfully used in her professional and personal life.

She currently lives in 'the best part of Victoria' with her fiancé Renee, daughter Ava, Charlie the dog, and cats Caesar and Max.

You can find Belinda on the following social media platforms: Instagram (belindagharrison), Twitter (beharrison78) or Facebook (Belinda Harrison Author). And don't forget to leave a review on Amazon or Goodreads to help spread the word.

www.ingramcontent.com/pod-product-compliance
Lightning Source LLC
Chambersburg PA
CBHW031720170626
46808CB00005B/1823